HORIZONS COLLIDE

HORIZONS COLLIDE

A NOVEL

J.E. RECHTIN

NEW YORK

LONDON • NASHVILLE • MELBOURNE • VANCOUVER

HORIZONS COLLIDE
A NOVEL

© 2019 J.E. RECHTIN

Published in New York, New York, by Morgan James Publishing. Morgan James is a trademark of Morgan James, LLC. www.MorganJamesPublishing.com

Publisher's Note: This novel is a work of fiction. Names, characters, places, and incidents are either products of the author's imagination or used fictiously. All characters are fictional, and any similarity to people living or dead is purely coincidental.

ISBN 978-1-64279-200-3 paperback
ISBN 978-1-64279-201-0 eBook
Library of Congress Control Number: 2018908361

Cover Design by:
Christopher Kirk
GFSstudio.com

Interior Design by:
Bonnie Bushman
The Whole Caboodle Graphic Design

In an effort to support local communities, raise awareness and funds, Morgan James Publishing donates a percentage of all book sales for the life of each book to Habitat for Humanity Peninsula and Greater Williamsburg.

Get involved today! Visit
www.MorganJamesBuilds.com

This book is dedicated to my wife,
my best friend and my personal cheerleader.

Acknowledgements

This book could not have been possible without the care and good will of the following people.

Whitney E: You provided blunt and sometimes brutally honest reviews of the work. Thank you for not letting me become lazy.

David J: Your opinions about story-flow were certainly appreciated.

Laura Helming: I will never forget your efforts to drive the manuscript and polish it into a thing of beauty.

Aubrey Kosa: Without your guidance, no one would see this book on a book store shelf.

David L. Hancock: Your vision is amazing, and I am honored to be part of this incredible family.

My Creator: I am ever thankful for the talent you gave me.

Preface

God works in mysterious ways and I believe this story was inspired by God. I say that because the story was given to me over three separate visions. The first time, I thought the tale was interesting, but I had no time or talent to bring such a project to fruition. The second vision appeared several months later and was a much clearer and detailed, almost a theatrical trailer-like, preview. This got my attention and I went to my best friend—my wife. She had suggested it was potentially a good story but kindly let me know science fiction wasn't her cup of tea. The third time is the charm, as the old saying goes. Almost one year later and very early one morning I was greeted with a movie playing in my mind. That movie was the story that would become known as *Horizons Collide*.

And so, I began to write the movie in my mind and months later I had assembled a story that was well over three hundred thousand words deep. There was a great need to trim this monster to a workable and marketable size and God once again began to slip-in suggestions; edit and re-write became a second full-time job.

So, why was this book written? There are people out there sitting on the fence about their faith and need to be reassured the message of faith is real and is as current today as when Jesus walked this earth. I believe in God and as a Christian, I believe in Jesus Christ and accept what is printed in the Bible. Jesus himself stated, he is the only way to the Father. While there may be only one way to the father, I believe there is more than one way to find Jesus.

What better way to find Christ than to follow a story of a person from modern time, a person whose life has been filled with pain and loss and watch them do what we ourselves might do—give up on our faith. It is a fair question to ask, what would you do if your plan had been scuttled and you had been accidentally sent to be in the presence of Jesus? If all things familiar are gone, how would you react?

This story is religion meets science fiction, medicine wrapped in chocolate. I realize some people don't like apple pie and a few will read this story and walk away spiritually untouched but I also believe the clear majority will be touched and may put this story into the hands of someone at that pivotal intersection. It is for them, God had inspired me to write this book.

CHAPTER 1

E arly March had always been a time of transition in the midwestern part of the country and particularly in Sycamore Illinois. The harsh cold of the winter had started to retreat as warmer temperatures brought forth the first signs of spring. Subtle and sparse speckles of green began to appear in the brownish gray of the dormant lawns of the neighborhood while the buds on trees had begun to swell. The longer days welcomed boys and girls to the streets to toss balls with their fathers.

In the recent past, Billy Thompson and his father had joined them and as he watched from his bedroom window he wiped a tear that rolled down his cheek. Not quite a year ago, the doctor diagnosed his father with cancer. He stood helplessly by, as the man he held closest to his heart slowly vanished from his sight. He kept vigil at his father's side as did his mother and most of the time they prayed.

The family was deeply rooted in Christian faith and very active in the church they attended. Billy had been going to Sunday classes since the age of five and the nearly seven years of Christian education taught him to trust that God had only their best interests in mind. His twelfth birthday was only weeks away and he would be promoted to a group of students that would be baptized later in June.

Billy had inherited his mother's intellect, her stunning blue eyes and her mannerisms while he took on his father's handsome features. He was an excellent student in any classroom he sat and was particularly gifted in the Sunday classes. His advantage was provided in part by his intellect but to a greater extent, his grandmother on his father's side. Velma Anne Thompson was a strict woman and believed children should be taught the Bible from the moment they could walk. Since James's mother watched Billy for the first five years of his life, she made certain he would enter Sunday school well read on the subject matter.

But prayer didn't seem to be helping. His faith was being tested and he was failing. He started to question God's will and the plan of God … even the existence of God. The filtered laughter of the neighborhood children seemed especially cruel and as he looked beyond the roof lines of the neighboring homes, the steeple of the church his family attended was in plain view. In the past, this sight gave him peace and hope but now it stirred feelings of distrust and anger.

As another tear dripped from his jaw, he took a breath, collected himself, stood and walked out of his room. The distance between his room and the bedroom of his parents was not long, perhaps ten feet at the most, but the walk seemed to be the most difficult journey he could take. He stood at the open door and looked upon an all too familiar sight, his mother sitting by his father's side, praying and lovingly stroking what little of his hair remained.

The deterioration of his father was certainly taking part of his mother with him. Kathleen was quite a beautiful woman however the stress of caring for her husband had begun to rob her of her kind features. She had always worn her long blonde hair parted down the center and partially pulled back into a flowing mane Today, like most of the days in the last six months, her hair was not as kept and bordered on shaggy. Her Blue eyes were surrounded by flesh that was red and puffy, worn raw from an endless stream of tears.

Billy said nothing as he leaned on the door frame. His arms were crossed as he pondered her actions. Surely, she too knew his father was dying and all the prayers and Bible reading produced no positive change. How could she do this? Wasn't she angry like he was?

His thoughts were interrupted by his father coughing violently. He took a step forward and froze as the latest turn for the worse became visible His mother reached for a tissue and began to wipe the pick phlegm from around his father's mouth. The cancer was now in his lungs and destroying them, slowly and probably painfully Billy winced at the sight but stayed in the room because he knew the end was coming soon.

With great effort, his father raised his hand, motioning Billy to come to him. A strange feeling stirred in his stomach as he walked to his father's bed. He paused for a moment and then took the final step to stand by his father.

"Don't worry about me." James said as he labored to get a breath to speak. His father's voice was raspy like his Grandmother's before she died of pneumonia. "I'm going to a place where there is no pain, no cancer and no death." The few words took so much effort but Billy knew his father needed to say them. "Take care of your mother. You're going to be the man of the house now and remember you need to get baptized … I'm sorry I won't be able to be there to see it."

Billy wasn't going to tell his father anything that would upset him, but he was not going to go through with the ritual. The events of this last year had steered him from his faith and only the miracle of healing his father would bring him back. More tears began to fill his eyes as he bent down to kiss the forehead of the shell of a man that once was his father.

Pastor Mark Jackson and his wife Judy, had been stopping by the Thompson house after the service ever since the first prayers for healing had been asked seven weeks ago. Opening the picket fence gate, they walked in silence toward the front door. As they reached the porch, they both looked upon the gardens Kathleen had planted and James had often admirably described. The green sprouts were bringing new life in the shadow of impending death and gave Pastor Mark and Judy the strength to proceed. She put her arm around her husband's waist and her head against his shoulder.

"Mark, I hope I can do this." Judy said as she dabbed the corners of her eyes which started to fill with tears.

"My Dear, we will rely on the Holy Spirit to guide our tongues." The pastor seemed less confident than his words. "Let's go."

After a deep breath, he knocked on the front door, turned to watch his wife perform one final wipe of her eyes and stow the tissue in her purse.

Upstairs in the bedroom, the situation was mercifully interrupted by the sound of a knock on the front door. Kathleen asked her son to see who was there so Billy backed out of the room, his face showing fear and a host of other emotions. When he reached the front door and opened it, he looked blankly into the faces of the pastor and his wife.

"May we come in please" asked the pastor.

Without speaking, Billy opened the door fully, to invite them in. The pastor and his wife could not help but notice the silence and the growing look of deepening sorrow on the boy's young face.

The Pastor spoke to Billy, "We came to see your father. Would it be alright to go up to his bedroom?"

Billy looked at the floor and replied shrugging his shoulders, "Sure". Since the Pastor and his wife had been there several times before, they knew their way to the bedroom but Billy still climbed the stairs to deliver them to his parent's bedroom door. Once they arrived just outside of the door, the Pastor whispered to Billy.

"May I talk with you privately before we leave?"

Billy nodded yes and made his own bedroom his destination. He closed the door behind him and he fell onto his bed, crying into his pillow.

He wiped his eyes and sat up. Crying didn't seem to be doing anything so he knelt on the floor by his bed. He believed prayer was a waste of time, but then what did he have to lose? After a sighing breath, he began a desperate prayer.

"Jesus, don't let cancer take my dad from me … please." He stopped to wipe his running nose on his sleeve. "Misses Jackson always said you protect us from evil … cancer is evil." Sorrow wrapped its cold iron fist around him and he once again began to cry.

Regaining some composure, he looked around his room. He had managed to undo all the efforts of his mother's latest cleaning. Billy tried to pass the time alone by looking at his collection of old toys he had out grown. Suddenly, out of nowhere his eyes found and stopped on his own study Bible. His nearly 12-year-old eyes narrowed angrily and he came to his feet. Walking inexorably toward the book, he grabbed it, squeezing it hard, hoping in some way deep inside of himself, it might get the attention of God.

There was a book marker at JOHN 3:16. He read the verse aloud: "For God so loved the world that he gave his only begotten Son, that whosoever believeth on him should not perish, but have eternal life."

Reading the verse gave him no peace at all and actually angered him. The Bible verse was taught in Sunday school and quite often referenced. He knew it was speaking about eternal life in Heaven. Unfortunately, he felt cheated and wanted to have more life with his father here, now … not who knew when.

"Why won't you listen? Don't you care about us?" Billy spoke aloud, demanding an answer from Jesus. All the Sunday school lessons and the countless times he and the other children were told that God loves, he began to believe God didn't care. He, his mother and father were not important to God and they didn't matter at all.

Again, the tears streamed down his young cheeks. As he wiped them away, a soft knock interrupted his angry thoughts; Pastor Robert was at his bedroom door. In a quiet reassuring voice, He asked if he could come into the bedroom. Billy offered a one-word reply, "Sure". The hinges squeaked as the Pastor gently pushed the door open.

He walked into the bedroom and closed the door behind him. "Billy, I know you are very upset right now, but God has a plan … a plan … we can't or don't always understand." He continued after a short silence. "You're almost12 years old and none of this seems fair but…"

Billy cut the Pastor off before the next words came from his struggling mouth.

"We all have prayed" Billy began sobbing. "The whole church prayed! Why didn't God fix my Dad? Why is he getting even sicker?" He threw himself back onto his bed, face down onto the pillow.

The Pastor tried to console Billy but the more he spoke, the more and louder Billy cried. The Pastor turned to leave the room but before leaving, he told Billy, "We will continue to pray to ask God for mercy and strength, but his will shall be done".

Without watching, Billy knew the Pastor had left the room. The squeak of the door hinges, announced the closure of the bedroom door. Subtle indistinct voices grew further away, giving clues, the visitors were leaving. Billy caught his breath, wiped his eyes, stood from his bed and walked to his father's doorway. Through swollen eyes, he gazed silently at the shrinking shell of the man that was his best friend and his father. The longer he looked at his father, the angrier he became.

Kathleen walked the Pastor and his wife down the steps and showed them to the front door, bidding them goodbye. The Pastor's wife gave a hug giving her assurances that the church family loved them and would do whatever they could to help Kathleen and Billy. Tears flowed from her tired eyes, as she closed the front door and watched through the small window, as the Pastor and his wife walked down the sidewalk to their waiting car.

"This is very hard on all of us but it's destroying Billy." Judy Jackson said to him as they opened the doors of the car to get in. "He's too young for this to happen to him".

"Yes, it's hard but there is little we can do". He replied as he sat down heavily in the driver's seat; both car doors closed at the same time.

"I don't think you handled the situation with Billy very well" She began. "I heard his crying." She said as she looked away from her husband out of the side window at the Thompson home.

"I simply told the boy, God is in control of the situation and we don't always get what we want in life" He changed the subject. "Fasten your belt – we need to go to the market"

The engine was started and the couple drove away.

Back in the house, Kathleen turned her back to the door, leaned against its cold wooden surface, placed her face in the palms of her hands and cried heavily. The stream of tears rolled down her forearms, dripped onto the floor and onto her shoes.

She hadn't noticed her son walking down the steps until she heard him call out to her. "Mom, Dad's going to die, isn't he?"

His mother looked up trying to regain control over the tears. "Billy, I don't know. But it's not my decision, it's up to God".

Billy looked at his mother with a blank stare and asked, "Is there really God mom? Why did he let Dad get cancer? He let Granny Velma die and took our baby too."

"That's a terrible thing to say, Billy." she told her son. "I believe God has a plan and his will shall be done on Earth as it is in Heaven." She continued as she sniffed the tears back. "We don't always get what we want in this life, but we will be given a great reward when we see Jesus in our next life." Her voice pitched to a squeak as her last words were choked out by tears.

Billy ran to his mother, wrapped his arms around her, and buried his face into her shoulder as they both cried.

CHAPTER 2

Two weeks later, two days after Billy's twelfth birthday, James Thompson died in his home while his wife, son, the Pastor and his wife stood by his side. Pastor Mark offered the prayers of the sick and dying while Billy stood stoically behind his mother. Once the prayers were finished, the pastor moved out of the way. Kathleen lifted the lifeless hand of her husband and held it as the tears from her blue eyes dripped onto his face. She said she would love him forever and then let Billy have his turn.

Billy couldn't speak. There was so much he wanted to say but most of it was aimed at the one who let this happen. He knew his mother was hurting at least as much as he was, if not more and vocalizing the anger he held for God now would be cruel to her. He turned and walked away.

Billy felt disembodied as he walked through the door of his parent's room. After entering his own, he quietly closed the door. He walked to the window and knelt, not to pray but to watch and listen as other fathers played with their children. Anger grew within him and the hollow platitudes offered by the pastor and his wife were no match for the inferno behind his bright blue eyes.

The following day the funeral had been arranged and Kathleen's family had come to town from Florida. That night, Billy couldn't sleep and had been tossing in his bed. His mind replayed the voice of his grandfather's incessant critiquing of his mother and him. He was a bitter old man, Billy thought, and he didn't really care what the man said about anything.

Though the night, the television was on but the sound was down and odd flashes of color bathed the walls of his room. Blues seemed to be the dominant color when the light of the screen was at its brightest, he thought. It certainly set the mood for him and he found himself thinking back to a time when he was younger—before his father had cancer. He watched the movie of his life with his father play in his mind remembering how he waited for his car to come around the corner as he came home from his job at the accounting office. He remembered the excitement of trying his new hunting rifle and how his father was there to share and enjoy every moment. He tried so hard to find peace in his heart, but only anger and distrust could be found.

A knock at the door brought him back to the crushing reality of the present. The sky was beginning to brighten. His mother asked if she could come in. She slowly opened the door, walked over to the edge of his bed and sat down. He looked at and into her swollen eyes.

"I don't think there's enough makeup to hide these bags." His mother said attempting to lift both their spirits.

"Mom, I don't think I can look at the casket ... I don't think I can do this."

"Billy, I know you think of me and your father as just your parents but we were actually best friends and lovers. We had a piece of each other's hearts and that made me feel special. So, when you say you don't think you can look at that casket, what do you think is going to go through my mind ... my heart?

He paused before speaking again and when he did, it was with serious conviction. "I'm never going to go to church again Mom. I'm done with it."

"What are you talking about? You are not positioned to dictate terms. Besides, your father would never let you stop going ... remember when your grandmother passed?"

"Grandma took some of my heart with her and everyone at church lied to me. They said it would be alright if we prayed. They said God would make it all right. Well, he either didn't listen, didn't care or isn't even there to hear anything. I'm not wasting my time and breath on something I can't see and certainly doesn't seem to care."

"Billy, please let's not do this, and certainly not today. It's going to be hard enough to keep myself together without needing to worry about fighting with you over the existence of God! Now please get cleaned up and get dressed for your father's funeral!"

The last words his mother said burned through him like a hot poker. He was nearly sick from his stomach twisting. There were so many "Last times" to be experienced today and he didn't want to take part in any of them but ... he had no choices remaining.

After arriving to the church, Billy and his mother gathered with her family. Grandpa Harvey shot a menacing stare across the aisle. If the old man wanted to fight, he would certainly accommodate him, Billy thought. But his grandfather didn't seem to be paying attention to him. It seemed his laser-like gaze was aimed at his mother. He started toward them and was stopped by Sally, his grandmother. Billy thought, perhaps the man was still irritated about the answer he gave about the reason for Christmas when they had visited Florida four Christmases ago. In his mind he replayed the moment and the look on his grandfather's face when he told Harvey Christmas was about getting presents from Santa.

Of course, he then recited the passage from Genesis verbatim, but he did so with a certain arrogant flare.

The church was overflowing with people. Every bench was filled with those wanting to show their respects to James and his family. Kathleen's sister, her husband and her parents, sat in the benches near the front of the church while Kathleen and Billy sat on the other side. James's casket rested in the center of the aisle, between them.

The service was a difficult one for the Pastor to get through. He had broken down several times which caused the service to run a bit longer. Kathleen didn't mind, because it was a little more time she would have with her husband. Even though he was gone, his body was close. She knew it was odd to think this way but so long as that casket was there, she could still feel some connection to him. The church service ended and the casket was loaded into the hearse and the short journey to the cemetery had begun.

The grave side service was more difficult than the church service. The final prayers were said and this was it— the end of his time with his father and the end of his mother's marriage. Billy tried to refuse to accept the finality of it all, yet there it was, indisputable as the gray clouds in the sky. He felt numb as he watched the casket be lowered into the ground. It was as if he was outside his body, perhaps having a horrible dream that would suddenly end ... but this was no dream. As the top of the casket disappeared below the surface of the ground a wave of emotion and desperation came over him and he made one final, futile and agonizing plea. He broke from his mother and rushed to the open grave, stopping just short so he didn't fall into the gaping hole.

"No Dad, don't go! You can't take him ... God, please no." He cried out as his mother and aunt pulled him away from the opening in the ground. Harvey and Sally stood and watched their grandson's grief explode. Sally wiped tears from her eyes while her husband stood emotionless. Billy's last gasp and pleading prayer touched almost everyone at the cemetery. His knees buckled from the sudden and intense grief and he knelt in the mud and cried. He felt the cold, muddy, water seep through his pants but he didn't care. His heart was being ripped from his chest and all he cared about was his dad … his best friend … a man he would never see again.

Pastor Mark tried to regain his composure to let everyone know the church fellowship room was ready to accept them. The crowd in the cemetery started back to their cars. Kathleen's sister Sandra and her husband Charles had driven separately while Billy and Kathleen decided to ride to the church and cemetery with her parents. It seemed like a good idea earlier in the day when her mother had suggested it but the ride back to the church would prove to be anything but easy. Billy's pants where muddy from the knees down and before his grandfather allowed him into the back seat, he took a towel and handed it to Billy, telling him he needed to wipe as much mud and dirt from his knees as he could. Kathleen's mother informed her husband that it was a rental car after all and the dirt didn't seem to pose any more harm than the fast food he had gotten all over the seat after they picked up the car at the airport in Chicago. Harvey started the motor and began the drive through the narrow roadway to leave the cemetery. Before they exited, they passed a newer grave where a woman and three children were placing flowers at a head stone.

"I guess God didn't care about them either." Billy said in a cry-worn voice.

Harvey took immediate umbrage to his statement. "Young man I will not have you blaspheme in my presence." He then started on Kathleen, suggesting her dress was too tight and she was leading her son down a path of destruction. "My goodness child, you can clearly see everything your mother and I provided you."

"Dad, this is not the time for this. In case you weren't paying attention, I just buried my husband, and the father of my son. I just can't argue with you right now."

"I raised you better than this Kathleen, I raised you to be a good Christian woman … and now I see before me a woman of loose morals and a son who disrespects God."

Sally tried to disarm the situation. "Harvey, Kathleen, Billy, all of you, please shut up. I just lost a very special person and I don't want to listen to any of this!" She looked very sternly at her husband and said nothing but her eyes telegraphed so much. She began again. "Harvey, you fall back on being God's protector every time. God is all powerful and while I'm sure he's flattered, he doesn't need your help. Lashing out at Billy and Kathleen is NOT going to help anyone get through this." She then addressed Billy directly. "William Thompson, you listen to me. It might be a good idea to learn to keep your thoughts to yourself and avoid these kinds of situations. It hurts to lose people close to you. At my age, they're starting to die on a regular basis. Unfortunate and as bad as this is, it's part of life. Kathleen, your dress looks very nice and I wouldn't change a thing." Sally turned her angry eyes toward her husband as her last comment registered in his ears.

Billy said nothing in return, he simply sat there looking out of the window and shared in the misery that each stone represented. Did they pray? Did they cry? *Did they question?* He decided to keep his mouth shut and his resentment for Grandpa Harvey to himself.

Once they got back to the church, Billy opened the car door and got out quickly. He ran into the church to put distance between himself and his grandfather. His mother caught up with him inside the church. She found him sitting on the floor where his father's casket had been just an hour earlier and he was crying.

As she approached Kathleen broke the silence. "I need to be careful sitting down in this dress … it might rip apart because it's so tight."

Her attempt at sarcastic humor had no effect on Billy. She sat down next to him and put her arm around him and rocked back and forth. His blue eyes met his mother's and as she held his hand he began to describe his feeling for his grandfather.

"How does he get off describing your dress as slutty? Aunt Sandra's dress was shorter and tighter than yours." He finished.

"My dad has always been there for me. I was his favorite daughter. That was one of the reason's Sandra didn't like me when we were children. So, he has a higher level of expectation from me."

"That doesn't make any sense mom … what does any of that have to do with your dress?"

He got up from the floor and started to walk away but then stopped, turned and walked back toward her. He held out his hand and helped her to her feet.

"It's just us now Mom." Billy said as he hugged her tightly and sniffed his nose which had been running from the months of crying.

Billy was just twelve but he had grown to be almost as tall as his mother. His voice was starting to change and he was experiencing some odd squeaks and breaks when he spoke. His boyish looks were disappearing and the body, face and attitude of a teenage boy was emerging. He told his mother he would not be finishing Sunday school and he would not be getting baptized. She looked at him with a suspicious eye, but she didn't argue.

"Mom, I've come to believe, none of this really matters." He said as he pointed to the church and its decorations. "I put all of my trust into this, my heart … everything. And what do I have to show for it? Grandpa hates me, he thinks you're a prostitute and Dad's dead." Billy wiped at the tears that came from his eyes. He had been wiping tears for the last six months and his eyes hurt which did nothing for his mood or give him a reason to stay associated with church. "I'm having trouble adding up all of the positives I tried to tell you this, this morning."

It was clear, he had been thinking about this for some time. As he looked at his mother's face, he could see she was struggling to form a thought that would be the correct response to what Billy had said.

"Honey, God works in mysterious—"

"—Ways." Sandra finished her sentence as she walked up behind them. "Kati, everyone's looking for the two of you. What happened in the car? Mom and Dad aren't speaking … they look like they're on the verge of divorce." She joined them where they stood in the church.

Billy started to explain but a look from his mother suggested it would be best if she did the talking. "There was a difference of opinion based on something Billy said as we were leaving the cemetery."

"Mom said Dad went nuts on both of you."

"He essentially told me I dress like a whore, and Billy is a blasphemous child who has been raised to be a heathen."

"Dad hasn't been right lately." Sandra said. "Mom told me he's been wetting the bed and had an accident in the parking lot of the grocery store the other day." She paused as tears started to fill in her eyes. "The doctor said he as a brain tumor."

"Wow more cancer … case and point." Billy injected.

"Billy, knock it off!" Kathleen scolded She then turned her attention back to her sister. "Why didn't mom call me?"

"She knew you had enough on your plate with James and Mom's been in denial. Kathleen, today's funeral was a dress rehearsal for Dad's funeral." Sandy finished speaking as she tried to hold back the tears. Kathleen reached for and held her sister.

Billy decided he needed to go apologize to his grandfather, if for any other reason, to sooth his grandmother's nerves. He excused himself from his mother and aunt and returned to the fellowship room searching for Harvey Tropher. When he found him he was talking to folks he hadn't seen in years. Outwardly there seemed to be nothing wrong with the man. Billy waited for the conversation to end so he couldn't be called rude as well.

"Grandpa, I wanted to apologize for my tongue in the cemetery." His grandfather looked at him with skepticism, wondering who put him up to this. "I was wrong and I wanted you to know before you and Grandma go back home."

"Thank you, Billy." Harvey said to his grandson as his wife quickly approached, undoubtedly to pry the two apart should round two of a fight commence. "Hello Sally, Billy here has just apologized for his comments. Perhaps there is hope after all. If you two will excuse me, I need to use the restroom."

Billy noticed the look of pity mixed with fear, in his grandmother's eyes. She looked at the floor and then to Billy who had grown as tall as she. You've gotten so big. I remember when you were a baby. Your Dad ... I'm sorry."

"It's okay Grandma. Aunt Sandra told us about Grandpa. I'm sorry."

"It seems this family hasn't had enough pain." She touched a tissue to the corners of her eyes. "I'll continue to pray for strength." Billy thought it best to simply smile and nod approvingly at her last statement.

Three exhausting days later, Kathleen and Billy waved goodbye to the family as they departed to return to Florida. The house was quiet. Billy went to his room and Kathleen sat on the couch. It seemed only weeks ago, she and James had sat in this very spot as he told her he was dying from cancer. The weight of the loss of her husband began to settle upon her and as she looked around the room, her eyes fell upon a full can of paint. She could hear his voice in her memory's ear, lovingly telling her the painting would get done. She took a deep breath and forced back her tears.

Moments later, she stood and walked to the wall of memories. There were pictures of different sizes, of the stages of their lives. She looked at and touched the pictures as the feelings they invoked paraded through her mind. She climbed the steps and went to her own room, lay on her bed and cried herself to sleep.

CHAPTER 3

N early three years had passed since James death. Billy had made good on his promise to stay away from church. His attitude toward anything to do with faith was to say the least, not complimentary. He began to associate less with his friends Christopher Wayne Seekers and Bob Stanton and started spending time with some unsavory types at school.

He rarely went to visit his father's grave and the relationship between him and his mother had become adversarial. Kathleen tried to reach him but he shut her out. She had suggested he should council with Pastor Mark but was told to mind her own business. When she told him he was her business, he became enraged and stopped short of hitting her.

The people he had begun to spend time, had much looser morals, if any at all, and he found himself in the company of several young women who were older than he was, by several years. It didn't seem to matter to them he was under age and they stole his innocence from him. He began to experiment with alcohol which further clouded his judgment and led him into circumstances that threatened to send him to jail should he get caught.

One very late evening, shortly before the sun began to brighten the skies, he was dropped at his house by a woman several years older than he. Reeking of alcohol, he staggered toward the front door of the house. Upon reaching his bed, he peeled off the clothes he had worn, climbed between the fresh, clean sheets and passed out. The next day his mother had found evidence of his encounter with the woman the night before. It sparked yet another argument with his mother.

"Billy, I found dried ... stuff on your underpants."

"It's called seaman. I know you can't bring the word to your holy lips." Billy said with as much disrespect as he could bring.

"Listen to me, please. You want to leave this town, this life and all of the misery and pain, I understand that, but if you get yourself in trouble with the police or some girl, your life and plans are over."

He looked directly into his mother's eyes and took a menacing step toward her.

"I told you to stay out of my life and I meant it." He said dangerously.

After a short stare between them, Billy turned and stormed out of the house and started to walk. He had no idea where his feet would take him but it was better than being in the house with his mother.

It was almost evening and soon the sun would be setting. His walk delivered him to the base of his father's grave. The low angle of the sun caused the stones to create long, almost foreboding shadows. So many emotions passed through his mind as he sat onto the recently cut grass. His mother must have visited because fresh flowers had been placed in the vase at the foot of the headstone. Birds chirped in the background creating a natural, soothing music. There was a peace in this place but even the bird's songs could not erase the pain the stone monument caused him. He wished he could speak to his father ... he needed him. He needed him to set him straight and to keep him from making more stupid decisions. He needed to know if God really did exist.

It was dark by the time he had returned home from his walk and once he reached the top of the stairs, he heard his mother crying in her room. The door to her room was closed and the muffled sound of her crying didn't seem to faze him at all but when his eyes caught sight of an empty bottle of sleeping pills sitting on the bathroom sink, his stomach fell to his feet. Suddenly, all the anger and frustration of the last three years evaporated. Guilt and fear took over and caused a crushing feeling inside his chest. He moved quickly to his mother's closed bedroom door and burst into her room. She was startled by his entrance. He found her lying on her bed, crying. She looked at him. In his thoughts, he took complete responsibility for what he was seeing before him. His eyes must have telegraphed his thoughts to his mother. She smiled at him and he began to panic. This was it, he thought, he had driven his mother to suicide. But why did she smile? Was this her love for him, to free him from the guilt of driving her to this point?

"I can't take this anymore Billy ... I can't do it." Kathleen said as she looked up at her son.

"Mom, let me get you to the hospital, they can get the pills out ... I'll get a pan and you can stick your finger down your throat and throw up and get them out of your stomach!" There was panic in his voice as well as tears in his eyes.

She started to laugh. "You saw the empty sleeping pill bottle on the sink." She began to laugh harder.

Embarrassment came over him. "What's so funny?" He asked, as anger had invaded his voice.

"Those pills were your father's. I flushed them down the toilet and forgot to put the empty bottle in the trash." She stood and then walked over to Billy. "You came in to rescue me ... you thought I was going to die." She put her arms around him and whispered, "Thank you, Jesus."

Billy had no choice but to surrender to the truth. He was worried his mother was going to die and leave him alone and that it was his actions that would have been the cause of it. His relief was unburdening and allowed him to understand what love was. Love over-took his anger and his self-pity, and made him act. It was a moment of epiphany for him, one that not only opened his eyes, but also his heart. With this sudden bearing of his soul, he also realized he would have a lot of apologizing to do for the brutal treatment he had given his mother over the last three years. As he stood, embraced by his mother, Billy was feeling so many emotions and didn't know what to do, but then, slowly and with some reluctance, he put his arms around his mother. Within moments, his arms held her tightly, as if he would never let her go.

Billy had apologized to his mother but there were some other people he needed to speak to. The end of the school term was approaching and he wanted to make things right with Christopher and Bob. They had been his friends since elementary school and were with him through the decline and death of his father. He knew there was a chance they would tell him to leave them alone, but he had to tell them he was sorry.

He walked into the cafeteria and found his friends at a table exercising the same ritual he had been part of for so many years. Tammy, Christopher's girlfriend, was at the table seated next to Bob and was the first to notice his approach.

"Look who it is, the bad-boy of Sycamore High." Tammy said sarcastically. Her gaze was less than compassionate and left Billy with no doubt, the low opinion she held of him.

"I came to apologize for my behavior and walking away from all of you." Billy said as he fidgeted nervously.

At first no one said anything but then Bob stood. Christopher followed almost immediately. Both teens smacked him on the shoulders and welcomed him back to the table. Tammy was a little more reserved and demanded an explanation. Billy gathered his thoughts before he spoke, but when he did, he delivered his heart. Once he finished, Tammy stood and hugged him. Tears glistened in her eyes as she welcomed him.

Over the next few weeks, Billy and his mother talked out the last three years. In an act of self-sacrifice, Billy agreed to return to church and get baptized. It was, in his mind, a high price to pay but he reasoned the amount of pain he had caused his mother, it would be his penance.

The first Sunday back to church left him a little nervous. He expected that everyone would be in his business and start preaching to him. Billy was pleasantly surprised when this didn't happen. Pastor Jackson and his wife Judy offered a simple welcome back and nothing further. Kathleen brought Billy's attention to a sign that was just inside the door. The second point down announced registration for Adult Baptism and the preparation classes would begin in two weeks. With some reluctance, he followed his mother into the church office and watched her complete the form. The look on Billy's face clearly showed what his mouth didn't say. His mother looked at him and smiled. After all, a promise is a promise he thought.

CHAPTER 4

The first class was scheduled to begin in about half of an hour and Billy's mother got her keys so she could drive him to the church. He told her he could walk there but she suggested he might get sidetracked and miss the class. She was quite aware that he didn't care if he was baptized and could easily find any excuse to prevent him from going to the classes. After reminding him of his agreement and the difficulty he put her through during the past three years, he had little choice but to accept the ride.

He may have made-up with his mother but he still wasn't quite settled when it came to the opinion he held about religion. As his mother drove, he was creating a scene in his mind about the classes he was being forced into. He was envisioning sitting in a cramped room surrounded by people who were make-believe Christians. Some had likely memorized a hand full of scripture verses and therefore were experts and holier than everyone else. The only reason they were getting baptized was because it soothed their pathetic consciences. He knew all too well if he voiced his opinion, it would cause a lecture, no, an argument with his mother. His grandmother was correct, sometimes, silence is the best policy.

As his mother turned her car into the parking lot of the church, Billy looked at the small group of men and women standing at the base of the church steps talking and smoking. They were there for the class as well and were simply getting that last cigarette in before entering the building. The car stopped near the small knot of people and Billy got out. He told his mother he would see her in about an hour and a half and started for the front door of the church. He waved to her as she drove away. Once he reached the base of the steps, his head bent down and he let out a sigh. He forced his feet to move and climbed the steps, walking slower than normal, asking himself why he agreed to this stupid process.

He passed through the open doors of the church and once inside he saw a sign that directed everyone to the Sunday school classroom. It was here the prep classes would be held. As he entered the room he looked around. It was the first time he had been here in three, almost four years. Little, if anything, had changed since then. Two of the walls were decorated with pictures of characters from the Bible the younger students had colored and the same large Bible Mrs. Jackson read from still sat on the same podium.

Billy noticed the desks the children used had been pushed to the sides of the room and chairs suitable for adults were situated in a semi-circle in the center. On each chair sat a small pile of papers and a pen. He counted a total of ten chairs and figured that was how many people would be coming. The room seemed so cluttered and tight and he wondered how uncomfortable the space would become once the class began.

No one had yet come into the room so he had his choice of seats. He decided to take the center rear chair. To keep himself busy until the class would begin, he looked over the provided materials. He had read and studied everything that was in the handout several times since he was five years old and Billy resigned himself to a sentence of boredom and futility.

He didn't look up as people started to come into the room he simply heard the feet of the chairs scrape along the tiled floor as people took their seats. Their unintelligible murmuring whispers touched his ears. Next to him, one man wondered aloud when the next smoke break would be and a woman seated by him handed him some chewing gum to help. He turned his attention back to the printed material he held in his hands. Once again, he was determined this was going to be the most boring waste of time.

Moments into creating his list of miseries, something derailed his thoughts. The scent of a woman's perfume caught his nose and he looked up. His attitude made a 180-degree turn. There off to his left and ahead of him a young woman had just sat in one of the chairs. His eyes were drawn to her like a moth to flame. She had very long straight black hair, green eyes and was well blessed in the female shape. Her blue jeans fit her perfectly as did the blouse she wore. She was stunningly beautiful, perhaps more beautiful than any girl he had ever seen in his life and when she flashed a smile at him, he abandoned his misery-list project.

She reminded him of Linda Williams, the girl he accompanied to the fifth-grade dance, years ago, but this girl was more elegant and had more modesty about her. He wanted to talk to her and to get to know her. Just as he decided to stand to begin a conversation, the pastor came to the front of the class and brought things to order.

Throughout the pastor's lecture, Billy's attention was focused on the young woman. From time to time the pastor would ask a question about the material covered in the lecture. He would choose randomly among the students and even though Billy hadn't been following the monologue, he provided a correct answer when he was called. Midway through the class, Pastor Mark called for a break. The assembled students could use the bathroom, stretch their legs or smoke. Billy stood quickly and had intended to talk with her but he was too late.

Another young man from the class apparently had the same idea and was in a better position and got to her first. He seemed to be making some progress with this young woman. She smiled at him while they talked just outside of the women's restroom door. The girl was moving from foot to foot and appeared to be in need to use the toilet. Billy thought his chances were scuttled, but then something changed and she abruptly sent the young man off.

Billy began to wonder if the girl had dismissed the boy because she already had a boyfriend. He figured it wouldn't hurt to at least say hello and introduce himself. He waited outside the women's room for her, but then decided to back away. He needed to be careful how he approached her because he didn't want to appear as though he was going to ambush her but he still wanted her to know he was interested.

Fortune came his way in the form that one of the men from the class dropped a large cup of water onto the floor directly in front of the door to the women's room, causing the floor to become very slippery. The door opened and the girl stepped out. He called out for her to be careful. The girl looked down at the wet floor and then smiled at him.

"Thank you for saving me from the embarrassment of a wet stain on my butt." She looked at him and smiled. Their eyes locked and neither said anything for a few seconds. The young woman spoke first. "Hi, I'm Lori Spencer." She said as she held out her hand in greeting.

"Hello, I'm Billy Thompson." His eyes stayed locked onto hers … blue into green as he took her hand and shook it.

"Isn't Billy a kid's name?" She asked as she smiled at him.

"Well, it kind of stuck when I *was* a kid and never went away. Maybe when I get into college in a few years, I'll change it to Bill."

"I'd keep it right where it is … it's kind of cute." She started to giggle and played with her long hair. "I could call you Billy the kid, or better yet, I'll just call you cowboy."

He had never been shy before but for some reason, this girl caused him to feel, almost, uncomfortable. His eyes were still locked to hers and his heart seemed to forget how to beat properly. He knew his mouth needed to start moving but for some odd reason it refused to form words. Finally, he regained control of himself and he spoke.

"I don't recall seeing you in church before … I think I would have remembered you."

"I've been here only a few months and really haven't been to too many services, and actually never to any at this church." She said as she continued to smile at him.

"What made you come here … not that I have any problem with that at all."

"I don't know. I was driving through the area and saw this small church and something just told me to pull in the lot and check it out. I read a sign that indicated they were having classes for baptism and I decided to enroll and now I'm glad I had."

Their conversation continued through the remaining minutes of the break. Billy happily escorted her back to her seat. Before the class resumed, they managed to exchange enough information about each other and their lives to guarantee another conversation once things wrapped up for the evening.

On schedule, Pastor Mark called the class back to order. Billy was flirting with her with his eyes and he felt she was doing the same to him. They continued to trade smiles with each other being very careful not to disrupt the class or draw the attention of the pastor in the front of the room.

Billy's internal antagonist began to spread inverse ideas. Were the feelings stirring inside of him valid or were they simply a response to hormonal stimulation? Rushing into something could have devastating results. It was true that he had spent time with other girls but never in his life had he ever had a reaction like this in his heart.

Something about this girl was different. Cupid may have found him and perhaps had shot one of his arrows into his heart. He found himself hoping the love inspiring cherub many have aimed one at hers as well. Pastor Mark continued the lecture. His voice was only a faint echo in Billy's ears as he found himself paying attention only to the girl named Lori. He watched her as she involuntarily spun her hair around her fingers. He leaned forward in his seat, trying to lessen the distance between them and cursed the clock that seemed to move too slowly. Finally, Pastor Mark brought the class to closing and he reminded them they needed to attend the next two classes to qualify to be baptized. He ended with prayer and dismissed them until next Wednesday evening.

Lori stood, grabbed her purse, placed the long strap over her shoulder and flipped her long hair over her other shoulder. Billy watched, captivated by each movement she made. He then stood and tried to walk quickly so he could talk with her as they left the classroom. She looked back at him and waited for him to catch up. As they talked, they discovered they each had a common denominator in that both had lost a parent when they were younger. Billy told her that his father passed from cancer and how difficult things had been for him emotionally. She shared her mother had died in an accident and how it too had changed her and her life. Her voice broke while speaking of her mother. Billy could see the glistening evidence of tears forming in her beautiful green eyes. He thought it would be best to change the subject.

He looked at her and reached out and held her hand. It was completely involuntary and realizing the impropriety, he apologized immediately. She looked back at Billy, said nothing but more interestingly she didn't try to pull her hand from him. A strange sensation seemed to pulse through him as they once more, looked deeply into each other's eyes. Reluctantly, Billy broke the contact and looked at the floor.

"Hey, I'm sorry I didn't mean to get all in your business. It's … well I know it isn't the easiest thing for me to talk about either."

"No, don't worry, it's really sweet. I don't get much of that in my life." She said as she firmly squeezed his hand.

They came to the door of the church and walked down the front steps. Lori invited Billy to walk her to her car and he accepted her offer. As they walked into the parking lot, Billy noticed the young man who Lori had dismissed earlier, was back for another try.

"You know, I'm sorry but you didn't let me explain earlier, I already have a boyfriend." She said to the young man as she grabbed Billy's hand and lifted it into the air. "And before you ask, our parents told us we were not allowed to sit together."

The young man wrinkled his face in dissatisfaction but walked away without saying a word.

"So, I'm your boyfriend now." Billy said as he smiled widely.

"I guess we could try that if you feel up to it and you think you can handle me." Lori said jokingly.

"Why would you choose me … why not him?" Billy asked her as they stopped at her car. Lori became serious and any trace of a smile left her face.

"I could tell all he wanted was these." She said as she placed her free hand under her breast and pushed one of them upward. "The entire time he talked to me he kept looking down there and not at me."

"How do you know that's not what I'm all about?" Billy asked.

Lori looked off to the horizon and then slowly faced him. "I looked in your eyes and felt something and just before when you touched my hand, I felt it again. She shook her head and laughed. "Billy, I know you see these things … it's hard to miss them but when you first talked to me you spoke to me, not what is inside of my shirt and, you shared something very personal with me." She paused and looked him deeply in the eyes. "I see something wonderful behind those gorgeous blue eyes and I'd like to get some of it." She paused again. "Maybe God told me to come to this church, maybe I was supposed to meet you."

She still held his hand from moments ago when she dispatched the would-be Romeo as they stood next to her parked car. As the conversation continued to unfold, Billy discovered Lori was one year older than he and her birthday was in November. He discovered her favorite color was Blue and she loved sarcasm.

Lori looked at her watch and noted the time, it was getting late. They would have more time to talk before and after the next class, they would make sure of that. Lori asked him if he needed a ride home and he told her his mother would be there to pick him up but thanked her for the offer.

"You know my Mom's going to want to meet you, don't you? Because she will know something is up with me."

"That'd be great!" Lori said. "I'd like to meet the woman who raised such a wonderful son."

Billy blushed at the compliment but also felt a cringe in his gut as he remembered the last three years and how he was far from a model son. He told her goodbye as she got in her car.

"Maybe you can give me your number and I'll call you?" Billy asked.

Lori quickly opened her note book to a blank page. As she sat behind the steering wheel she wrote her name in a large cursive script and her telephone number below it. She drew two hearts beside the number and handed the page to Billy.

"I'll talk to you soon cowboy." She said as she started the engine. "Oh, and don't call me when my Dad's there, he gets upset because if the line is tied up and a sales call is missed, I get in trouble. You can call me on Thursday and Saturday after 4 o'clock." She backed out of the parking spot and drove away.

Standing alone in the church parking lot, he watched as she drove away. He looked down at the piece of paper in his hand, lovingly touching the letters of her name with his finger. He folded the paper and put it in his pocket. Within seconds of Lori's departure from the parking lot, his mother's car stopped next to him. He walked over to the passenger side and got in. Once inside he couldn't contain his excitement.

"I met a girl tonight Mom." He said very excitedly.

"That certainly explains why you're all perky. I didn't think it was because of the lecture. So, tell me about her."

"Her name's Lori Spencer, she has long dark hair and she is the most beautiful girl I have ever seen … except for you, Mom."

"Let me pull over so I can put waders on. What do you want?" His mother asked as she laughed.

"She said she'd like to meet you next Sunday at the service and fellowship."

"Well, if she's there, I'll be happy to meet her."

They continued their conversation about Lori Spencer throughout the short trip home. As they pulled in the driveway, Kathleen stopped the car so Billy could get out and open the garage door.

"Mom, don't you think it's time we got a garage door opener?" He had asked her each time they stopped at the closed door. "It's like were the only family in the free world that still needs to open a door by hand."

"Your incessant whining doesn't change the fact those things are expensive to have installed. I need to spend that money on important things like food and clothing for you."

"You could buy the thing and I can put it in. It doesn't look that hard to do. I saw one down at grandpa's old hardware store for less than fifty bucks!"

"First of all, things are always more difficult than they seem and secondly, you my dear, did not inherit your father's mechanical aptitude. I seem to remember your attempt to fix your bicycle." She looked at him with her head cocked to one side. "Now if you'd please open the door before I idle the gas completely out of the car."

Billy reluctantly got out of the car, walked to the door, dutifully reached down and pulled the door upward. The stagnant air from the garage punched Billy in the face as soon as the door was opened. His face registered the foul odor as he moved out of the way and next to his father's car. His hand rested on the rear fender, disturbing the dust that had gathered over the last three years. He watched his mother guide her car into its place. As he looked down at his hand print he thought that perhaps his father's car would become his next year. He presently imagined driving Lori to a date. His mother shut off the engine and the sound of her opening her door brought him out of his daydream. Billy closed the garage door and he and his mother walked to the house. All he could talk about was this girl named Lori.

Kathleen knew by the sound of his voice and the look in his eyes, this girl was not going to go away, at least for a while. She remembered how he was with Linda and how crushed he was when they broke up and hoped this wouldn't follow the same path. But she also saw something in her son's eyes that reminded her of her own life when she was her son's age. She remembered how James consumed her thoughts. But they had known one another since they were five and it was a completely different situation. It was true, love had to start somewhere but she worried for her son's heart and believed this was only a teenage boy's crush.

She cautioned her son that 15, year-old boys tend to get excited about girls quite easily and while he may feel like she's the one, she may be only the first one in a long line of girls. The more he talked about how a strange feeling came over him and how her eyes seemed like a magnet to his own, Kathleen began to wonder if this was simply a short infatuation or something more serious. Could lightning strike again in that church? She would know better the answer that question Sunday after meeting and speaking with this girl named Lori.

Sunday mornings had become busier in the last several weeks because Billy was once again attending the service. But this Sunday was different because this was the day Kathleen would meet Lori. So far all she had to go on was what her son had told her and the way she heard him carry on while on the telephone with her. None of this was extraordinary, so she figured meeting the girl was going to be the only way to determine the longevity and potential depth of this relationship.

Kathleen was having a difficult time deciding what outfit to wear. She had dresses, skirts and blouses covering her bed. She finally decided on a nice skirt and blouse she often wore to work. It showed confidence and professionalism, something she wanted to convey to the girl who was interviewing for the position of her son's girlfriend. As she stood in front of the mirror applying her makeup, she thought she may be overreacting to all of this and once again believed this will turn out to be a quick fling, lasting a month, perhaps two at the most.

"Billy, are you almost ready?" She called down the hallway. "It's almost time to leave."

Billy bolted from his bedroom and bounded down the steps. He couldn't wait to get to church and did everything he could to get the car loaded with the food his mother prepared the day before. Kathleen descended the steps in a lady-like manner. Her shoes made that sound that only high heels make as she walked across the wooden floor on her way to the kitchen door. He waited as patiently as he could and held the kitchen door open as she approached.

"Billy, we'll get there, I promise … so please stop rushing me."

As an afterthought, he looked at his mother and offered a compliment. "You look terrific Mom." He said as they reached the garage. He went straight for the garage door and lifted it open.

"No complaint about opening the door by hand. You seem to be incredibly happy today." Kathleen said as she looked to the ground with an obvious smile occupying her face as she passed him to get to the driver's side of the car.

As they pulled into the parking lot of the church, Billy scanned the parked cars for Lori's but couldn't locate it. They parked and Billy quickly got out of the car, removed the basket of food and very quickly delivered it to the fellowship room. His mother began to unpack the basket while he became fidgety and impatient. She smiled and suggested he should wait for Lori near the church's front door. Without hesitation, he departed her side and rushed to the entrance. Billy looked around at the surrounding people, searching for Lori. He didn't see her in the crowd and was worried she wasn't coming back. Thoughts passed through his mind thinking that he was too forward with her and he may have scared her away. Then he saw her. His heart skipped a beat as he watched her make her way up the steps to the church. She had chosen to wear a nice light blue dress and heels. Her long black hair was pulled to one side so it flowed over her left shoulder. He waved to get her attention and once she recognized him, she approached with a smile on her face.

"Good morning. It's almost as pretty a day as you." Billy said as he held out his hand for her to hold. "My Mom really wants to meet you."

Billy and Lori walked together while holding hands and they found his mother speaking to the Pastor's wife. Kathleen's attention was turned to her son and Lori as they approached. Her eyes scanned her son's girlfriend and she started making mental notes.

"Mom, Misses Jackson, I'd like to introduce you to Lori Spencer."

The pastor's wife excused herself from the conversation and went off to the Sunday school classroom.

"Hello Lori, it is a pleasure to meet you. Billy has been gushing about you and I can see why… you're quite a beautiful young woman." She said as she reached out to shake Lori's hand.

"Hello Mrs. Thompson, it's my pleasure as well. Billy never told me you were so pretty." She then added, "I see he has your eyes."

Kathleen thanked her for the compliment and offered to direct her son and Lori to their seats in the church. They started into the benches, Lori first who was followed immediately by Billy and then herself. As they sat through the service, Billy's hand always seemed to be next to or on top of Lori's. Kathleen watched them closely and was ready to react to anything beyond them touching hands. Her mind turned to James. She wished he could have been here to experience this and wondered if he would have even permitted them to sit together at church. An insult her father had issued three years ago about her not being a good mother played through her memory. Once the service had ended, Pastor Mark stood at the door of the church wishing all well and offered an invitation to fellowship.

Two lines formed the food queue. Billy and Lori chose one side and his mother took the other. He could tell she was watching them, but for reasons he couldn't explain, he didn't care. Anger didn't come as it had in the past. It was almost as if Lori was some calming force. Once they had filled their plates, Kathleen led them to a less crowded section where they could talk while they ate.

"Lori, I noticed your father isn't here—unless I missed him. Did he drop you off?"

"No, I drove. My Dad doesn't feel comfortable in a church setting. According to him, that was my mother's thing."

"So … you have a car. That's nice."

"My Dad is a salesman and he bought it for me earlier this year after I got my driver's license. He's always traveling and doesn't have time to drive me to places I want or need to go. He said he's far too busy with his customers that he can't take time from them to take me all over creation."

"Billy says you've moved a lot. Where are you from, originally?"

"I was born in Ohio and grew up in a town called Lebanon. It's between Cincinnati and Columbus. I loved it there. We were really close to an amusement park called *King's Island* and we went there all of the time. Mom loved riding the roller coasters with me. When Mom died … let's just say things changed. We moved to Indiana, then over to southern Illinois and now to here." As Lori spoke of her mother her eyes became glassy from tears.

Lori answered all of Billy's mother's questions and she responded with a few of her own for Kathleen. Overall, it seemed to go well. He breathed a sigh of relief when his mother invited her for a cookout one evening and suggested she bring her father.

After they finished their lunch, Lori and Billy excused themselves from the table. He and Lori left his mother to spend some time together alone. She held his hand as they walked about the church property but was quiet. Billy broke the silence.

"What's wrong? Did my mom cross a line?" He asked tenderly.

"No, she didn't say or do anything wrong. Your Mom's a terrific woman, you're lucky to have her." Lori stopped and pulled her hand away from Billy so she could wipe the forming tears from her eyes. "She makes me miss my mom." The tears continued to increase and began to spill down her cheeks. "Look at me, a fool crying over my mother. It's been almost ten years since she passed … I should be over this by now."

"You never get over it." Billy said as they resumed their walk. "I don't know if I'll ever get over my Dad's death." Guilt from the treatment he gave his mother over the last three years was beginning to bother him. He took a chance telling Lori about that tumultuous time. "You know, you're right. Mom is a terrific woman and I'm not this saint you think I am. I have been as cruel to her as I could be all because I felt sorry for myself about my dad's death."

Lori reached out, took his hand and held it firmly. She looked at him directly into his eyes and said nothing for several seconds but then spoke just above a whisper. "My dad and I don't get along too well either. Look your mother is very pretty and she's very smart. I wasn't just being polite or trying to score points. It's very clear she loves you and I'm a threat to her little boy." She smiled at the phrase. "So why didn't you tell me she was gorgeous?"

"I know my mother is an attractive woman. Everywhere I go with her, I see the guys looking. Even a couple of guys in my class have said she's hot. I thought it would be weird if I told you I thought my mom was pretty ... and why are we whispering?"

"Because Cowboy, I can't talk loud whenever I'm on the verge of tears." Lori said. She paused and after clearing her throat, changed the subject in her normal voice. "Remember when I told you were different? And I told you I could tell by your eyes?"

"Yea, I remember you saying that. Why?"

"It's true." She turned to face him and reached out and took his other hand. "The eyes are the gateway to the soul. If you had something to hide, or a hidden agenda, I'd see it there. "You're different than any guy I've ever known." She cut off her own words and nervousness set in as she let go of his hands.

Billy noticed the change and thought he'd redirect the conversation. "We better get back Lori before Mom sets out the dragnet." He looked at his watch and realized the day was moving far too quickly. "Can I call you in the morning?"

"How about I call you when my dad leaves the house?" She asked.

"Yea that's fine." Billy answered.

"Look, I have to go. Tell your mom I think she's great and I'll talk to you tomorrow." She hugged him and kissed his cheek and told him goodbye. He stood on the steps of the church and watched her walk to her car. As she drove away, he lifted his hand and touched his finger to where traces of her lipstick showed the touch of her kiss.

Billy walked back into the fellowship room to find his mother. He was confused about what just happened. Questions and panic were filling his mind: Did he upset her? Is she breaking up with him? Will she be back? Why did she kiss him on the cheek?

His mother met him as he walked back into the kitchen area. She looked at him and knew something was troubling him. She remained quiet until they were seated in the car but once underway, she began to talk about his mood change.

"Lori seems to be a nice girl. She's very smart, very pretty and she has a car ... which concerns me a little."

"Why?" Billy asked as he looked out the side window of the car. His chin was rested in his hand and he had a look of sadness on his face.

"For openers, a car means freedom to go to places that would otherwise be out of reach and she's older than you ... and it has a back seat."

"What's that supposed to mean?"

"We both know you're not that naive." He knew she was reminding him about the stains in his underpants from not too long ago. She let a few seconds pass before she spoke again. "Why are you so quiet?"

"Lori and I were walking around the church and when we were heading back in, she told me she had to go. We were talking about her mom and the next thing you know she's telling me bye."

"She was crying, wasn't she?" Kathleen asked.

"Yea but we—"

"—No, you don't know anything about the emotions of a girl." His mother cut him off mid-sentence. "She was upset about her mom. She probably told you I reminded her of her own mother." She looked over at her son and reached over to touch his hand. "Don't worry, she's not breaking up with you, she's probably just feeling how much she misses her." She looked at her son and added, "Welcome to love. It makes your heart soar one second and rips it to pieces the next. Oh, and by the way, are you going to keep her lipstick on your cheek all day?" She smiled as his face turned red and he began to wipe at the red lip-shaped mark on his left cheek.

Over the next two weeks, Billy and Lori spent as much time together as they could. He got to the church earlier than required and stayed a little longer after the classes and logged plenty of time on the telephone, something that was beginning to annoy his mother. She sat down with her son and set the rules for how she felt the relationship between he and Lori should be managed. Billy understood his mother was only watching out for him but he believed her meddling was completely unnecessary and overreaching.

The night before their baptism, Billy and Lori went out their first real date. That day though, at Lori's house, her father began to question her about something he had heard from someone at the church.

"I understand you've been seeing some boy there at the church. Why didn't you tell me?" Her father asked.

"I think you already know the answer to that Dad." She said with a cynical tone to her voice. "You know that every time I get a boyfriend we move?"

"I ought to smack your face right now for your disrespect."

"It wouldn't be the first time would it Dad." Lori replied.

"Have you told that boy all of your stories about my brother or are you afraid he'll drop you like a hot potato?"

"If you mean have I told him about being raped by my uncle, no I haven't—not yet anyway."

There was a great disparity between their versions of the story. According to her father, Kevin was having flash-back episodes from Viet Nam and was unfortunately, self-medicating with alcohol. When Lori came home from school, attired rather provocatively, he mistook her for someone else and tried to have sex with her. He returned to reality and realized the woman he was trying to hold was his niece and not some Vietnamese prostitute.

"Where's Uncle Kevin … he's usually sitting at the table getting drunk?" She asked.

Before her father replied, his eyes narrowed and his hand tapped the papers that sat on the table before him, indicating his frustration with his daughter's attitude and comments. "Kevin got into some trouble today down at Bernie's tavern. Allegedly, he had too much to drink and he allegedly, touched some man's wife and a fight broke out." He began to wring his hands as he spoke. "Kevin was given two choices: Jail or rehab … he chose rehab for three weeks."

Lori shook her head in disbelief as her father continued to think of his brother as the victim. At least she would have three weeks of no fear or worry of her uncle sneaking up behind her and putting his hands on her. She turned away from her father to get ready for her date with Billy.

"Lori, you're walking away from me before telling me about this boy." His tone was very serious. "I need to know who is spending time with my daughter."

She turned around to face him and took a step in his direction; her hands were balled into fists. "Really Dad, you expect me to believe you have this deep sense of protection? You're hardly here and when you are, your face is buried in those … sheets of paper and you don't pay any attention to me."

"These sheets of paper as you call them are profit and loss statements. My customer base keeps you in nice clothes and a car. You need to show some appreciation."

Lori bit her lip and took a cleansing breath. "Okay Dad, thank you for all you do for me and his name is Billy Thompson. He is a year younger than me, he lives with his mother and they go to church. I met him in our baptism prep classes. He lost his father three years ago to cancer and he is very intelligent, has blue eyes, sandy brown wavy hair and he's about six feet tall. His mother is a gorgeous blonde woman who is also very intelligent and caring. She is very conservative, takes her faith seriously and likes to have order in her life. Now, I need to get ready for my date with Billy, so if you'll excuse me, I'll be heading to the shower."

She and her father looked at each other for a moment before she turned to walk away.

"You have your mother's sarcastic streak." He said to her back as she disappeared into the hallway.

CHAPTER 5

K athleen insisted that Lori would come into the house to get her son. There would be no blowing the horn and waiting in the car. When the doorbell rang, it was Kathleen who answered and invited her in. Her eyes took in the full view of Lori as she stood in the living room. She was wearing a close-fitting navy, blue skirt and a nice blouse. Kathleen asked questions about where they were going and what time they would be back, all of which made Billy terribly uncomfortable. But Lori stood toe to toe with Kathleen and left his mother with a little more ease as she and Billy walked out of the house.

They had planned to see a movie at the Egyptian Theater near Dekalb Airport and afterward walk around town. About ten minutes into the show, they got bored and decided to walk along the streets. The thick, humid, summer-night air made them both sweaty and Billy suggested they drive back to Sycamore to Ollie's for some frozen custard. Both were a little over-dressed as they sat on the picnic benches enjoying the cold snack. Billy had, more than once, placed the cold plastic cup against his sweating forehead. Lori smiled at him and noticed they were collecting a stare or two from parents and their children. Since Lori had already seen the movie she described it quite well. Billy knew his mother would be asking questions, so he listened closely to Lori's synopsis of the story as he stirred the spoon in the now, nearly melted, liquid custard. Lori looked at her watch and then to Billy and announced a new plan for the evening.

"You want to learn to drive?" She asked.

"Yea but, I don't have my learner's permit yet."

"I know a place we can go."

She was holding his hand but started to pull him along as she started to run back to her car. She drove eastward well out of town on route 64 until they came to the Sycamore Speedway. After she turned into the parking lot, she stopped the car and suggested they switch places. For the first time in his life, Billy sat behind the wheel of a car to drive. Before they began, Lori suggested a route to follow. In the parking lot stood concrete posts that on event days were joined by chains however, now they were open and were spaced wide enough let him try parallel parking. Billy was quick to learn how to control the vehicle through the necessary maneuvers and easily could have passed his test.

Throughout the lesson, they talked and laughed. Billy parked the car and suggested they switch places before they got caught. Lori agreed and after taking over drove further east to another small town called Wasco.

Billy had been there with his father on several occasions to hunt and those memories caused him to fall silent.

"Are you Okay?" Lori asked.

"Yea, I was just thinking about my dad and how we came here to go hunting."

Lori steered the car into the parking lot of the post office on the main road, shut off the engine and suggested they get out and walk around. They were a little over dressed for a walk along the road but the nervous energy this town caused Billy had to be expended.

The air was warm and the humidity was very noticeable as were the mosquitoes. They decided to walk along a side street where there were a couple of small restaurants ... places his father called greasy spoons. Although they hadn't walked more than a block or so, Lori saw a bus stop bench and decided to rest her feet as the heels she wore where digging into her ankles. As they sat down, one of those odd periods of silence fell upon them. Billy broke the silence with a question.

"Whenever we're on the phone, you always seem distracted. Do you hate to talk on the phone?"

"No, it's ... it's what goes on at home. I told you my dad's a salesman and travels a lot and ..." Lori's voice trailed off. Something seemed to be upsetting her. "You know, I want this to be a great night. The instant I first started swimming in your blue eyes, I've wanted to go on a date with you." She stood to face him and he stood to join her. "Look at me and tell me how you feel about me." She said in a seductive whisper.

"Lori, is something going on in your house that's bad or dangerous?" Billy asked.

"Look this is our night. Please, look into my eyes and tell me what you see."

Billy let out an exasperated sigh but looked deeply into her green eyes. Moments later as a smile came to his face he told her he saw love, beauty, compassion and hope. She returned his smile and pulled him close to her and she kissed him. It began so innocently but quickly the kiss turned passionate. His tongue touched hers. When they broke apart, both were sexually charged. Billy put up his hands for her to stop.

A familiar feeling from the recent past began to surge inside of him. He forced himself to resist the boiling caldron. We need to talk about this." He said as he fought to clear his mind of the thoughts that had filled it.

"Why did you stop? Don't you want to make love to me?" She asked.

"Yea I do and it's taking everything I have to stop this." He shook his head in disbelief at what was to come out of his mouth next as he took a half step backward. "When we make love, I want it to be something special, not just a heated moment in your back set." Lori looked at him with the slightest hint of a grin. He continued. "Lori Spencer, I want to see if you're the one. Like my mom was to my dad, the one that no one can pull me away from. Since I looked in your eyes on that first night, you hooked my heart and I don't want to ruin it by jumping onto something."

At first, Lori said nothing but looked intently at the young man standing before her. Her subtle grin became a laugh.

"Billy Thompson, you passed the test. I thought you might actually try and make love to me. You know we've only known each other for three weeks and I'm not ready to cross that line yet."

"Then why did you just do what you did?" Billy asked with a very confused look on his face.

"I needed to know if you really like me or if you just want these things." This was yet another reference to her breasts. "You're smart and very charming. I would have hated to tell you goodbye." Lori stirred the ground with her foot and she worked through her thoughts. "But you ... you are so different and I wanted to make sure you're being honest with me." The smile fell from her face and she became serious. "You want to make sure you love me before we have sex ... I'm perfectly fine with that." Lori closed the distance between them. "When we're ready, we'll make love and not a moment sooner. So, can you handle that?"

"You bet I can." Billy answered as he gave a quick kiss on her cheek.

The time was getting on and Lori suggested they get going or they would be super late getting home. The drive home was filled with further discussion of *their* future which unfortunately led her to one dangerous topic: her uncle.

She needed to be honest with Billy. After what transpired in Wasco just minutes ago, she knew she couldn't hide the truth from him—not if she was to have a real relationship with him. But she was worried that when she told Billy what her uncle did to her and what she believed he did to her mother, she would be alone, just as her father suggested might happen. So, if he did love her, this wouldn't make any difference and instead of running away from her, he would run to her to protect her and make certain it could never happen again. Her sudden silence was noticed by Billy.

"What's wrong?" He asked.

"Billy there's something really important I need to tell you before you commit to a serious relationship with me. If I expect you to be honest with me, then I need to be the same with you."

Lori squeezed the steering wheel nervously as she began to tell Billy how her uncle raped her when she was 13 years of age and how her father covered it up, and continued to do so to the present. She explained how her father watches her closely and becomes very nervous whenever she starts dating. Certain topics of conversation can have deep consequences in her family.

"Dad always uses the excuse that the current market becomes saturated and he needs to move to new territory to find new sales. I accepted this would be my life until I turned 18 and if I kept his brother a safe distance from me, I'd be alright. And then, we moved here, I found that church, decided I would fulfill my mother's wish of getting baptized and then I meet you … probably about two years too early." She stopped to wipe tears that began to fill her eyes. "You crossed that line in my heart. I tried to keep it from happening but for some unknown reason, the harder I resisted the further and faster I fell."

There was an awkward silence in the car. Billy looked shell shocked. His mind was trying to process everything Lori had said and he weighed his options, which were few. He could accept her and this situation or he could walk away and possibly walk away from the deepest love he could ever experience in his life.

"Let me get this straight. Your dad is doing everything he can do to hide a criminal and enable him to continue to do what he's been doing. Lori that could put them both in jail … aiding and abetting is serious stuff.

"I think he killed my mom." The words came out with malice. "I think he raped and drown her in our pool so she couldn't turn him in. He was at the house that day. When I came home from school, I found my mom floating face down in the water." She began to cry. "The police and my father said she fell into the water while she was trying to save a dog." She tried to get control of her emotions. "Billy I'll never get the sight of her hair floating around her face … her arms stretched out. I called to her but she didn't answer and when I jumped in the water to help her I noticed her eyes were motionless and when I turned her over … it was obvious she was dead. Then my uncle came out of the house. He was soaked so I knew he had been in the water and the look on his face said he was guilty and up to no good. I yelled for him to call the ambulance and he just stood there. When he wouldn't do anything, I got out of the pool and ran into the kitchen to make the call myself. Like I said, the police called it an accident and the marks on her neck and arms were caused by my uncle trying to rescue her."

"So, you believe your dad used money and position to get his brother off and will move again if he finds out about us." He paused. "You know there's no statute of limitation on murder?" If they or can prove he did it, he could still go to jail."

"There will be no further investigation, too many people will get in trouble if the truth comes out and we both know hush money is money well spent." After a brief pause, she added, "Please don't share any of this with your mom … please."

Billy agreed to keep the secret but also wondered what he was getting himself into. He really felt something wonderful when he was with Lori and didn't want it to end but at the same time, getting mixed up in this dysfunction, was it worth it?

As he looked at Lori's profile, his answer came. His heart had begun to write a list that his head had better pay attention. He needed her touch, to smell her perfume to hear her voice and to feel her lips against his. His heart would break without these things. He asked himself: How do you fall in love with someone you've dated just once? It was the question his mother had asked and now he was asking it to himself. He cared more for Lori and her feelings than his own. She caused him to peel the layers of his emotions, to go deeper into himself causing him to want to protect her and protect the feeling he got whenever he looked at her or when they touched. His answer was an overwhelmingly strong yes, this was worth it.

When Lori pulled into the driveway of Billy's house, they both noticed the light was on downstairs and the television turned on. Billy said goodnight and promised to see her tomorrow at church, kissed her once more and waved goodbye. After her car was no longer in sight, he turned and started for the front door.

The revelation Lori presented was still playing in his mind. He was sworn to secrecy so he couldn't talk to his mother about it. She would have been able to offer some advice to them both, perhaps even stop this danger from going any further. But then there was the other danger as well and that was she would forbid him to go anywhere near Lori. He slid the key into the lock and slowly turned it. A squeaky door hinge announced his arrival and woke his mother who was sleeping on the couch.

Kathleen stirred and came to her feet. She could smell Lori's perfume on his clothes but also noticed he was very reserved.

"You're awfully quiet. When I got home from a date with your dad, I was always bubbly and gushing. Did your date go alright? Do you want to talk about it?"

"I'm just thinking about tomorrow Mom."

"Not buying it. Something happened tonight ... something's eating at you,"

Involuntarily it came out. "If Lori's dad finds out about us, he'll move again."

"Billy, he already knows. He knows because Judy Jackson likes to talk. Lori is a minor and he needed to sign a permission form for her to get baptized. And, while the two of you were on your date, he called me on the phone to talk. I invited him and Lori to a cookout tomorrow to celebrate your baptisms. Besides, how are you going to be able to hide your enthusiasm when the two of you get next to one another tomorrow?"

"I know you're going to think I'm crazy but ... I think I'm falling in love with Lori."

She didn't overreact, she knew this might happen and was prepared for it. She slowly sat down on the couch, placed her hands on her lap, looked at her son and began. "Billy, you're 15. When your father and I were this age, we started to get serious, so I know it's possible. But we knew each other for ten years, you've know her for all of three weeks. It's a bit of a difference, wouldn't you agree?"

"I knew you were going to say that. I'm not saying we're getting married any time soon, but we want to be exclusive to each other. I'm thinking like you and Dad through high school and maybe getting married after college."

"Well I'm glad you've though this through." She said with a touch of sarcasm. "Billy in just one year, things can change, you might not feel the same about her. What happens when another pretty girl comes along and wants your attention? What happens to Lori then? I don't think it's

a good idea for you to put all of your emotional eggs in one basket …
at least not at your age." The memory of her mother giving her the
same lecture years ago suddenly played in her mind. She had cautioned
her about putting too much of her heart into James Thompson. As a
teenager, she thought her mother was meddling, much like her son
probably did now, but she, like her mother, was only looking out for the
best interest of her child.

Lori parked her car in her driveway. The house was dark except for a
single light in the kitchen and the porch light next to the kitchen door.
She entered the house and as she walked through the kitchen, on the
table, was a note from her father.

> *Lori,*
>> *We've been invited by Kathleen to a cookout. I plan to*
>> *Attend so there's no need for you to drive. Mrs. Thompson*
> *suggests you*
>> *Wear dark clothes that dry easily or bring others to change into.*
>> *Hope your date went well.*
> *Dad*

The note left her confused and guarded. There was no sarcasm,
no threats, nothing that was usually present in their conversations.
She knew if her feelings for Billy were made known, it would be only
a matter of time before a FOR SALE sign would be planted in the
front yard. She walked to her bedroom and quietly got herself ready
for bed. Before she could sleep, she needed to make an entry into
her journal.

> *Tomorrow is the day I get baptized. Not only do I start a new life*
> *with my faith, I take another step forward in a life that may bring*
> *me closer to Billy. I don't understand why I have been so drawn to*

him in such a short time but the fact remains I can't imagine my life with anyone else.

Tonight, he told me no to sex because he wants to make sure he loves me. My heart beats stronger for him now more than ever. I want to tell my dad that I think I have found my one but I know he will end this relationship as he had the other. But Tom Yelton, in Indiana, was nothing compared to Billy

The next morning the alarm clock sounded, Billy got out of bed and headed for the bathroom. Kathleen was up earlier and had already gotten herself bathed but had not yet gotten dressed for the service. While he was in the shower, she pulled some clothes out for her son to wear. Recalling her baptism experience, anything made of cotton would stay very wet and become cold, so she had chosen pants and a shirt that were lighter and would dry quickly.

At 40 years of age she was still a very attractive woman and could have worn anything she wanted. She had gone through several outfits before settling on what she had chosen to wear. Once she had herself dressed, makeup and hair in place, she turned her attention to the kitchen downstairs and the food she prepared last night. It was packed up in the refrigerator and would be easy to carry to the car when they left the house, which would be very soon.

"Billy, come on, we need to get moving. You know you take longer to get ready than a woman?"

"My hair is screwed up Mom." He said from the top of the stairs. The cowlick nemesis had returned. He held a brush in one hand and a spray bottle of water in the other. "I need to look good today."

"Billy, you're going to be dunked under the water. I don't think it's going to make a difference what your hair looks like."

Once the challenges with his hair were overcome, Billy and his mother arrived at church, bringing with them their contribution of food for the Fellowship meal after the service. When the food was properly stored, she went into the main sanctuary and caught up with her son who was speaking to Lori. Kathleen's eyes took in Lori's appearance and began to wonder if she might have chosen the wrong clothing for the occasion. She was wearing a green, form-fitting dress. Her long dark hair was in such contrast it made her seem to glow. The color of the dress also brought out the color of her eyes. She could not deny that Lori Spencer was indeed a beautiful young woman and judging by their glances, several of the men seemed to agree with her.

"Hello Lori and congratulations on the day." Kathleen said. "Is your father here yet?"

"That's him just coming in now from parking the car."

She waved to a man a little more than six-foot-tall and of slender build. He had a polished appearance and a general air of confidence as he walked through and around the small groups of people that stood between himself and his daughter. He stopped when he reached Lori's side and his eyes quickly scanned Kathleen and Billy.

"Dad, these are the Thompsons ... Kathleen and Billy." Lori said.

He shook Billy's and Kathleen's hands as calmly and as easily as could be. His experience from the years of selling provided him a calm and confidence as he announced his name. "Hello, I'm Tim Spencer."

Billy looked at her father and a sudden wave of anger came over him. How dare he look at them and pretend that he had done nothing wrong. Lori's father picked up on the attitude, hidden behind Billy's eyes. Thankfully the music started to play and this was everyone's signal to be seated in the hard, wooden benches. Those who would be baptized were seated on old wooden fold-up chairs near the front of the church.

Lori's father sat in the group of benches opposite of Kathleen. He positioned himself so he could monitor Billy, his mother and his daughter. Judging from Billy's reaction earlier, his daughter told the young man something.

The service went on as scheduled and when the time came, Pastor Mark and one of the church elders, climbed into the baptismal pool, waiting at its center. One by one, children first, they would walk into the water and be baptized. Kathleen had noticed the process hadn't changed at all from when she was baptized. Off to the side of the pool was a place for parents or other family members to stand to take photos of the person as they were baptized and offer congratulations after they climbed the steps out of the water.

Slowly the queue moved forward and it was Lori's turn. Kathleen had moved to the viewing area and wondered why Tim had not joined her. She readied her camera and decided to capture Lori's baptism for him. Pastor Mark motioned for her to enter the water. Billy watched with attention as she descended into the pool. He watched as her hands pushed the dress down as it attempted to float to the surface of the water as she moved deeper. A few steps and she met the two men waiting in the pool. She turned, faced Billy and those awaiting their turn. The Pastor and his assistant lowered her beneath the water and baptized her. When she surfaced after her immersion, she stood looking directly at Billy and grinned. After turning toward the exit steps and before reaching them, she went below the water again, surfaced with her head tilted back to straighten her long hair. As she climbed the steps to exit the pool, Billy's eyes took note of how everything glistened as the water cascaded down her hair and over the darkened green dress which was now painted to her body. She was quickly covered with a towel to provide modesty and to prevent an unwanted spectacle.

Unfortunately, the woman who had been distributing the towels wasn't quick enough. A barrage of flashbulbs from cameras captured Lori's assent from the water. Billy watched the men who had gathered near the front and registered an opinion about their lack of morals. In front of the group was Kathleen Thompson and her eyes displayed disappointment and irritation.

Billy was welcomed to the water next. He stood with his hands in front of him, slightly below the belt. Lori's turn in the water had aroused him and he tried to hide the embarrassment that was presenting itself. As the cool water soaked into his clothing, his concern was vanishing with each step he took. After he was baptized, he climbed the steps to exit the water and was, like all those before him, covered by a towel. His mother was close to the exit of the pool, took his picture and congratulated him with a kiss on his cheek. As Billy walked to join the others, a smug grin covered his face. The iniquitous men with their cameras seemed to help solidify his position with organized religion. As he approached the old, wooden fold-up chairs set aside for them his eyes caught sight of Lori directing him to the seat to her right. After he eagerly accepted it, she leaned over to him and whispered in his ear, "Congratulations cowboy, I love you." Billy smiled responded in-kind and held her hand. The anger he held for her father and the men with their cameras, had suddenly vanished.

Once the service had ended, everyone went over to the fellowship room. Most of those who were baptized had changed clothes and they sat comfortably while they accepted congratulations. Neither Billy nor Lori had brought a change of clothing with them but their clothes were light and dried quickly. As the fellowship ended Lori and her father were once again invited by Kathleen to come to the house for a cook out. Tim Spencer was more than happy to accept the invitation and let his daughter know that she would be riding with him to the Thompson's.

As preparations were underway at the house, Billy asked his mother what she and Lori's father were discussing at fellowship. His anger toward Lori's father was not well hidden.

"We were just talking about the past and the future." Kathleen said. And why do you have this subtle dislike for Tim?

"You didn't suggest to him that Lori and I might be getting serious, did you?"

"What difference would that make anyway? And please answer my question."

"Mom, we talked about this! He has a history of moving whenever she gets serious with someone!" He avoided the second part of her question.

"Listen to me. I know you're all wrapped up in Lori and believe every word she says is true … I get it. But there are two sides to each story and honestly, from what I heard today from Tim, her math doesn't add up."

"What math … what story?" His insides seemed to be collapsing.

"The story where she claims Tim's brother raped her." His mother looked at him sternly. "I know you've been told. And to be honest, I must ask, why would you get involved or stay involved with that kind of mess?"

The story was now public knowledge, at least to the point where his mother knew about the topic, so he could discuss it without breaking his promise to Lori. He started to boil inside and as much as he wanted to engage his mother, he knew he would do well to keep his mouth shut. Unfortunately, his eyes spoke as loud as his mouth could.

"You disagree, that's fine." Kathleen said. "You don't know this girl well enough to choose sides in this fight so I'd be really careful what you say young man."

"You're right Mom I don't have a long history with her but let me say this. While she told me about the attack, her entire body became stiff and it was almost like fear gripped her. So, she's either telling the truth or she's one great actress." He then turned away from her and started with the preparations for their guests. Unfortunately, his mother wasn't finished talking about Lori.

"I would have thought Lori would have chosen a different dress for her baptism."

"What's that supposed to mean?" Billy asked with an obvious edge to his voice. He didn't want to renew the war between them that had lasted almost three years, but his mother was attacking the woman he loved and he would not let that go unchallenged.

"Billy, she chose that dress for a reason and that reason was to get your attention. Well it worked. I could tell that … everyone in the church could tell that! Your hands didn't hide everything you know."

His face blushed with embarrassment as he fidgeted while he tried to produce an answer that was both intelligent and battle-worthy. Finally, he replied to her volley. It was a question that was weak but it was all he had.

"Yea Mom, let me ask you this. What about all of the dirty old men that seemed to be standing by the baptismal pool?" He responded to her with the same anger he held just months ago. "They didn't seem to be too interested in the other people from the class."

Kathleen, like her son, had no desire to relive the past three years and decided to back down. "Look, your right, I suppose I'm just trying to protect you from getting hurt."

Her surrender calmed him and his anger diminished. "Mom, I know that and I appreciate that, but we're not doing anything, we've talked about it. We decided to wait to cross that line until we're ready and not a moment sooner." Billy said as he placed his hand on his mother's shoulder.

"Let's just hope you're not ready for a while. I'd hate to see you both, compromise your futures because it seemed like a good thing to do at the time." She said as she looked at her son and feigned a supportive smile.

A few hours after church, Tim Spencer turned his car into the Thompson's driveway. He surveyed the house and neighborhood. "It's a little smaller than I expected. Don't you think you might want to shoot for someone a little … better off?"

"Dad, Billy will be going to college, probably on a full ride. He's very smart ... and some people don't need to show off with a big house." Lori said in the defense of the home and its occupants.

Billy opened the door to let them in. He didn't kiss Lori when she said hello, he wanted to hide that from her father. He next greeted Tim Spencer and welcomed him to the house. Billy had reminded himself to keep his feelings about Lori's father well-hidden or there would be trouble. Luckily, his mother stepped in to greet them, and invited them to the back of the house where an umbrella and chairs offered shade from the hot July sun. Conversation began, most of it between Kathleen and Tim, and before long they were talking about family and how they had struggled through life after the death of their spouses. As Lori's father spoke of his wife, Kelly, he appeared to become emotional. Billy looked over to Lori. She had never seen her father fill with emotion so this was new to her. Billy knew Tim was a salesman and wondered if what was playing out before them was real or an act.

Tim began to explain he had never shown these emotions to anyone because they were simply too difficult to process. As Lori's father spoke further, her eyes became wet with tears and Billy had noticed his mother's eyes were sparkling as well. Still this wasn't a clear indication of the truth, not to Billy anyway.

Kathleen wiped at her eyes, stood and excused herself. An awkward silence fell over those seated at the table. Billy wanted to hold Lori's hand or show some support and affection but he knew he could not. Thankfully, moments later Kathleen returned with several photo albums and placed them on the table. Tim and Lori viewed pages of photos, some of them going back to when Kathleen and James were dating. They progressed through the albums and the life of the Thompson family up to right before his father had gotten sick.

Emotion was rising in Billy and as a tear rolled down his face, his mother had mercifully suggested it was time to begin cooking. Billy volunteered to work the grill. Unfortunately, he had no talent for cooking and after converting the first three burgers into hockey pucks and immolating a few hot dogs, Lori stepped into help. "Someday I'll teach you to cook Billy." Her guard had fallen and the words that had just left her mouth let everyone at the table know there was a connection between them. But it was the way she rested her hand on his arm and stood next to him that made the bolder statement.

There was no denying it and it was in full view of both of their parents. The closeness between him and Lori could be seen by even the most unobservant person in the world let alone someone as keen as her father. Oddly Tim Spencer seemed to be relaxed and even pleased that they were together. She had seen this before in her father, his tacit approval but then out of nowhere the moving trucks come. Lori realized what she had done and was convinced she would soon be packing her belongings to move to another town.

Time passed quickly and soon evening had arrived. Billy's animosity toward Tim Spencer had softened a bit and when her father showed some affection toward Lori, he felt better about their chances of staying in Sycamore. The Spencer's thanked their hostess and got into their car and left for home. On the way Tim began a conversation that was not exactly what Lori expected.

"Kathleen is a very likeable woman. She's pretty and very smart too and she thinks a lot of you." Her father said.

"Okay Dad, so when are we going to move?"

"I never said anything about moving. I'd like to stick around here for a while and see how things might work out with your boy-friend's mom."

"So, what happens when your brother gets out of rehab and starts nosing around?"

"I think you need to drop it about my brother. Everything will be fine."

Her father's behavior was very unusual. He had been exposed to attractive women in the past but he never made any effort to cultivate a relationship. He was too busy protecting his brother and rationalizing his actions. Was this a game, a way to break down her walls and admit how close she was getting to Billy? She worried she had already exposed too much of her true feelings for him. But there were other questions surfacing. After meeting Billy's mom, did he finally reach a breaking point with Kevin and was ready to move on? How would Kevin react to being set aside for some woman?

Over the next weeks, Lori's father did spend time with Kathleen and had even taken her out to dinner on a Saturday evening. This did not sit well at all with Billy. His anger and distrust for Tim Spencer had returned in full measure. He talked about it with his mother and it started an argument.

"Mom, you of all people ... Ms. Rationality, the woman with the *true moral compass*, can stand here and accept the fact that he hid what his bother did to his own daughter, and knowing all of this, go on a date with this man!"

"I am your mother and I will NOT be lectured by you! I told you before, there are two sides to each story and frankly, I tend to lean toward an adult whose judgment isn't clouded by hormones!"

"Have you ever met his brother? Because, you know, from what I've heard he's a real piece of dirt!"

The argument continued for a bit longer and eventually they went their separate ways. She got ready for her date with Tim and Billy was getting ready for his date with Lori. Once they had both gotten dressed, they met once again in the hallway at the top of the stairs. Billy looked at his mother and started to laugh.

"Mom, I'm sorry. I have my feelings and so do you. By the way, you look very nice. Tim's a lucky guy to have you on his arm."

Kathleen looked suspiciously at her son. "I'm not sure how to take that." She said.

"Look, I know I said some things I shouldn't have said and I'm sorry. I still don't like her father, but that's my problem."

Kathleen stepped toward her son and hugged him. "By the way, you look nice too. I'm not saying Tim and I are getting married but I do enjoy spending time with him. I'll tell you this, if I do find out he's a scoundrel, I won't spend another second with the man."

A short time later the doorbell rang. Kathleen opened the door and met Tim on the porch. She didn't invite him into the house she simply walked with him to his car. Billy watched through the window and shook his head, trying to accept what was happening.

About half an hour later Lori arrived to pick up Billy and as she had done before, she walked to the front door and rang the doorbell. When he greeted her to let her in, he couldn't help but notice she was wearing the same dress she did when she was baptized. His anger with Tim Spencer evaporated.

"You look terrific." Billy said has he put his arms around her and kissed her.

"I have plans for after dinner … I think you're going to like them."

Billy was very curious and tried to get an idea about what was in store but she wouldn't say. She had an impish grin on her face which did nothing but make Billy even more curious.

They drove to a newly opened hotel on the west side of town. It housed a very nice, highly rated restaurant where Lori had made dinner reservations. He had no idea where his mother and Tim had gone and he hoped they didn't cross paths. As they enjoyed dinner and conversation, the stress of Lori's father's indiscretion, faded.

Billy didn't know it but Lori had reserved a room and after they had finished with dinner, she led him to the elevator. Once the bell chimed and the door opened, she took him by the hand and led him through the hallway, stopping outside of a very beautifully decorated door.

She dangled a key from her fingers and after opening the door, she kissed him and suggested he should enter first. After she followed him into the room, she closed the door behind her and leaned against it, posing very seductively. She looked at Billy and asked him to sit on the edge of the bed and wait for her. Moments later, she returned from the bathroom. Billy could clearly see she was no longer wearing anything beneath the dress. She approached him and he stood. He leaned in to kiss her but she held her hands up to stop him.

"Have you decided if you love me or not?" She asked as their eyes came together. Her pretty features showed so many emotions. Her green eyes were locked to his blue and after a moment he answered.

"With all my heart, I love you."

"Then I won't tell anyone if you don't."

They made love and spent every minute they had available to them in passion. Lori had earlier set the alarm clock to alert them lest they would be late getting home. After making love, she was restless as she lay next to him but Billy seemed to be content and not nervous at all. She decided to get a shower and rolled away from him. Lori reached for her dress and walked to the bathroom.

Billy was confused. Her sudden nervousness was beginning to cause him some concern. He stood from the bed and stopped at the bathroom door. It wasn't locked so he cautiously went in. The water was running and she was in the shower but she hadn't closed the curtain completely. Her dress had fallen from the hook and lay on the floor in a puddle of water. He announced his presence, startling her and she shut off the water.

"Hey, you know your dress is soaked?" He asked, attempting to start into a conversation about his uneasy feelings that had been brewing since she left him alone in bed.

"Oh no, I thought it was on the hook." She said as she quickly pulled the curtain to the side. "Billy, get your shower while I take this thing to the laundry room! She immediately began drying herself with the towel she had hanging by the shower and in moments, she had her undergarments in place. She borrowed one of the large plush white robes in the closet and dashed out of the room.

He was now alone and his mind began to create a host of reasons why Lori may have had this change of heart. Did his mother say something to her or did he move too fast toward the prize of making love to her? A flash of guilt came over him and he wondered if what he told Lori was true or, did he say it so they would have sex. He did love Lori, more than anything—or at least he thought so. The voice of his mother could be heard echoing in his mind's ears ... What happens when another pretty girl catches your eye? But there would be no other girl. The thought of not having Lori by his side was like a death sentence. His heart belonged to her and this gilt, well that was an obstacle his mother placed in his way. No, this was not a mistake, and some day, those around him would raise a glass of champagne at their wedding. As he processed those thoughts, he finished his shower and got dressed.

Lori had returned to the room, kissed him, and suggested she needed to dry her hair. Billy watched her pull the brush through her long hair as the hair dryer evaporated the moisture. He approached her, put his arms around her waist and asked the question that had been forming in his mind since she had left the bed so abruptly.

"Is something wrong ... Did I say or do something wrong?

She shut off the dryer and turned to look at him, eye to eye. A smile came to her face as she placed her palm against his cheek.

"No, my sweet cowboy, you haven't done anything wrong." Her smile widened as she paused. "You know we're running out of time and the last thing I wanted to do was to be late bringing you home ... your mom would kill me." She leaned toward him and kissed him. "Could you check on my dress while I finish my hair and makeup?"

After returning to the room, they gathered their few belongings and they left. The material of her dress was still slightly damp but at least it wouldn't be dripping as they rode the elevator to the main floor. Once they were in the car, the ride back to his house was filled with conversation about her uncle and father.

"Billy, I told my dad I forgive him for what he did … for all of it."

"Lori, are you crazy? The man is harboring a fugitive from justice and as you said before, he may do it again."

"Look, I didn't want to ruin our night talking or arguing about this but I need you to understand me. Since I have been going to church and reading the Bible, I have been feeling like I need to practice forgiveness." Billy looked across the car at her as if she had completely checked out of reality. "What does it say in the Bible about forgiveness? Jesus said if you forgive, the Father will forgive you and if you don't forgive, you won't be forgiven. It's all over the place Billy … we're supposed to be Christian people. So, if I can forgive my father then I think you can too. That alone could go a long way to keeping me and Dad here—and us together."

"What about Kevin … are you going to forgive him too?" Billy asked with a touch of sarcasm.

"I'm still working on that one."

Billy began to laugh and almost immediately, Lori joined in. As her car came to a stop in front of the Thompson home, they noticed her father's car was there. The lights were on in the front room and it was obvious that someone was moving around. Billy's animosity toward Lori's father returned but not as strong. He figured his mother was a smart woman and would handle the situation the best way possible.

He once again suggested Lori to speak to his mother and give *her* side of the story. At first Lori said nothing but after a moment she began.

"Billy, I understand you want to protect your mom." She paused to choose her next words. "I'll talk to your mom and let her know my side of the story … I promise."

"Lori, she already knows your side of the story based on your father's version. She needs to hear yours."

They walked to the front door of his house. He took a cleansing breath and with some trepidation, turned the knob and slowly opened the front door. The squeaky hinges announced their arrival and drew the attention of the two adults sitting on the couch watching a rented movie on the television.

"Hello …won't the two of you join us?" Kathleen asked through a smile. Billy and Lori slowly walked over and sat together on the couch. Billy could tell that Lori was a little concerned about leaving a damp spot on the couch cushion but her dress had dried enough it wasn't a problem.

Without warning, the rented movie's video cassette had some issues and the picture became jumbled. There was an odd sound that came from the VCR and suddenly the TV screen turned blue. Kathleen jumped off the couch pressed stop, followed by the eject button. The door opened and the plastic cassette popped out. As she removed the cassette, the ribbon of crumpled video tape reluctantly followed from the player. Tim suggested the cassette was old and probably worn out. Billy and Lori didn't care about the movie anyway they just pretended to be interested.

Tim decided it was getting late and took his leave of Kathleen. He offered her a peck on the cheek, told Billy he would see them tomorrow and reminded Lori to be home soon, then opened the front door of the house and left them.

This was Lori's opportunity to tell Kathleen her side of the story and suggested to Billy that he might need to find something in his room and leave her and his mother alone so they could chat privately.

Kathleen could tell something hid behind Lori's green eyes as she watched Billy walk up the steps to his room. Once she heard the door close, Kathleen began.

"You're going to tell me your side of the story, aren't you?"

"I'm going to make this very quick." Lori took a deep breath. "My uncle has a long scar on his penis that goes from the tip to half way up its shaft." She looked directly into Kathleen's eyes as she spoke. "I know the only way to prove that is to have that piece of dirt drop his pants in front of you but ask yourself, how disturbing is it why I would know that?" She continued. When he's around and I'm alone, I am scared to death. I know it's only a matter of time before he does it again."

Kathleen looked down at the floor after Lori had spoken. She could read people well and she could tell, what Lori was telling her was the truth. Questions began to play in her mind but she didn't ask Lori any of them.

Lori was visibly shaken by what she had said and Kathleen reached out to hold her. After a brief silence between the two women, Lori asked to have Billy come back down so she could tell him goodnight.

CHAPTER 6

Tim Spencer drove to the church separately from his daughter. After arriving he immediately sought out Kathleen but when he found her, she was cold and distant.

"What's going on?" He asked

"We need to go someplace private." Kathleen stated curtly. Tim was surprised by her sudden change of attitude toward him, but led her back to his car and suggested they could talk there. After looking around to make sure no one was near, she began to speak in a hushed voice. "I spoke to your daughter last night after you left and she had a much different version of the story about what your brother did to her." She again looked around to make sure there was no one close to them as they talked.

"Kathleen, Lori loves attention and she'll sometimes exaggerate things to get it." Tim said as he nervously played with his hands, something Kathleen easily noticed.

"So, is she making up the part about the scar on your brother's privates?"

The color ran out of Tim's face and he became even more nervous. "Look, Kevin saved my life in a bar-fight a few years ago and I owed him."

Kathleen's face changed with Tim's last statement. He could tell by her expressive eyes, Vesuvius was about to erupt.

"Your brother raped your daughter you hid it from the police and still let him come around her, that's criminal Tim." She spoke in a very dangerous whisper.

He tried to plead his case but every one of his reasons seemed hollow. Kathleen had heard enough.

"You sold out your own child—the product of your love for your wife—to hide a man who had your back in a bar!" She shook her head in disbelief. "You disgust me! I can't believe I actually considered continuing our relationship!"

She turned and walked away. Tim watched as her long blond hair trailed behind her, suspended in the wind caused by her quick pace. He looked down at the ground feeling shamed and as he watched Kathleen walk away, he thought of chasing after her but knew she would not listen to a word he said. He made one terrible mistake years ago and was now paying a huge price for that mistake in the present. There was nothing to do now but to return home to start over.

Kathleen came back into the church and was visibly upset. Billy knew something was wrong as soon as he caught sight of her. As Lori stood by his side, he asked why Tim wasn't with her.

"Let's just say I don't think he'll be back to church again." She told them both what happened. Lori began to panic.

"Oh no, I've got to fix this or we're going to move away." Lori said as she looked around wildly. "I've got to go home and talk to him." Tears were forming in her eyes. "Love you Billy." She said as she turned and quickly walked out the door.

Billy's worst fears were unfolding before him. His relationship with Lori had just developed a rapidly approaching expiration date. His panic turned to anger which was directed toward his mother. He was so incensed that he walked out of the church. His mother ran to catch up with him. She grabbed his arm to stop him from leaving.

"Why do you want to involve yourself in this mess? She asked.

"Because Mom, I'm the one that's supposed to save her."

She shook her head at her son. "Billy, you were right. The man is a horrible person. I can't believe I actually let someone like that in my home."

"Mom, I don't understand how all of this works out but he seems to like you."

"I don't believe my ears! For the last few weeks, you have been suggesting … excuse me, demanding, I stay away from him because of what he allowed his brother to do to Lori, but now you're defending him. You're so blinded by what you feel for that man's daughter you're doing essentially the same thing … looking the other way so you get what you want!"

"Mom, what he did was wrong and I don't like it any more than you but he was trying to apologize and he was trying to do the right thing. What's faith say about forgiveness … hate the sin not the sinner."

"Billy, you said it … he's a salesman and he can sell anything to anyone. I'm sorry Billy, he lied to me and everyone else and I don't believe it's in *your* best interests to be tangled up in this … this mess."

"What about my feelings Mom?" Billy asked with a hint of a whimper in his voice.

"Yours, what about my feelings … don't they count for anything?"

Let's talk about your feelings Mom. Ever since you and Tim started seeing each other, you've been undeniably happier. Yea, you're right. I pitched a fit about him, but Lori and I have been talking it through. She told me, if *she* can forgive her father, then *I* should be able to do the same and move on." He was breathing hard and began to pace. "I was going to tell you all of this later today, after church ... actually Lori and I had planned to tell you together."

Kathleen looked at her son. He was trying everything he could to save his relationship with Lori. Why was this so important to him? She thought back to James and their brief break up in their senior year in high school and how James had worked so hard to get back with her. Maybe Billy did love her. But still there was the fact Tim Spencer lied to her. Hate the sin not the sinner, the words passed through her mind again. She decided she would try to apologize to Tim and convince him to remain in Sycamore, for her son's sake. Maybe in the future she could grow to forgive him, but now that wasn't a possibility.

"Billy, where is Lori's house?" She asked.

"They live in Hannover on Templeton Court. The house number is 1959." Billy said with some irritation in his voice

"Billy, can you walk home after the service? I'm going over there now to see if I can apologize and smooth this over."

Kathleen didn't wait for an answer. She turned toward her car in the parking lot and once moving squealed the tires as she sped off to the address on Templeton. Billy stood alone as he watched her car disappear around the corner.

Lori parked her car in the driveway, next to her father's and quickly came into the house. As she entered the side door a foreboding feeling came over her. She saw her father sitting at the table with the phone book open and a pad of paper. He was compiling a list of realtors ... they would soon be moving. An intense urgency filled her once she began to speak.

"Dad, we need to talk about this, please!" Lori voice cracked with tears.

Her father looked up at her and could see the droplets begin to stream down her cheeks.

"I'm sorry honey, but I can't do business where I've been embarrassed. My customers will start to leave me and new ones won't come." He let out a sighing breath. "It's too bad too because this area was good for me." After another pause, he looked at his daughter. "You know this is your fault. If you had kept your mouth shut about my brother none of this would have happened. We wouldn't need to move. Billy and you would be together and Kathleen would still be with me."

Lori's sadness suddenly turned to anger. "This is not my fault! Your brother is an animal and predator and should be put in a cage to protect women who live in a civilized society!

Lori's response was interrupted by the sound of the doorbell. Tim stood from his seat at the table, stared at Lori as he walked past her and preceded to the front door. After he opened it he came face to face with Kathleen Thompson.

"I suppose what you said to me at church wasn't enough." He told her.

"Tim, I came to apologize. I let emotions get the better part of my judgment, and I broke the first rule I was taught about management: weigh all of the evidence before acting." She looked at him for a second. "Can we talk?"

He opened the door and invited her in, suggesting they go to the kitchen to talk. Tim asked Lori to give them some privacy. She went to her room and slammed the door behind her.

"Well it seems everyone is angry with me." He said as they sat at the table.

"I didn't come here to continue our argument. I've already expressed my opinion."

"So why are you here?"

"Our kids seem to be very close to each other. Billy says he's in love with your daughter and Lori seems to feel the same about Billy." She nervously shifted in her chair. "I was lectured by my son in the parking lot about forgiveness and turning the other cheek. I sometimes forget he was one of Judy's best Sunday school students and he knows scripture better than some preachers."

"What are you getting at?

"Simply this Tim, your daughter and my son have forgiven you for what you did and they have asked me to do the same."

A moment of quiet fell between them. It was Tim's turn to move uncomfortably in his chair. "Are you telling me you're here to forgive me, or that I should pack my bags for hell?"

Kathleen began to laugh. "Probably a little of both, Tim,"

Tim looked across the table and took in her beautiful smile and suddenly calm filled him inside and could once again gain some control over the conversation. Kathleen could tell he was changing the subject in his head as she detected a slight smirk on his face.

"So, are you going to tell me what's on your mind or do I need to play twenty questions?" She asked.

"Do you think you could ever forgive me enough to go on another date with me?"

"Not right now … I still need to process this in my mind. Besides, as I said, I'm here to apologize and to try and save a relationship, our children's relationship.

Tim sat in his chair with his arms on the table and his hands resting on the list of realtors, listening closely to her words. "You know I can't set foot in that church again, not after what you said openly in the parking lot."

"No one was there to hear it and if you recall, I wasn't yelling."

"You expect me to believe that. Come on Kathleen, this is a small town and an even smaller church. Everyone knows everyone's business … you can't sneeze without everyone knowing." He looked away from her gaze and began again. "I'll tell you this though, your right about my brother, he needs to see a shrink. I've been …" He stuttered through his words.

"You've been what?" Kathleen asked tenderly as she placed her hand on his wrist.

"You'll just think I'm making excuses."

Tim went on explaining that since Kelly died a huge hole was created in his heart. As Lori got older, she looked more like her mother every day and was a constant reminder of the person he loved the most. As he spoke, he pulled a photo of Kelly from his wallet. He said it had been taken two weeks before her death; the photo was well worn. Kathleen was amazed at the resemblance. Had she looked at the photo without introduction, she would have assumed it was a photo of Tim, Lori and some young girl with dark hair.

"Tim, running away isn't the answer. I have the same issue with Billy. He looks almost like his father. There are times he stands in a room and my eyes tear up because I miss James too." Tim had brought his eyes back to her. "We have a lot in common, just the same as our kids." She broke her gaze for a moment to collect her thoughts. "When we went out the other night, I felt happy and alive. But when I got home, I— "

"—Felt like I cheated on my wife." He finished.

They both laughed at each other.

"Kathleen, I know I made a mistake, I know what I did to Lori was wrong and I'm sure I'm going to pay a price for that someday. But the fact is, we both had a great time that night and I had hoped we could build onto that."

"Stay in Sycamore Tim. Do that for your daughter. Show her you really do care and you are repentant. Show me, you're repentant. When you do that, *we* can move forward."

They spoke a while longer. Lori had been held up in her room for the entire time and was getting anxious. She looked at her watch as she paced about the room. She figured the service was now over and Billy would be home any time. She tried to call him but there was no answer. She tried again after a few minutes and this time he answered the phone.

"Your mom's over her trying to talk Dad out of putting the house up for sale and moving. I told you this was going to happen. I just can't have a relationship." Her voice broke off as she struggled to fight off the tears.

"Lori, there's got to be a way to convince him to stay, and my mom can find it."

"Billy, he already has a list of realtors written down. We're about two to three weeks before a sign is planted in the front lawn."

The tension didn't ease at all through the week. Lori's father told her he wouldn't be at church Sunday because he needed to go out of town for business. She knew he was looking to relocate but where would they be going. Perhaps they would move an hour away, she could still make that work but when he said his destination was Seattle, her heart sank to her feet. She made a very emotional entry into her journal.

My worst fears have been realized. The love of my life will be ripped from my arms because I had to share something from my past. It's my fault. I love him so deeply my heart is breaking.

The following Sunday Lori arrived at church and met Kathleen and Billy inside. Billy kissed her and whispered in her ear how good she looked. His eyes caressed what his fingers had better not touch and followed every line of the close-fitting jeans she wore. She smiled and reminded him they were in church. The music began and they took their seats. Once the service concluded, they went to the fellowship room to eat and share conversation.

Three elderly women came to Kathleen and offered their opinions of Lori's father and his actions. Kathleen wondered how they knew. She thought she and Tim were alone when they talked and she defended him telling the women they didn't know the entire story and shouldn't be so judgmental. They began to offer their opinions to Lori as well. Billy came to her rescue and suggested they needed to read their Bibles more and judge less.

Kathleen watched as her son defended Lori and was immediately reminded of her late husband. James always stood between she and trouble and it seemed Billy would protect Lori as James had protected her. A sense of pride grew inside of her but Lori was clearly irritated with the women, so much so, she told Billy and Kathleen she was leaving. She kissed Billy goodbye and started for her car. Vexation grew inside of Billy and he prepared to deliver a mighty blow to the women but his mother strongly suggested he let go of his anger because it would only cause problems. He clinched his teeth and went to follow his girlfriend to the parking lot.

Lori stood at the back of her car. She rummaged through her purse looking for her car keys while she uttered unflattering words about the women she left inside. Her attention was focused on that task and she hadn't seen a man approaching from her left. Once she found them, she placed the key in the lock of the car door. A raspy voice called out her name. She turned … terror filled her eyes and her body shook with fright. Billy was only about a dozen or so feet from her and saw what was happening. He ran to close the distance between them so he could protect her. Although he didn't know it, his mother had also left the fellowship room to offer some additional kind words of support and was not far behind. Lori appeared to fear for her life as she pressed her back tightly to the side of the car.

"Hey Lori, come give your uncle a kiss and hug." The man said as he staggered toward her and grabbed her pulling, on her blouse. She started to scream but fear choked her voice. As Billy quickly approached her from behind, he could see a dark stain traveling down both legs of Lori's jeans. The man was becoming overly interested as he looked at her.

"Get away from her!" Billy yelled out as he finally reached her. Deep loathing for Kevin Spencer filled him as he stood by Lori to protect her.

He was primed for a fight. His fists were ready. All he needed was one simple excuse to unleash his judgment and fury to punish the man who raped Lori.

"You must be the boyfriend my brother talked about."

Her voice finally returned "When did you get out … and why are you drunk?" Lori asked. Her face showed discomfort as she picked at her jeans which were now soaked and smelled of her urine.

"I got sprung today." Kevin said as he laughed at the sight of his niece.

"You need to leave her alone." Kathleen said as she caught up to the group.

"Oh wow, a pretty blonde woman." Kevin said as his eyes took in the sight of Kathleen.

"You're drunk Uncle Kevin, you just got out of rehab and your drunk again. You need to go back until you're sober." Lori said as she began to cry.

Three adults were standing on the steps of the church, smoking and talking; two men and one woman. The noise coming from the area around Lori's car caught their attention.

"I suggested you leave her alone." Kathleen said again as she stepped between Lori and Kevin.

"What are you going to do about it Blondie? Kevin taunted her. "I'll knock you out if you don't let me get to my niece."

Kevin stepped forward and leveled a quick but strong punch that landed on Kathleen's face. She fell against the car and slid to the ground, landing in the puddle of Lori's urine. Billy had his trigger and immediately began punching Kevin in the stomach, the face anywhere he could land a fist. Kevin fought back and before long both were on the ground exchanging blows. Billy's youth and sobriety provided him a little bit of an advantage but Kevin was trained as a soldier and he used that training to deliver a few heavy blows to Billy's face and stomach. Two of the men who had been watching from the steps had arrived to offer aid. They picked up Kevin and held him fast by his arms. Within seconds, two police cars quickly turned into the parking lot. They stopped just behind Lori's car. The flashing lights added to the chaos of the moment.

As the fight between Billy and Kevin ensued, Lori attended to Kathleen. She had gotten to her feet but the front of her blouse was soaked through by Lori's urine and splattered by the blood from her lip. Kathleen was nauseated by the odor of urine and irritated by the wetness of the material as it pressed against her skin. As she pulled at the wet blouse, Kathleen spit blood onto the ground. It was as much a need to empty her mouth of blood as it was an insult to the man who not only struck her, but raped Lori. Mrs. Jackson and the woman, who had been smoking, ran out with towels to help cover Lori's and Kathleen's wet clothing.

Two men were holding Kevin and the first police officer walked over to place him in handcuffs. Kevin broke free and punched the officer and attempted to take his gun. He was forcibly subdued by both officers, hand-cuffed with his arms behind him and placed rather firmly in the back seat of the police car. The first officer took the statements of each witness and carefully wrote every detail. He took photographs of the scene and several of Billy's face but needed to also get photos of the injury to Kathleen's face. Before the photos could be taken, the women helped Lori and Kathleen back into the church where they could get first aid and clean themselves

Billy had provided his account to the policeman as he and the officer walked back into the church. By now, a sizeable crowd had gathered as almost everyone from the fellowship room had come to the parking lot to see what was happening. Stories were starting to circulate and in the middle of all of gossip were three older women—the same women that verbally attacked Billy, Lori and his mother. Billy stared coldly at the women as he and the police officer walked past them.

The officer needed to speak to Kathleen and Lori to get their statements and to ask if Kathleen wanted to press charges for assault. Billy and the officer waited outside of the women's restroom. The officer was patient however, Billy was quite agitated.

Kathleen had rinsed her blouse and bra in the sink while Lori had found a garden hose and was rinsing her jeans and shoes.

It seemed odd that the women were laughing after what had happened. Billy knocked on the door and announced his and the police officer's presence. When the ladies walked out of the room, Kathleen was wearing her blouse but she had wrapped a towel around her so she could maintain her modesty. Lori walked out with no towel. Her jeans were completely soaked and glistened in the light. With each step, her shoes made flatulent noises and caused both women to giggle.

"Mom your face looks horrible. That guy's going to pay for what he did." Billy said through his swelling bloodied lip and painful jaw.

"Billy, please try to remember you're in church … remember forgiveness." His mother answered. Her face was swelling and made it painful to talk or move her mouth.

"Mrs. Thompson, I'm Officer John Phillips. Will you be pursuing assault charges against Mr. Spencer?"

Without any thought, Kathleen answered: "Yes."

"What happened to forgiveness, huh mom?" Billy asked as he smirked in his mother's direction.

The officer produced a form and began to fill-in each line. Once the information was recorded, he told her she would most likely receive a call from the County Attorney's office within three business days.

The police cars had left the parking lot and the crowd that had gathered had dispersed. Lori was walking to her car and was closely accompanied by Billy and Kathleen. As she reached the door of the car, Kathleen stopped her.

"Lori, are you going to be alright at home?" She asked.

"Yea Dad is out of town and won't be back until later in the week, but now that he's in jail, I'll be fine."

"Are you sure you don't want to stay with us?" Kathleen asked.

"Thank you, Mrs. Thompson but I'm sure my uncle will have the police department reach out to me to find my dad … I'm sure he'll want to have my dad bail him out again."

Kathleen reached out to hug her and Billy waited his turn. As she sat in the car, her wet jeans made a wheezing noise.

"Well, I think my pants just said it all, it's been that kind of day." Lori joked as she looked up at Billy's swelling face. "You know I really do love you." Painful as it was, Billy kissed her goodbye.

The telephone had rung in Tim Spencer's motel room. He answered it and the voice on the other end belonged to a member of the DeKalb County Sherriff's department. He was brought up to date with the information concerning his brother who was arrested and charged with, among other things, Felony assault.

Frustrated and angry, he quickly packed his belongings and caught the first flight out of Seattle to Chicago. He had several hours in the air to think about his brother and what Kathleen had said to him a week or so ago. When he arrived in Sycamore, he visited an attorney who he had made an appointment with before he had left Seattle. The meeting didn't offer much hope for Kevin. The attorney told him he would do the best he could with what he had to work with.

He next visited with his brother in jail. After the guard brought Kevin to the visitation area, he sat across from his younger brother.

"You going to spring me from this place little brother?" Kevin asked in his raspy voice.

"Kevin, I'm afraid you've gone too far this time. I've paid for your attorney but that's the best I can do. Unfortunately, you're going to go to trial at the end of September."

"This is about that blonde, isn't it?" Kevin spat out the words.

"You hit a police officer and tried to take his gun you idiot! I can't do anything to help you but get you an attorney. You've dug a hole too deep for me to get you out."

Kevin began screaming at his brother and attracted the attention of the guards. He was quickly subdued and taken back to his cell. Lori's father was visibly shaken by the meeting as he left the jail building. The memory of Kevin's eyes had telegraphed more than disappointment with him. He shook off the uneasy feeling and decided to go back home and check on his daughter.

Tim hadn't had a full night's rest and still wore the clothes from the previous day. The stubble of a beard had grown on his normally clean-shaven face and he had the appearance of someone who was down on their luck. He parked his car in its usual place but he didn't see Lori's car. He figured she was with Billy and Kathleen. He decided he would call Kathleen after showering and changing into a fresh set of clothes. As he suspected, his daughter was there. He asked Kathleen if he could come over and she said yes.

Lori was walking past the front door after using the restroom when her father rang the bell so she let him in. She was not overjoyed to see her father because she knew the purpose for the trip was to find a new home in Seattle. Tim quickly picked up on her displeasure and kept some distance between them as he followed her to the kitchen where both Kathleen and Billy waited.

After taking a cup of coffee, Tim asked for everyone's attention. He started to explain a couple of things, Lori's experience with his brother and the real story behind his wife's death. He knew he took a risk of reengaging Kathleen's anger with the former, but he needed to clear the air.

"Lori … actually all of you, I owe a huge apology and I suppose it's time to get this out. Kathleen, if you never want to see me again after this, I understand." He collected his thoughts and began. "When

I heard Lori crying in her bedroom, I wanted to know what had happened and she told me. My brother's soiled pants were still on her bedroom floor. I was angry. I grabbed them and then set out to find him, and I did at a bar. He was drunk and was bragging about having sex with a pretty, young woman. I confronted him and we got into a physical altercation. After I threatened to report the incident to the police, he reminded me of how he took a knife for me." He paused as he prepared the next part of the history lesson. "Lori, your mother and I met at a business function. We hit it off straight away. She told me she was separated and her divorce was pending. We spent several evenings together and I got close to her. I invited her to join me on a weekend trip to Toledo for a sales seminar. Several weeks later she told me she was pregnant and then confessed she was still married. I felt like I had been sold out. I sat on a bar stool drowning my sorrows and looking for pity when and Kevin came running in. He told me to get out and get Kelly because her husband was looking for she and I ... he was going to kill us both. The next day I got a phone call from the hospital that my brother had been brought in with a nasty cut on his arm. Her husband had come in with a knife and asked for the Spencer guy. He got Kevin instead of me. The only reason Kevin wasn't killed was because of his hand-to-hand training in the Army. If I had been there, I would have been dead."

"I fell in love with your mother on our second date. I would have taken that knife for her, that's how much I loved her. Kevin always told me I owed him for that and every time he had gotten in trouble, he played that card. So, when ... after he ... after he attacked you, I was told the same thing." Tim's eyes were filling with tears as he not only thought about Kelly but was being crushed by reliving the memory of the attack on Lori. "He said you came home from school that day wearing a short skirt and a tee-shirt and taunted him. He said you coaxed him into your room and then changed your mind at the last second. I didn't believe him but he had enough of a plausible story that the police would have believed him."

Kathleen entered the conversation. "What plausible story, I mean what could he possibly say?"

"He identified pieces of clothing she had in the laundry. He could physically describe things about parts of my daughter's body. It made me sick because I knew the truth."

"I still don't see why you let this go." Kathleen stated.

"Kevin said he had something to blackmail me with. He wouldn't divulge it but he said it would ruin me and destroy my life. I thought back and the only thing that I had done that was black-mail worthy, was my relationship with a married woman and that ship had sailed years prior."

"So, you never did hear what it was that he was holding over you?" Kathleen asked.

He then went on to describe how Kelly had died. "She was an animal lover and when the neighbor's dog had gotten tangled up in the pool cover, she jumped in to save it. Her dress and shoes made swimming difficult and after the dog was freed from the sinking cover, she had managed to get her leg tangled into one of the straps. The weight of the cover pulled her under the water. If she was by the edge of the pool, she could have held on and not be taken under but she was in the middle of the deep end. By chance, Kevin stopped by the house to drop off some papers he wanted me to look at and found her not moving beneath the water. He jumped in to free her but by the time he reached her and got her loose, she had already drowned. He got out of the pool to call the police and that's when Lori found her floating in the pool. Kevin didn't kill your mother. I know you and my sister think he did but he didn't. It did mess him up though; he was never the same after that. He turned to drinking and started having flash backs from the war. I should have gotten him help then and none of this other stuff would have happened." He paused for a moment and looked at everyone in the room, particularly Kathleen. "I didn't join you to take any photos of Lori getting baptized because seeing her in that pool reminded me of Kelly's death and I couldn't handle that, so thank you, Kathleen, for taking them for me."

Lori stood and hugged her father. She held him as he repeatedly apologized. Moments later, Kathleen stood to join her and offered a compassionate hug. Tim was surprised at her reaction because he thought she would have told him to leave for good.

After getting past the emotions, Tim changed the subject and began to talk about moving to Seattle. He said he wouldn't do anything to stop them seeing each other but they were still going to Seattle.

Lori looked at her father and then asked the question that was on Billy's mind as well. "Dad, if you want us to get together or let us do our thing, then why not stay here?"

Everyone agreed and waited for his answer. "I actually considered staying here but the long arm of Pastor Mark's gossip gang has caused me to lose two accounts and more are threatening to leave. I considered going to Champaign but they already have a strong representative in that region. And returning to Ohio doesn't work either for the same reasons. Because of the way things are structured, the only territory that I can grow is Seattle. This brings me to my next question for you Kathleen and Billy: Would you consider relocating in Seattle?"

Billy immediately answered yes but his mother was a different story. "Tim, that's something I would need to really think about. My job, my life, everything is here."

Tim began selling the idea. There were places that Kathleen could continue her career and even grow beyond the level where she currently was. He painted a wonderful picture that would have made most people jump aboard. Kathleen promised she would think about the offer and would get back with him.

As they were talking the telephone rang. Kathleen excused herself from the conversation and answered it. The look on her face told everyone in the room that the news on the other end was grim

"When did it happen … How's Mom … We'll be down."

Kathleen returned to the table and fell into tears. The call was from her sister letting her know her father had passed away that morning. Billy stood and went to his mother's side to comfort her. He was quickly joined by Lori and with cautious hesitation, her father.

"Can we go with you?" Tim asked Kathleen. "You obviously loved your father very much."

Kathleen looked at Tim with tear-filled blue eyes and thanked him for the gesture but he and Lori might feel out of place with her family.

"Kathleen, I'm a salesman … I never feel out of place and I'm sure your family has heard all about Lori."

Kathleen smiled at his comment and agreed to let them come.

"It will actually be a good thing. My sister and mother have wanted to meet your daughter for a while now." Kathleen said as she sadly wiped her eyes.

"You'll like Aunt Sandra and Uncle Charles, they're pretty cool." Billy said to Lori and her father.

They would be leaving for Florida in the morning. That night Billy lay in his bed, sleep was never going to come. The smooth darkness wrapped around him. The only source of light was the alarm clock that was set to go off in just a few hours. His mind kept playing the scene of Lori telling him goodbye and realizing they would never see each other again. The thought of Lori being ripped from his life was something he couldn't get past. There had to be a way. He thought about praying that something would happen, something that would keep her and her father in Sycamore, but his past experiences with faith seemed to be a path that would produce no results at all. September would be here quick enough and the month would evaporate as fast as a puddle of water on the roof of a car in the summer sun. He rolled onto his side and once again looked at the clock that taunted him.

He wasn't the only one who found sleep elusive. His mother knocked softly on his door. As she opened the door, the squeak of the hinge seemed louder than normal.

"I can't sleep either. Your father's funeral was probably the worst I've ever felt but I have to admit, laying my dad to rest is a close second." She looked at her son who was on the verge of tears. "You're upset about Lori leaving, aren't you?"

"Mom, I don't know what to do. I mean, why would God put her in my life and then take her out? This pattern keeps repeating itself in my life ... I get attached to them and then they get ripped from me ... Grandma, Dad, the baby and now Lori. You might not want to get too close to me, you could be next." As Billy recited the list of those taken from him by death, the mention of the miscarriage years ago, sparked the memory of Billy's grief. The loss of the baby hit him hard, almost as deeply as the loss of his father. Kathleen cleared her throat in an attempt to push back the avalanche of emotion that had threatened to spill out of her.

"Lori's sarcasm is rubbing off onto you, isn't it?" She forced a smile as she casually crossed her arms. "It's too late for me anyway ... I was hooked when you were born."

She moved to the side of his bed and sat down as Billy sat up. As a baby and small child, whenever he was hurting or upset she would wrap her arms around him and rock back and forth. This time it was no different. As she held him, he began to whimper and cry.

CHAPTER 7

The plane lumbered into its parking spot and stopped at the gate and within minutes the chime rang, the fasten seatbelt sign was turned off and everyone aboard quickly stood and walked toward the front door of the airplane. Most were patient but for some, the wait was getting to be too much to endure. The foursome traveled with the other passengers to the baggage claim carrousels. Most of their fellow passengers were there for vacation and couldn't wait to feel the ocean lap at their feet. Their lack of patience in the airplane was understandable but now those same people were becoming rude and forced their way to the front of the parade to the luggage recovery area. Tim traveled a lot and had experienced this more than once and had suggested they stay back and let the discourteous mob have first dibs at the luggage merry-go-round. After crossing the security line, they waited out the melee at the baggage claim, and it was there that they met Sandra and Charles. After a brief introduction by Kathleen, Sandra did a quick visual exam of her sister's face. The makeup didn't hide the cuts and swollen features as well as she had hoped.

"What happened, Kati?" She involuntarily touched her own lip as he asked

"I'll explain later at Mom's because she's going to want to know too."

Sandra then turned her attention to Lori. "So, you're the girl that has captured my nephew's heart. He obviously has great taste … we brunettes need to stick together." She said as she administered a crushing hug to both, Billy and Lori.

It was a typical day in Daytona Beach Florida, sunny with white puffy clouds dotting the blue sky. The air was hot and humid and one could smell the distinct scent of the ocean. The walk to the van was not that far but the humidity in the air caused everyone in the group to perspire. Charles was the heaviest of them all and by the time they had reached the car, the man's forehead was a dripping mess of sweat. The bags were quickly loaded into the trunk and Sally started the engine to get the air conditioning going.

The drive to New Smyrna Beach took about an hour. Tim used that time to get acquainted with Charles and Sandra and to learn about the family. It was nothing less than amazing how Lori's father could instantly fit-in to any group of people and act as if he had known them for years. Once they arrived at the Tropher home, they went in to meet Sally.

They found her at the dining room table surrounded by a pile of tissues she had used to wipe her eyes. Kathleen entered the room and without hesitation, she went to her mother's side and hugged her. Her tears began immediately as she held her mother who shook with grief as they both cried. Sandra joined her sister and mother and too began to cry. As he looked upon the three women, Billy felt the tug of emotion in his heart. He knew what loss felt like and it was for their loss he felt badly. But this emotion was not for his grandfather, for they had always seemed to be adversaries.

Her mother pulled herself out of her grief and because of the close proximity to her youngest daughter's face, noticed the cuts and bruises. "My word ... what in the world happened to you?" Her mouth fell open in shock.

"It's a story I don't want to get into right now ... maybe at dinner."

"No, you told me at the airport you would tell all of us when we got here." Sandra said, prodding her sister to explain the bruises.

"I got into an altercation at church. A man attacked Lori and I stood in to help. Billy had his lip bloodied in the same situation. The man's now in jail and is no longer a danger to anyone." She purposely omitted the specific detail that the assailant was Tim's brother.

Billy then came forward to hug is grandmother. He acted quickly so they could move beyond further discussion of the topic. Because he hadn't seen his grandmother since his father's funeral three years prior she was easily distracted. After he said hello, he looked at her and noticed the stress of going through the disease and death of his grandfather had robbed her of what little youthful appearance she may have had. Her hair was now solidly gray and the skin on her face was deeply wrinkled. He introduced Lori and after looking at her, Sally offered a quick assessment. "My goodness, you're a pretty thing."

She looked at Lori from the top of her head to her beautifully painted toe nails, but seemed to spend a little extra time just below her shoulders.

"My goodness child ... you have a bodacious set of— "

"—Mom, please!" Kathleen quickly interrupted her mother. "Some manners and a little modesty would be nice!"

"That's okay Mrs. Thompson, I'm used to it." Lori said trying to appear as though the comment had no effect on her.

Billy quickly took Lori by the hand and led her to the back of the house to a room that overlooked the beach and the crashing waves. Sandra quietly came next to them and apologized for her mother. Lori thanked her for her kind words but stared at the ocean. She was visibly upset that once again the size of her breasts overshadowed any of her other qualities.

"Hey, look at me." Billy said to her as he squeezed her hand. "I don't care if you have boobs or not … I'm a leg guy."

Lori shook her head as she smiled. "I love you." She said as she raised her hand to wipe the tiny tears that had formed in the corners of her eyes.

Attempting to break the tension, Sandra had suggested they walk along the beach to take a break from the crushing emotion. Sally agreed with Sandra, and everyone changed into swimwear, except Lori.

"You knew we'd be here all week … why didn't you bring a bathing suit?" Billy asked.

"I don't wear a bathing suit. It draws too much attention to me and I don't like that." She answered.

Everyone in the group was playing in the surf except for Billy and Lori. They walked in the shallow water while the surf played at their feet. There was quietness between them and the others assumed it was grief for Harvey. The truth was that the end of September was on Billy and Lori's minds and the struggle to stay together was a common problem that seemingly could not be solved.

Since Tim Spencer had announced the move to Seattle Billy hadn't been able to sleep. Every time he closed his eyes, he could see Lori getting into a car that would take her from him forever. His hopes to keep her with him took led him to some dangerous thoughts such as her becoming pregnant. He knew they would be forced to marry, but he also knew that would also destroy both of their futures. There would be no college, no chance at a career ... no, that was not the answer. Lori herself had even thought about that option but she, like Billy, knew that would probably tear them apart in the end. They continued to walk along, holding hands, mostly in silence.

The next morning, everyone rushed to and through the shower as they readied themselves for the funeral. They arrived early to pay their individual respects privately. The funeral home was no different than any Billy had seen back in Sycamore. It was a very large old house that resembled an old plantation home. The building was elevated on piers and white lattice covered the space between the ground and the bottom of the house. As he walked into the various rooms of the funeral home, the wooden floors squeaked beneath his feet.

In the center of the back wall was the casket that held the body of his grandfather. On both sides of the casket, dozens of flower arrangements had been carefully placed. A photo of Harvey was positioned on the right. It rested on an easel and showed his grandfather when he was much younger. Billy thought, even then, the man's face held that arrogant smirk.

The upper section of the casket was open so the visitors could see the deceased. Sally, Kathleen and Lori's father walked to the open casket first, followed by Sandra and Charles. Billy and Lori brought up the rear. Billy could hear his grandmother say something to her husband's remains but he couldn't understand her. His mother began to cry once she came to face her father. Tim held her hand, and then put his arm around her. She looked at Lori's father and shook her head yes and moved on. Sandra and Charles stopped next. She wiped at tears in her eyes, said good bye and they too moved on.

Billy then came to face his grandfather. "Hello grandpa. I'm sorry we always seemed to fight." He really hadn't much more to say. He wasn't expecting the emotion that had risen inside of him and caused tears to form in his eyes. Lori squeezed his hand and then tenderly put her head on his shoulder.

After the service concluded the family said one final goodbye. Sally Tropher kissed her husband's face one last time. The emotion was debilitating for his mother, grandmother and aunt. Billy came to his mother's side, held her and told her he loved her. He did the same for his grandmother and aunt. The guests said goodbye and it was finished.

After the funeral, it was decided that they should go to Sandra and Charles home which was another hour's drive. Once they arrived and settled in, everyone was talking and acting as comfortable as if they had been together for years. Billy's mind took a trip to a place in a future where this was his family. Lori was his wife, Tim and his mother were together and everyone was perfect. It was easy to get lost in that desire and certainly better than the reality of the end of September.

Sandra called his name and brought him back from his dream. She was taking Lori shopping and wanted to know if he would like to join them. He agreed but then everyone else decided to go too. The van his uncle and aunt owned was well appointed and had the room to accommodate everyone so there was no need to drive multiple vehicles. Billy began to feel both awkward and angry toward his family because he wanted time alone—or nearly alone with Lori. But now everyone would be there and any chance of a private moment with the woman closest to his heart was impossible. Lori seemed to be able to read his thoughts and offered a reassuring smile followed by a quick peck on his cheek.

Billy and Lori occupied the smallest back seat while his mother, Tim and grandmother took the center, larger, bench. With such proximity to Tim, Sally began another round of interrogation. She began to ask embarrassing questions and both Kathleen and Sandra turned toward her with shock.

"Mom, Tim and I are friends, we're not having sex and it's horribly improper for you to ask that question." Kathleen admonished.

"You always were so prim and proper. It's amazing that you managed to have Billy. You should talk to Sandra because she knows how to have fun."

Billy's face turned red. He didn't know if he was embarrassed for his mother or because his grandmother was a dirty old lady. Lori looked away from them to the side windows of the van, placed a hand to her lips, and failed miserably to stifle a laugh.

Charles managed to find a parking spot close to the building. Kathleen remembered this place from seven years ago when she, James and Billy visited for Christmas but it had grown and expanded a bit. As they entered the building, the expanse of the mall opened before them. In the center, a two-story tall waterfall provided not only a natural ambiance it served as a perfect backdrop for tourist photographs. Security guards stood close by to keep would-be thrill seekers from entering the fountain for that perfect photo.

They walked through the wide area entering several stores until they came across one Kathleen had been in not quite a decade ago.

"Lori, I think we can get you a bathing suit here." Sandra said. "Hey Kati, maybe you can find a new suit too, one that shows a little skin." Her sister added the jab at her obvious hyper-conservative style.

Kathleen wrinkled her nose at her sister's comments and decided against starting a playful war with Sandra.

They moved through the store and gathered plenty of things to try on. After several options, Lori settled on a bright yellow bikini. Billy had hoped to see her model it but was told he would need to wait until tomorrow.

By the time they had finished shopping, the quantity of bags they each carried bordered on excessive. Sandra managed to spend a fair amount of money on Lori, something that made her father feel awkward.

"Tim, if this plays out the way I think it will, your daughter is going to be my nephew's wife. This is how I roll buster so don't beat yourself up over it." Sandra said.

Tim could certainly see the difference between Sandra and Kathleen. Sandra could be as wild as Kathleen was tame, and as flamboyant as she was conservative. Sandra was also a little heavier than her younger sister, but that never stopped her from choosing clothing that Kathleen would never be seen in. Of course Charles enjoyed his wife's wardrobe choices and made that very clear as he would playfully spank her on her bottom as he followed her about.

After they arrived at the house, the booty was distributed. It was getting near dinner time and Charles suggested they cook on the deck and eat in. After dinner, everyone walked along the beach and Billy noticed his mother seemed to walk closer to Tim than she had on previous walks. He didn't say anything about it but Lori had. She smiled and suggested his mother may have found forgiveness in her heart and that could change the meaning of the end of September.

The following day, Billy got to see Lori in her new bikini. She had tanned quickly in the Florida sun and between her long dark hair and darkening skin she was quite striking. She was also catching more than the rays of the sun. Every guy that passed seemed to pay her a bit of attention as she walked next to Billy. He started to get angry but she laughed it off.

"I thought you didn't like all of that attention." Billy said as they continued walking. "They're undressing you with their eyes."

"Well there isn't a lot to take off." She said. "So long as you're with me, they can look all they want. I already have the man I want."

After she finished her statement, she became very quiet as she looked out at the ocean. The end of September was a mountain on the horizon and the source of insomnia for them both. It grew closer with the passage of each day and she, like Billy, knew that after Kevin's trial at the end of that month, they would be saying goodbye. Lori remembered what she had said the day before about Kathleen and her hope she had forgiven her father, but it was only hope. She stopped walking and wrapped her arm around his, and turned to face him. Lori looked in his eyes and kissed him. Their eyes were still locked and Billy spoke something he thought he wouldn't ask for at least six more years.

"Lori Spencer, would you marry me? I mean, not today or tomorrow but when we're ready?"

"Yes, I will." Her gaze never broke from his. "Billy, I give you my heart and soul forever … will you give me yours?"

"Yes, I do … forever."

They were lost in each other's eyes for a moment and then they kissed. A strange feeling came over them both. If love was a person, it had just wrapped its arms around them and joined them as one. They broke their kiss and stood quietly looking at each other. The sounds of seagulls squawking and a young man passing, telling them to get a room, brought them out of their dream-state.

After they returned from their walk, Kathleen quickly came to stand next to Lori. She asked her if she had enough left in her for another walk so they could talk privately. Lori looked at Billy as if he had some idea what she wanted to talk about but he shrugged his shoulders in silence. After they had walked clear of the house, Kathleen began.

"How did you do it? How did you forgive your father?" She had a tone in her voice that was not filled with malice but slight desperation.

"I decided that I needed to do what it said in the Bible and that was to forgive. I've never forgotten but after I told Dad I forgave him, this weight seemed to be lifted from me." Lori Explained. "Are you trying to forgive him too?" She asked with the faintest grin on her face.

After a second of contemplative silence, Kathleen answered. "I don't know yet, I'm on the fence." Another few seconds of silence she began. "If I did forgive him, maybe he'll stay in town."

"Mrs. Thompson, as much as I would love for my dad to stay in town, I'm not going to ask you to sacrifice yourself for us. You need to do this because your heart drives you to do it ... but thank you for considering it. And, before you ask, I won't tell Billy."

The week had come to an end. Charles and Sandra delivered Sally to her home and then drove their guests back to Daytona Beach so they could catch their flight. They said their goodbyes and waited for the call to board the plane.

Tim was watching his daughter and then looked at Kathleen. The bruising and damage to her lip and face was healing nicely. He looked at her as the sunlight beamed through the terminal roof windows, causing her blonde hair to glow. Through his smile, he spoke to Kathleen.

"You look like an angel sitting there in the sunlight"

"Is that your come-on line mister?" She laughed after asking.

It looks like you and I are going to be in-laws someday. I can see it in their eyes, and I'm sure you can see it too." Tim said as if he was talking through a dream.

Kathleen looked at Lori's father and smiled. "Tim, when we get back home, can we go on a date ... all by ourselves?" She asked. "I think it would be nice for us to spend some time together before you leave for Seattle."

"Kathleen, nothing would make me happier than to be with you. I'm sure our kids won't mind."

CHAPTER 8

The plane landed in Chicago in the early evening. After collecting their luggage and loading the car, they set off for Sycamore. Summer road construction easily added an hour to the trip. Lori and Billy had fallen asleep in the back seat and she and Tim could talk somewhat privately while they drove through the slow traffic.

"I hate this traffic. I think I need to work a little harder so I can hire a charter flight between DeKalb airport and Chicago O'Hare." Tim said and Kathleen then laughed.

"Tim you're going to be in Seattle so DeKalb is a little out of your neighborhood, isn't it?"

"I've been rethinking the Seattle move." Kathleen had a puzzled look on her face. "Our kids are trying to tell us something if we would just listen and open our eyes. Isn't that what you told me a few weeks back?"

"Okay, so then why the sudden change in direction?" Kathleen asked with a degree of caution in her voice.

"I think I can fix things here. Now that I've done the right thing by the law with my brother, people will notice." He looked over at Kathleen. "I'm also going to start going to church … with you if you'll let me."

"That all depends on your intentions and what your motivation is." She said to him.

"Do I need a motivation other than to be happy?"

"I make you happy?" She asked as she looked down at her lap, smiling and trying to hide her reddening face.

"Kathleen, I feel alive again when I'm with you. I want to stay home and not hide my feelings in my work." He knew he was taking a massive risk saying these things. "I'd like to explore a relationship with you."

"Are you sure this isn't about recovering from the embarrassment of your brother's issues?" She felt it was a valid question. "Tim, I don't want you to go out with me so you can save your reputation and your sales accounts."

"Look, Kathleen, a couple of months ago, I might have said yes that may have been my motivation. After I was invited to go with you to share your father's funeral I felt … I felt like I hadn't felt in years. I was part of a family again." Tim nervously drummed his fingers on the steering wheel and began to speak again. "When I held your hand it felt wonderful, as if I had a purpose other than keeping a roof over my daughter's head. I got to know your family and I think they're great people … and Charles, for a rocket geek, he's pretty cool."

The discussion in the front continued a little longer and Lori and Billy began to stir in the back seat.

"Welcome back to construction delays." Kathleen said to the backseat occupants. "We're only about a quarter of a mile from the exit of route 20 but we've been sitting still for the last ten minutes."

Half an hour later, they pulled into the driveway of the Thompson home. The luggage was sorted and those items that needed to go with Lori and her father were put in the car. Billy hugged Lori and kissed her goodbye and thanked her father for coming to Florida with them. Tim stood next to Kathleen and thanked her for a wonderful week. She hugged him briefly and gave a quick peck on his cheek and before he left her side he asked her to think seriously about what they had discussed.

As they watched the sedan drive away, Billy could tell his mother had something on her mind. Every crisis, every major decision and almost every bit of family bonding took place at the dining room table and that was their destination. It was a comfortable place for them to be, to talk about what was on her mind. After they both had a cup of coffee, the conversation began.

"Mom, I think you should go out with him. I mean it's not like you're cheating on Dad. Besides, they're going to be moving soon so why not?"

"There's a new wrinkle—they're not moving now." Billy's face became very expressive as it was covered with a huge smile. "And before you begin dancing around, we need to have an important discussion." She said as she placed an anchoring hand on his wrist.

Billy took a breath to get a little composure before speaking. "Mom, I saw the way he looked at you, I have seen the way you looked at him, and— "

Kathleen cut him off in mid-sentence. "—I've been alone for better than three years so the attention was nice."

"Come on Mom, it's more than that and you know it!" His blue eyes looked at hers; the fire behind them was almost palpable. "I miss Dad too but walking away from a chance to be happy or feel good for a while is not good and it won't bring him back. God knows I'm the expert on that!"

"Do not lecture me on love young man!" His mother fired back. "You think because you feel all warm and fuzzy about a girl you've known for two months, you're now an expert on love. You know little about love and commitment. Your father and I had years together and you can't just turn that off." Tears began to form in her eyes and she looked away from her son.

Their argument lasted a short time longer when Billy ended it by breaking out in laughter. Kathleen looked at her son as if he had gone completely mad. He offered one last observation and opinion.

"Listen to me ... Please ... you can't think, your stomach is in knots and you're incapable of winning this argument because your head is being beaten up by your heart. You're scared that you might actually fall for this guy ... Mom, it is okay to let go."

Kathleen's tears had won and she began to cry heavily. Billy stood to hold her and began to rock her as she had always done for him when he was hurting or upset.

"Mom, I know you love Dad. Your lives together are what a love story is all about. I know I've only known Lori for a short time but it has been the most incredible short time I have ever experienced in my life. I have no desire for anyone else ... she's the one." He paused to wipe a tear from her cheek. "Please give a new life a chance."

The discussion was a little different in the Spencer's car on the way home. Tim was doing most of the talking. He didn't tell Lori about his decision to stay until they got into the house. As he and Lori dragged their luggage through the kitchen, he offered the final point.

"We're not moving to Seattle." Her father said quickly.

Lori dropped her suitcase and ran toward her father, throwing her arms around him almost knocking him to the floor. "Daddy I love you!" She said as she covered his face with kisses.

The end of September had arrived. Since the decision to leave Sycamore was no longer in play, the only troubling experience the families needed to address was facing Kevin Spencer in court. Both families met outside of the courthouse and met with the prosecuting attorney. He once again went over the case and explained how the process would unfold.

One by one, Lori, Kathleen and Billy took the witness stand. The events of that day were described by each of them. The other witnesses also gave their testimony too, but the most damning words came from Officer Phillips. When the jury heard Kevin punched the officer and attempted to take his weapon, they quickly and unanimously decided, Kevin was guilty.

The judge initially sentenced Kevin to twenty years. His attorney asked for mercy to be shown. His client, he argued, was a war veteran and the war is what made him what he had become. The judge granted his request and gave Kevin only twelve years behind bars. The judge suggested that was the best deal he would give because of the assault of the police officer. As they led him out of the courtroom, he held an angry stare at everyone who had stood against him and especially to his brother, Kathleen and Lori. He said only one word as he walked past them: "Later".

The following Sunday in church, the bench was occupied by the Thompson family flanked on each side by a Spencer. Kathleen stood next to Tim and Billy next to Lori. From time to time Tim's hand could be seen touching or covering Kathleen's left hand. Billy noticed she had removed her wedding rings. Even after his father had died, the rings that still showed her love and commitment to his father were there. Today, only a sliver of lighter skin that had been shielded from the sun was present. His mother was moving on and appeared to be doing so with Lori's father. Billy wasn't the only one to notice either. Some of the gossipy types spotted the absence of the rings as well and would most likely tell the entire church before fellowship would end.

As the service began, they noticed Pastor Mark was not alone today. Another younger man, also wearing a minister's robe, sat on a chair. When Pastor Mark walked to the pulpit for the message, he announced this would be the final service he would be leading in this church. He and his wife were retiring but not before he would serve two more years at a church down in a small town called Cairo, just across the river from Kentucky. He introduced the new pastor, Thomas Singleton and his wife Maria. Pastor Mark thanked everyone for their support and friendship. He remarked how he had many fond memories of his time with them and was very happy to have been able to be part of some special moments in his church family's lives.

During fellowship time, Pastor Mark and his wife Judy stopped to offer a special goodbye to Kathleen and Billy. It was particularly emotional for them, considering the deep history the pastor had with them. He had buried James's parents, married Kathleen and James and sadly read his funeral. He had baptized Billy and now wished time would have allowed him to unite Billy and Lori in matrimony as it seemed they would indeed someday become husband and wife. After saying their final goodbye, he and his wife waved their hands to the crowd as they walked out of that church forever.

Change wasn't happening only in the church. Tim's sister, Lisa, had called to speak with him. She hadn't any contact with him since Kelly had passed away and the animosity she held for her brother Kevin prevented her from speaking with Tim. The police had been interviewing her about Kevin and since his incarceration, she felt renewing the relationship with her youngest brother was important. Several weeks after that phone call, Tim, Lori and the Thompsons went to Ohio to visit and catch up. Lori was introduced to cousins she didn't know she had. Tim introduced Kathleen and Billy and everyone seemed to connect. Tim laughed as it was now Kathleen's turn to be interrogated by his sister. Kathleen took it in stride and figured it was only fair considering what her mother had done to him in Florida.

Lori became friends with her cousins. So many years had gone by and they had a lot of catching up to do. There were those awkward moments that caused Billy to feel uncomfortable but like his mother, he figured it was payback for what his grandmother had said to Lori.

Overall, his time in Ohio was good and he could tell it was certainly cathartic for Lori. She borrowed her father's rented car and with Billy by her side, they left everyone at her aunt's house. She drove to the cemetery to visit her mother's grave. It had been a long time since she stood by her mother's headstone. It had weathered a bit since she last had visited. The shine of the granite had been dulled slightly by the effects of nature but she still felt it was beautiful. The engraved picture of a single rose next to her name was fitting because she always loved roses. As tears gently rolled down her cheeks, she introduced Billy as the man she was going to marry. After placing a dozen roses on the grave, they returned to the car and drove back to her aunt's house.

Tim and Lori introduced Kathleen and Billy to Kings Island. The amusement park had several roller coasters that were nationally known. As they rode them, the challenges of the past seemed to dissolve behind them and a brighter future was on the horizon.

CHAPTER 9

Seven years had passed since the day Pastor Mark said goodbye. Billy and Lori had attended and graduated college with both achieving honors albeit a year apart. Kathleen and Tim had been dating through much of that time and their relationship had deepened. Tim's business had also grown so much he needed additional representatives to cover the expanded territories.

Half way through college Billy began to work with Tim and quickly learned to sell and how the business worked. Together they expanded the line of product representation offerings to their customers and Spencer and Associates was founded. Lori and Kathleen joined the organization shortly afterward and soon the company began another expansion. The women brought their skills and talents and combined them with the Men's and that amalgamation was the catalyst for exponential growth. Territories were further expanded and the addition of even more associates was required.

Billy and Lori had always talked about getting married but held off until they finished college. They set a date in the spring of 1994. To add an exciting twist, Kathleen had accepted Tim's marriage proposal and the girls got together and thought a double wedding on the beach in Florida would be not only romantic, it could be historic.

With the date set, it was time to choose the members of the wedding party. As her Maid of Honor, Lori chose one of her closest friends from college, a young woman who was now in Law school. Billy chose Christopher Wayne Seekers as his Best Man, who was also in law school.

Tammy had been on Christopher's arm since the fifth grade. They were engaged and had planned to marry after Christopher passed the Illinois Bar Exam. He and Lori had double dated with Christopher and Tammy several times and everyone had become friends. They had all stayed in touch through their time through college but they hadn't spent any time together as a group. Tammy had grown into a very pretty, young woman and had developed a sense of propriety. Gone were the extremely short dresses and skirts but she did have a small tattoo of a fairy on her right shoulder blade. It was impossible to not see the large diamond engagement ring Tammy wore on her finger but Billy took a bit of pride knowing Lori's diamond was larger.

Tammy asked him if he realized his fiancé had a resemblance to Linda Williams, the girl he took to the fifth-grade dance. He was succinct in his answer and tried to be as proper and non-judgmental as he could be when he said that Lori wasn't a slut. Tammy laughed at his response and then informed him, his former girlfriend had become the single mother of two with a third on the way.

Kathleen had chosen her sister Sandra to be her matron of honor. Since Tim didn't have a close friend, Charles offered his services as best man. The remainder of the wedding party was made up of Lori's cousins and Billy's friends from college. One of the huge questions they faced was who would walk Kathleen down the aisle? It was decided that Lori's father would walk her down the aisle first, then Charles would follow shortly afterward with Kathleen. Another question was who would read the service? Initially, a local pastor would have sufficed but then Billy suggested Pastor Mark Jackson.

There was a connection to that man that seemed essential to make sure this chapter of his life would get off in the right direction. Everyone agreed and Billy began to make phone calls. He started at the church in Cairo Illinois where the pastor had been transferred but he would have been five years retired. Luckily the woman on the telephone remembered the pastor, found and provided him with contact information. Billy pressed the numbers into the phone. After the third ring, a familiar, but aged voice answered.

Mark Jackson had retired to Tampa Florida. Unfortunately, his wife Judy had recently passed and Billy offered his as well as his entire family's sympathies. After they had caught up a little, Billy got to the point with his former pastor.

"Pastor Mark, it would be our honor if you would officiate our weddings this coming spring." Billy said.

"What do you mean by weddings?" The pastor asked.

"My mother will be getting married to Lori's father the same time I get married to Lori. It will be kind of a historical thing when you think about it."

The pastor gladly accepted the invitation and suggested he would look forward to seeing everyone in the family again.

With so much to do, the list was split four ways. The colors for the Bride's Maids dresses were chosen, the styles for the tuxedos was finalized and the size and type of wedding cake was agreed upon. The only major thing remaining was wedding gowns and Sandra was taking the lead.

Since the wedding was to be held in Florida, the gowns would be purchased there. Kathleen and Lori went to DeKalb County airport and boarded a chartered business jet that took them to Coco Beach. They met Charles at the airport and after a brief drive to the house they gathered Sandra and her mother Sally.

Sandra brought them to a bridal shop that was in the mall they had visited when they were there for Harvey's funeral. Sally was getting on in age and needed help to get around but once she sat in the chair, she was a fire ball of attitude and opinion. An assistant met the women at the door and after a brief interview, she directed the brides to dressing rooms and began to pull and bring samples for them to try.

At 48 years of age, gray strands of hair were invading Kathleen's natural blonde color but this worked well with the headdress and veil the assistant had chosen. Kathleen's gown was not very elaborate and looked like something she would wear to work or out to dinner but she was still stunning.

"Katie, you look amazing and you'll make beautiful pictures on your wedding day." Sandra had tears in her eyes and Kathleen's were beginning to fill as well. "I wish I could have been there for the first fitting. I remember Mom saying that Dad drank all of the coffee in Sycamore that day."

"He had a horrible time. That man could not sit through anything without counting the costs." Their mother added.

"Costs, there were no costs. James paid for my wedding dress. It was a deal Dad made for getting him on at Peterman." Kathleen corrected.

"That cheap … he lied to me. He told me he would spend any amount of money on your gown … whatever made you happy." Sally said and then began to ground her teeth together in displeasure.

Lori was fitted next. Choosing her gown took a long time. She didn't want to look frumpy but she didn't want to look like a stripper either. After the tenth gown, she walked out of the fitting room. She was tired from all the dressing and undressing and as she stood on the dais the clerk adjusted the train of her dress. Once the veil and earrings were placed, silence fell on the room. The women's smiles and tears said it all; this was the dress.

Five months passed quickly. Tim, Kathleen, Lori and Billy boarded a private jet that took them to Coco Beach Florida. Upon arrival, they immediately began working through all the final preparations for the wedding. The contractors had finished the beach platform and boardwalk. The chairs for the guests were in placed on sheets of plywood covered with artificial turf and flowers and strategically placed shorter palm trees ringed the perimeter. Everything was now ready.

As the people arrived they were escorted to their seats by the ushers. Some wore dressier clothes while others arrived in nice shorts and button-down shirts with sandals. Pastor Mark took his place on the stage and music began to play.

Sally was helped down the board walk and to her seat. She was prepared for a lot of crying and carried with her, a box of tissues. The music changed and everyone's eyes looked behind them. Sandra walked down the aisle first. She took her place on the stage. Next Charles walked Kathleen down the aisle. Billy looked at this mother as she approached. She was a very beautiful woman and even though the gown she wore was much less glittery than the one she wore years ago, she still shined like a diamond in the sunlight. When they arrived at the stage, she took her place next to her sister.

The music changed again and now Lori's bride's maids began their journey toward the front escorted by each of the groomsman. The maid of honor came through the door next and was escorted by the best man. Once they reached the stage and took their places, the music stopped. All eyes looked to the door that was opened by two of the groomsmen who had circled back. The wedding march began to play. Through the door Tim Spencer walked with his daughter on his arm. Cameras could be heard over the music as father and daughter walked toward the front. Billy watched Lori as she approached. She was the most stunning and beautiful bride he had ever seen. Once they arrived at the stage, Tim and Billy shook hands. Lori stood next to Billy and Tim stepped next to Kathleen. The pastor looked at the people standing before him and began.

It was not a church service but the pastor treated it as if it was. He asked for the blessing of God to be upon them. The exchange of vows came quickly and the ceremony of the rings was completed. Minutes later he pronounced both couples husband and wife.

"It is my honor to be the first to introduce to you, Mr. and Mrs. William Thompson and Mr. and Mrs. Timothy Spencer."

The guests stood to applaud and the group of people that had been walking along the beach clapped and cheered. After a minute Billy raised his hand requesting they become quiet.

"There's something I want to tell my wife, something I've been working on for almost a decade." He turned to her, looked deeply into her green eyes. She smiled back at him. "Lori, since I first looked at your eyes, when I met you outside of the restroom door, I knew you were something special. I've heard it once or twice from someone, God works in mysterious ways." Pastor Mark chuckled. "You came to that class because you, on a whim, decided to do that for your mother. No one believed us when we said we were in love, but I guess we proved them wrong. I love you Lori and I always will." He leaned into her and gently kissed her. She wrapped her arms around his neck and kissed him, pressing her lips tightly to his. The guests cheered as some whistled and clapped.

The reception was held in a rented space that was decorated to the rafters. In all the excitement of the wedding, Billy hadn't had a chance to congratulate his mother and Tim. Lori's father now had two titles: Stepfather and father-in-law. It was a humorous moment when Billy asked Tim what he should call him. But Billy still wanted to see his mother privately. She had put her life on hold and endured the tumult he had caused, always loving him and he wanted to thank her. They finally had a quiet moment as they stood alone in a hallway.

"Your father would be very proud of you Billy." She looked at her son who had grown into full adulthood and looked so much like his father. "I'll never forget your dad and I'm sure Tim will never forget Kelly."

"Thanks Mom, I know you won't."

"I guess you did prove me wrong." She smiled at Billy. "I should have known when you rattled on in the car after the first night of baptism classes."

Sandra came around the corner and ruined the moment. "There you are we've been looking for you everywhere. We have pictures to take, cake to cut, toasts to make … you're screwing up my itinerary!"

Kathleen and Billy returned to the party. Lori grabbed Billy's hand and as the music began to play, they came together on the dance floor for their first dance as husband and wife. Kathleen and Tim stood on the sidelines and had to be reminded that this was their wedding too and they also needed to be on the dance floor.

Sally made sure she danced with Tim. She said she always danced at least once with her daughter's husbands and at her age, she didn't know how many opportunities she might have remaining. She also danced with her grandson who seemed to be stepping on her feet more than he should.

"I'm just a little out of kilter Grandma." Billy said his face red with embarrassment.

"No, the problem is your wife has boobs and mine are hanging down to my belly button … it's throwing you off." Billy offered a slight chuckle at his grandmother's turn toward tawdry humor.

After all the pictures were taken, the cake was cut and the garters tossed. Their wedding day celebration was coming to an end. Christopher

Wayne Seekers approached Lori and Billy. He was accompanied by his fiancée, Tammy.

"Hey, Billy, Lori, congrats to the both of you." Christopher said. "You guys came a long way from that first Baptism class. Tammy offered her well wishes and then they announced they would be leaving.

"What ever happened to Bob? I tried to find him but it was like he didn't exist." Billy said.

"He went into the military and as far as I know he works at the pentagon. Maybe after law school we'll get together."

"We'll look forward to the reunion." Billy said as he pulled his wife close to him.

Billy and Lori said goodbye to everyone but before they left, he made certain he spoke to Pastor Mark.

"Billy, Lori, the two of you, take care of yourselves and each other. I had no idea the mischief you two got into during your baptism would lead to this … but I'm glad I was part of it. God bless you both with love and someday children."

Billy shook the pastor's hand and Lori leaned over to kiss his cheek. The pastor smiled as his cheeks turned red. As Pastor Mark Jackson walked away, Billy had a feeling that he would never see the man again.

CHAPTER 10

Three years had passed since the weddings. Kathleen and Tim had sold their current houses and combined their assets to build something they would be able to call theirs. Lori and Billy had built a home of their own on one of the larger remaining lots of the Hannover neighborhood. Lori loved the landscaped hills and walking paths as well as the other amenities. She believed it would be a wonderful place to raise a family.

They had planned to hold off for at least five years before having children, but the vacation in Puerto Vallarta had other ideas. One month after returning, Lori broke the news to her husband they were going to be parents in eight short months. Kathleen and Tim were excited by the news and started preparing for their new grandchild.

Kathleen began to make plans for the child's education, both in faith and secularly. This placed her son at odds with her because Billy had still not quite returned to his trust of those of faith and faith in general. They never had an open argument, but it was clear he didn't want his mother making decisions that should belong to Lori and himself.

The June weather was warm and Billy sat alone on the deck that overlooked the back yard. He thought of his father and an inconsolable mood had cast itself over the best of news. He had rewound the earlier conversation with his mother and as he struggled internally with the feelings, Lori came out to sit with him. She could tell he was dealing with something. As she placed her hand on his shoulder, Billy closed his hand around hers.

"Hey cowboy, what's eating you?" She asked.

"I was thinking about dad … my dad. He's never going to be able to see his grandchildren."

"Yea, I know how you feel. I have the same thoughts about my mom. But you know they can see them. It's true, they won't be able to pick them up but they'll still be able to love them."

"Mom wants me to enroll our kid into Sunday school classes. I told her I didn't know yet."

"You know she just wants what's best for the baby." She paused and then smiled. "I'll bet that went over well."

"She crossed her arms and tapped her foot at me." Billy said as he gave up a short laugh. "I told her we have better than five years to decide."

Kathleen's life with Tim had caused her to abandon her strict conservative nature. She and Tim still attended church but she began to dress differently. At 51 years of age, she was still quite a head turner and the wardrobe of her past life was not going to work. The current styles of clothing worn by women in Chicago were beginning to fill her closet. The business meetings they attended found her attired in clothing that she would have never been seen in a decade ago.

Because of the business, they had to host parties and attend parties and alcohol was often part of those gatherings. Billy reminded his mother of her first encounter with alcohol many years ago and how she missed church that day because she was so hung-over. Eventually she had built a tolerance for alcohol but getting through that period was sometimes punctuated with embarrassing moments.

At the office, Tim and Billy managed the salespeople while Kathleen managed the internal office operations. Lori contacted product producers to expand the product lines their company offered. She would negotiate the details of sales and distribution and would present this information to the Billy and her father. As she was working at her desk the telephone chirped.

"Good morning, thank you for calling Spencer and Associates, my name is Lori, how may I help you?"

A raspy voice on the phone said only one word … *Later*. The call terminated immediately afterward. Fear struck her deeply. She knew the voice was of her Uncle Kevin. She hadn't heard his voice in over ten years and now it had returned.

Lori stood from her desk and went into her husband's office. She shut the door behind her. Billy looked up at her and could tell she was upset.

"What's wrong Lori?" He asked. Billy never used pet names when she was like this. He knew something was seriously wrong.

"I just got a call from my uncle." She said as she sat down in a chair, her face had turned pale.

"He's not scheduled to be out of jail for two more years." He reached into his desk drawer and pulled out a telephone directory.

"I'll call the courts and see if he's still in jail." As Billy was looking up the number in the phone book, Tim came into the office. He held in his hands a handful of papers to go over with Billy. He could see the serious look on both of their faces.

"What's going on?" Tim asked as he shut the door behind him.

"Your brother just called Lori."

"Lori, are you sure it was Kevin?"

"Dad I'd know that voice anywhere." Lori answered as she nervously rubbed her hands together.

"Look, I'll take care of this ... he's my brother and my responsibility."

Billy had written the number for the court clerk onto a piece of paper and handed it to Tim. Lori was upset and with tears starting to form in her eyes, she began to plead with her father.

"Dad, I'm worried. I think maybe we should get out of here ... all of us ... for a while anyway. Your brother has been silent for ten years and now suddenly he's making calls. I'm telling you he's out and he's coming to take revenge on all of us." She patted her slight baby bump as she talked.

Billy sided with Lori and called the police department. He explained the situation but was told that unless Kevin was there and an immediate threat existed, they could not station an officer on site. Billy offered to pay the officer's salary to offset the burden to the city but the voice on the other end of the telephone explained they didn't have the depth of personnel to station an armed guard at their location. The voice told him the best they could do was to have an officer drive by regularly to check the area. They were disappointed with the answer from the police department. Tim looked at the number for the courts on the paper in his hands and quickly left Billy's office so he could make the call.

They needed protection and Billy remembered he kept a pistol in his desk drawer. He was an excellent shot with a rifle but a fair shot with the pistol. Both he and Lori had worked with the weapon at the practice range so they each knew how to aim and fire it. Billy handed the gun to his wife.

"Lori, put this in your desk and keep it with you."

With some defensive measure in place, he and Lori felt a little better. He stopped by his mother's office and explained what had happened. Kathleen's face showed she was uneasy with the information and suggested as Lori had, that it might be wise to leave the area for a while, at least until they knew where Kevin was and threat he posed was neutralized. She also suggested that perhaps, as a precaution, they should send everyone home. Billy had suggested they should first wait until they heard from Tim.

According to the court records, Kevin was still in jail so Tim decided to visit his brother. When he arrived to set up the visit, the guard told him Kevin was no longer there and that he had been released yesterday, two years early, based on his good behavior. The clerk explained because of outdated systems, the county inmate information was often a week behind on updates. Panic began to form in his gut. Tim knew he needed to call the office immediately to alert everyone that Kevin could show up at any time … he feared the worst.

He doubled back to see if he could use one of the telephones in the jail but the guard at the front told him civilians were not permitted to use their phones. Tim tried to reason with the guard but his persuasion failed and was told he would need to use the phone booth outside. Irritated and nervous, he walked out of the jail building and started for the phone booth across the street. After only a few steps in that direction, he heard the voice of his brother calling his name.

"You look surprised to see me little brother." Kevin said in his wheezy voice. His walk had a sway in it and as he got closer, Tim could smell his brother's breath had the distinct odor of alcohol. "Let's take a ride." Kevin showed Tim a pistol in his belt and ordered him to take him to his car. Tim was reluctant to comply with his request and felt doing so was the worst thing he could do.

"You've got a lot of nerve doing this in front of the jail." Tim told his brother as he started for the car. "Where are we supposed to go?" Tim asked.

"You're going to take me to your office so I can get caught up with my family."

"No, I'm not doing that. You're not going anywhere near them or touch anyone in my family again."

"Is that any way to treat the man that took a knife for you in that bar fight?" Tim was no longer imprisoned by that threat and Kevin could see by the lack of fear in his younger brother's eyes. "I suppose you'd hate to have that pretty little daughter or that new wife of yours to find out the real reason you and Kelly got married

"Kevin that debt had been paid many times over ... besides, they already know." He then changed the subject. "When you raped Lori, I had the police look the other way. There was just enough reasonable doubt and they bought it. I had to make a huge donation to the police scholarship fund so they would stop considering the case. But it never ended with you Kevin. I was always bailing you out of trouble, paying your legal fees. Lisa wrote off Lori and me for helping you!"

"Our sister is a spoiled little twit that hung out long enough to get her a doctor. She's nothing but a whore the way she threw herself at him." Kevin again motioned for Tim to move toward the car. Once they stopped, Kevin made note of the vehicle his brother was driving. "Wow Timmy, you must be doing alright. BMW's don't come cheap." He walked to the passenger door and tried to open it. "Unlock the door before I blow out the window."

"Go ahead, blow out the window. You'll be back in your cage faster than I can blink an eye"

Tim had stalled for as long as he could. He was amazed that not one police car came to or from the jail building while he stood there. The doors were unlocked and both men entered the car. Once inside, Kevin pointed the pistol and ordered his brother to start driving. Tim watched his brother closely, trying to gauge how drunk he may have been. He was hoping Kevin's reaction time was lessened by the alcohol in his blood. As he drove away from the jail, he noticed Kevin had returned the pistol to his belt. Kevin was right handed so the pistol was out of his reach. He needed to do something to get control of the situation. He would not deliver this maniac to his wife and daughter and if it cost him his life, it would be the payment for what he had done to Lori.

He ran through a red light and turned the opposite direction of the office. He was driving erratically, hoping to attract the attention of a police officer but to his disappointment, no police car was in sight. Kevin was onto his plan, pulled the pistol from his belt and pointed it at his brother, demanding he take him to the office immediately or he would shoot. By that time, they had traveled out of Sycamore and were getting close to the area where Billy's grandparent's farm had been. Along the side of the road was a deep ditch. Tim hit the brakes and turned the wheel sharply hoping to crash into it. The car spun to a stop, just at the edge. Kevin was momentarily disoriented and Tim reached over to grab the pistol. A fight for the weapon ensued. There was a shot. Brother looked at brother and without a word Tim slumped over the center console.

With no remorse, Kevin pulled his brother's lifeless body out of the car and dragged it to the edge of the bank. With a firm push of his foot, he rolled the body of his brother down the hill. It splashed into the water at the bottom of the hole. It would be discovered at some time but not before he administered his revenge. He climbed into the driver's seat of his dead brother's car, paying no attention to the blood that covered much of the front interior and he drove toward the offices of Spencer and Associates.

Billy needed to get some things from the store and asked Lori to go with him. She told him she would be alright now that she was armed. The fact that he hadn't heard back from Tim left him uneasy. He should have called by now. He thought. "Are you sure, because I don't feel right leaving you here alone, are you sure you won't come with me?" After Lori gave him several reassurances, he kissed her and left the office.

Kathleen had stopped by Lori's office and was going to go over some numbers from the last quarter's business. The pistol Billy had given her was sitting on the top of her desk and she presently made the decision to put it away. The barrel of the pistol hit a coffee cup on her desk and knocked it over. Some of the liquid splashed onto Kathleen's white skirt. As Lori apologized and Kathleen wiped at the coffee stain, a noise from the front of the building caught their attention.

A man walked through the front door of the office, turned and locked the door. He pulled a pistol from the right side of his blood covered pants and demanded that Kathleen and Lori be brought to him. No one moved at first but then a young woman reluctantly and nervously stood and complied with his request. As she walked he told her if she tried anything funny, he would start shooting people. One of the salespeople thought he could over-power the man. He was not athletic but Kevin was slightly intoxicated and he took that advantage. Unfortunately, his timing was off and Kevin quickly turned and shot him. The man fell to the floor dead.

"Don't get any ideas about calling the police because the phone line's been cut outside." He held a piece of wire in his hand so everyone could see it. The people that remained in the front of the office huddled together fearing for their lives.

The young woman who stood to get Kathleen and Lori was followed closely by Kevin. Fear gave birth to tears and she paused to wipe at them. Kevin believed her crying was a way to alert Lori and Kathleen about him and he shot her in the back. She fell to the floor bleeding heavily. Kevin stepped over her with the same dispassionate ease as if he stepped over a log in the forest. There was no room in his heart for anything but hate and revenge.

As Kevin passed through the archway the surviving people ran to the door, unlocked it and went for help. Three men stayed and attempted to take Kevin down. He was ready for them and shot each of them dead.

He had one bullet remaining in his gun and he had two targets. He chose Kathleen to receive the round.

Inside the office, Lori had removed the pistol from the drawer of her desk. She was not as experienced with firearms and fumbled as she attempted to load the bullets into the chamber. She wished Billy was there because he would have had it ready moments after her uncle's voice was detected by their ears. The sounds of gunshots and people screaming further hampered her inability to load the weapon. The sound of a young woman crying just outside of the office and the crack of a pistol shot told them Kevin was close. Lori placed the pistol back into the drawer, but did not close it.

Within seconds, he reached the two women and found them huddled together in fear. The lifeless telephone receiver lay on the desk and as his eyes rested upon it, he laughed at their futile attempts to call for help. He rushed toward Kathleen, pulled her away from Lori and punched her in the face with his fist. Lori tried to engage him but he pushed her away and she fell to the floor. His fury completely consumed him as he turned his attention back to Kathleen. He raised the pistol and struck Kathleen with the grip. She fell to the floor as blood poured heavily from the wound in her scalp. She tried to recover from the pain and as she got to her hands and knees, she raised her left hand to press against the blood and pain that flowed from her scalp. Kevin uttered something unintelligible and then kicked her in her side.

"That was for sending me to jail!" He kicked her again, this time in the face. Her nose had broken and she recoiled in intense pain. Blood was coming from her mouth, nose and head. Her blonde hair was becoming matted by her own blood and was splattering onto her light colored, blouse and skirt. "This one's for taking my little brother from me!" His shoe came to rest on her ribs several more times, breaking them and driving their jagged spear-like edges into her lungs and other organs. She was bleeding heavily both inside and outside her body.

Lori once again tried to stop him and as before he pushed her away. A third time she tried ... this time he shot. The bullet hit her in the chest and she fell to the floor. Kevin returned to his punishment of Kathleen. He hadn't seen Lori crawl to the desk nor did he see her pull the pistol out of the drawer.

Seated on the floor, Lori aimed the pistol at her uncle. "GO TO HELL KEVIN SPENCER!" She yelled as she fired every round the pistol held. His upper body absorbed three of the bullets. He was still on his feet and ran out of the hallway but he was bleeding heavily. He tripped over the body of the young woman he had murdered minutes before. He tried to get up and leave but the bullets Lori had pumped into him spelled his doom. His legs would not answer the call from his brain. Seconds later, his arms could not support his weight and he collapsed onto the hard tile floor. Kevin Spencer died in a puddle of his own blood.

Lori pushed her hand over the bloody wound in her chest and started for Kathleen's bloodied body. The bleeding was heavy and the blouse and hem of her skirt dripped blood onto her legs and down to her shoes. She knelt next to her friend and mother-in-law.

"It's Jimmy, I see Jimmy ... his hand is out." Kathleen said through a gurgling and whispering voice. Seconds later, she died.

Lori was much too weak to cry for the loss and managed to prop herself against the near wall. The sound of sirens could be heard along with the voices of people rushing to help. It was getting difficult for her to breath and her vision was getting blurry. She knew she was in trouble and probably would die soon but she had to hold on to see her husband, the only man she ever truly loved ... just one more time.

Billy turned the corner and a block away, directly in front of the office, several police vehicles with flashing lights clogged the road. His heart started to beat rapidly and fear gripped him so tightly he could hardly breathe. After parking his car as close as he could, he abandoned it and forced his way through the crowd of people that had gathered. They were saying things he didn't want to hear and terrible images played through his mind. He reached the front of the building and two police officers blocked his way.

"My wife and mother are in there!" He yelled. One of the officers opened the door. He quickly scanned the scene. Blood was everywhere and the bodies of people he had worked with lye motionless on the floor. The survivors had walked out and were being tended to by the ambulance crews. He saw Kevin dead on the floor and hoped his mother and Lori were safe. As he walked into the hallway where their offices were located he stopped at the sight of his mother's bloody and motionless body. Her hair and clothing were soaked red. His lip began to quiver and he started to cry. But he needed to find Lori. He quickly stepped past that horrible sight and found Lori sitting on the floor, leaning against a wall, bloodied and barely alive. The officer who had been trying to help her stood aside.

Billy knelt next to her. The knees of his pants began to absorb her blood. She looked at him, her green eyes into his blue. Her face glistened by sweat, she was in shock and needed medical attention immediately or she would not survive, nor would their child.

"I got him ... I'm sorry Billy ... I love you cowboy." Her voice was raspy as her lungs had begun to fill with her blood. She reached to hug him and as their lips touched, her arms fell to her side. As he looked into her eyes, he watched the blackness dilate into the green, he cried out.

"No Lori no ... Please God no!" He cried harder than he had ever cried in his life. The death of his grandmother, his father, the baby and his mother, the sum of all that pain was nothing to what he felt at this moment. Two police officers stood by as he cried and sat on the blood-soaked carpeting holding his wife's lifeless body, rocking her back and forth as her arms extended outward keeping time like some gruesome metronome.

Five days later, the funerals for his wife and mother took place. His mother and Lori's service would be held together. Tim's sister Lisa had requested his service be held back in Ohio and one week later so she could attend both. Lisa also took responsibility for Kevin's remains. Instead of a burial, she donated his body to the medical school at Ohio State University. Billy's aunt and Uncle arrived from Florida as did Christopher, Tammy and Bob Stanton, Billy's friends from high school.

Billy purchased two plots close to his parent's graves and not too distant from his grandparent's graves. It was impossible for him to be at both gravesites at the same time, so a service with two caskets, side by side, was performed in the chapel on the grounds. Lori's casket would be lowered into the ground first and then everyone would walk the short distance to Kathleen's burial.

As he stood before Lori's casket, watching it be lowered into the ground, the memories of his father's burial played through his mind and like then he fell to his knees, crippled with the excruciating pain of loss. He asked how a loving God could cause one person so much pain. Hadn't he had enough pain in his life? Why did God need to rip away everyone he loved? Why did *he* need to suffer so much?

As he cried from the crushing pain in his heart, his family and friends tried to console him. Every nerve in his body reacted to the grief. His body shook uncontrollably and he began to vomit. Christopher and Bob stood next to him and placed their reassuring hands on his shoulders as he attempted to gather himself for the next burial. The crowd moved to the next casket. It was positioned on its mechanical sling and was moments from being lowered into the grave. Once everyone had assembled, the final words were said and the casket began to move downward. Billy watched as his aunt's grief overcame her ... she became faint and collapsed. His uncle needed help carrying her to the car and Bob was there.

One month after the funeral, the head stone that Billy had ordered was delivered and was placed on the grave. As he stood before the black granite stone, it was the inscription in the center that pulled strongly at his heart:

I love you cowboy.

Kevin Spencer's revenge was complete. The company was destroyed, his life was destroyed. Three of the four principal members of the company were gone and all but one of the top managers was killed—the company was dissolved.

Billy tried to find solace in faith. Kevin would stand in judgment before Jesus for the evil he unleashed—that is if Jesus and God existed. He imagined a scene in his mind of Kevin being dragged to hell by demons so unimaginably horrifying ... it offered no peace.

Depression overtook him and almost convinced him to take his life. Their home, the town were filled with memories of her, and their lives together and each memory ripped at his heart. He hoped the sorrow would go away but the hole deepened. He became jaded and hard. He resented God, Jesus and anyone who professed faith. His pain would never go away and his distrust and distain for his creator grew ever deeper.

CHAPTER 11

Nine years had passed since the day he buried his family but in the earlier days of that time, the estate of his mother and father-in-law had been settled and Billy found himself a very wealthy man. But all the money in the world couldn't fill the hole in his heart nor stop the resentment toward God from growing deeper. On several occasions, Pastor Singleton had tried to invite him to church but Billy was less than kind to the pastor.

He would often go to the cemetery and sit on the ground in front of Lori's headstone. His love for her would never end and neither would the torment in his heart. The shiny black granite stone that bore his wife's name was nothing more than a source of pain. When his aunt would call from Florida to check on him, the conversation would always go back to stories about Lori or his mother. Grief impaled his heart and he lashed out at Sandra. He demanded she stop calling him and refused to answer the phone whenever she did call. He was alone and turning into a miserable human being.

He needed to get away from Sycamore or he would go insane so he contracted a real estate agent to sell everything. Billy kept only the photo albums and presented Tim's sister Lisa, a check for the proceeds of the sale of her brother's house. He packed his belongings and moved to Chicago.

Billy purchased a condominium in a secured upscale building near downtown Chicago. The space overlooked Lake Michigan and was perhaps one of the best units in the entire building. He secured a position with an advertising company and soon began to build accounts. His charm, confidence and good looks put potential clients at ease and helped him close many deals that might have otherwise gone astray.

He buried himself in his work because it kept him from dwelling on the loss of his wife. But there were women in the office that reminded him of her. There was no one person that was the complete package, but pieces of Lori's personality and physical attributes, were found. Loneliness had begun to pull at him like a pack of wolves ripping the flesh of a fresh kill. One evening after a long and difficult day of work, Billy accompanied a young woman from the office to a bar for a drink. After several glasses, Billy escorted her back to his condo. He discovered the intimate company of a woman and alcohol removed the pain from his life. He had become a womanizing man. His office mates seemed to approve of his behavior because when they accompanied him to the taverns and saloons, they too could find themselves nightly companionship. In his professional life, Billy's confidence, charm and good looks, provided him success and those same attributes awarded him a different woman in his company nearly every night of those last six years.

As was often the situation, Billy and his posse, entered one of the many bars they would frequent. His eyes landed on a woman with long straight dark hair. For a moment grief was laced with fantasy and he thought Lori had somehow returned. Reality forced the apparition from his mind but still, it tainted his judgment. He abandoned his pseudo friends and walked over to the woman and introduced himself. Her name was Kelly Anderson and she was five years his junior.

As they spoke, he learned she was from a suburb of St. Louis and was in town applying for a job at a competing marketing firm. He discovered she was a woman of faith and had recently been divorced. Billy used his knowledge of the Bible to ease her into a false sense of trust and security. He was intoxicated with the memory of Lori and in his mind this woman was becoming her. The way she flipped her hair, the way she stood … he was going down a path from the past. The young woman was slightly inebriated and was easily manipulated to be led back to his home.

The combination of alcohol, fantasy and grief brought the mirage back to the forefront of his mind. As the elevator climbed, her alcohol induced clumsiness caused her to fall against him. He caught the woman as he had caught her. The lines of reality and dream were beginning to blur and he was put off his routine and had even called the woman, Lori. Once inside the condo Billy began to kiss her … she responded and became impassioned. Kelly was a surrogate for Lori, more so than the dozens of women before her. He had let down every defense and he foolishly dove into the deep end of passion.

Several hours later, in the early darkness of the new day, sobriety had returned to Kelly and she realized what she had done. She slowly left his company and silently walked to the bathroom. In the dim light, she began to cry and prayed for forgiveness for her weakness. Kelly quietly dressed herself and left him sleeping in his bed. She walked through the quiet and deserted hallway, hoping no one would see her waiting for the elevator. The bell announced the arrival of the car. But before stepping into the elevator, she looked back through the hallway, to his door, feeling ashamed and confused.

One year of misery and self-destruction later, Billy was standing in his kitchen looking through the mail determining which envelopes should be thrown in the trash. The front door buzzer sounded. He wasn't expecting anyone and asked through the microphone who was calling. On the other end was a voice of a man who said he had a delivery. Billy pressed the button to unlock the door. A couple of minutes later, there was a knock on the door to his condo. When he opened it, a young man was standing before him. The man spoke with a very heavy Bronx accent.

"Are you William Thompson, and is this your driver's license pitcher?"

"Yes, and who are you?" Billy asked.

"Bill Teedle. I'm from the law offices of Brandy, Coyle and Harden." He produced an identification badge. "I have papers of a child support suit for you … please sign here." Billy signed the form. "You have been officially served sir." The young man said and then turned away.

Billy stood in the doorway of his apartment his mouth had fallen open from the shock. He regained his composure, closed the door and stared at the thick envelope he held in his hand. Billy began to ask questions in his mind and he couldn't come to any easy answers. He walked into the kitchen still holding the unopened envelope. He started for the refrigerator but decided he wasn't hungry. Billy then sat down at the table in the dining room and opened the envelope. He took a deep breath, removed the folded papers, opened them and began to read.

The suit was brought by a woman named Kelly Anderson. She was the woman with dark hair he met in a bar a year ago. The more he read from the paper the angrier he had become. His thoughts were not kind and he began to think terrible things of the woman as he rationalized his behavior. She could have been with other men, he thought. She had told him she was recently divorced and could have been with other men to taste her new freedom. As he paged through the legal papers, he came across an order from the court to submit to a blood test for paternity.

Billy retained an attorney to attempt to limit the financial exposure he faced. Several weeks after he had complied with the court order to provide a blood sample, his mailbox contained an envelope with the results of that test. He reluctantly opened the letter and began to read. There was a 99 percent probability that he was the father of Kelly Anderson's baby girl.

Billy paced about his living room, puzzling over what to do next. The television was on but he wasn't paying it any attention. He had to figure a way to get out of this. Billy tossed the letter onto the small table next to the couch and decided he needed a drink to help calm him. He returned to the couch and once again picked up the letter. No matter how many times he read it, the words never changed.

Ten years ago, when he wanted to be a father, it was ripped away from him by a lunatic. Now he didn't want the job. Thoughts of his past were being interrupted by the movie on the television. A teenage boy accidentally goes back in time. He had seen the movie several times and he knew how it ended. He mused having an inventor-friend with a time machine would be very convenient at this moment. He brought himself back to reality by reminding himself movies aren't real and time travel isn't possible … or is it?

He began to seriously think about the entire time travel possibility. Einstein had theorized it was possible. His mind raced with the possibility that someone in the future may have indeed figured out how to do it. If he was successful, he could stop himself from meeting Kelly Anderson preventing this pregnancy. But then he began to think on a grander scale. What if he could go back to Sycamore, ten years ago and stop Kevin Spencer? This decade long nightmare would not be and instead of defending a child support lawsuit, he would be celebrating his son or daughter's birthday with his family.

His eyes watered as the memory of Lori filled his mind. His love for her never faded nor did his anger at God for taking she and his family away. His obsession brought a plan to mind.

He stood from the couch and quickly went to his den where he composed a letter on his computer. It was an ad to be printed in the local paper. He hoped, if time travel was ever realized, someone from the future might see his ad and respond. He began to write.

Time traveler wanted to help with personal strife ten years in my past. I will be sitting on a park bench, ten feet from a mailbox outside of Ben's Pizza Emporium. I will be wearing a Blue Chicago Cub's Baseball hat. I will be there at 11:00 am Central Time on Wednesday May 16, 2008. I will answer to the name Samuel.

He included a cover letter directing the printer to list the ad exactly the way it was. Do not make any changes to any of the provided information. Billy folded the papers and placed them in an envelope and applied the postage stamp. In the morning, he would place that envelope in the mailbox by the park bench.

The next morning, he readied himself for the possible journey to the past. He called into the office to say he wouldn't be in. After leaving his apartment he went to the mailbox, deposited the envelope and sat on the bench.

Moments later he heard a voice.

"Excuse me, are you Samuel?"

Billy was startled. He didn't expect someone would appear. When a man called out his name, hope filled him. Billy jumped to his feet, shook the man's hand. He began to talk but the man held his hand up and suggested they walk in silence. The man asked him to follow him.

They entered a very expensive hotel and went to the top floor. After entering the room, the man closed the door behind them. It was then he began to speak.

"My name is Smith." He went on to talk about the dangers of time travel and how small changes that seem insignificant can have enormous consequences. "The fee is $100,000.00. You can transfer the money into an account I have already set up."

Billy began to ask the questions that had surfaced when the two men met by the bench and the man named Smith answered some of them.

"I am a graduate student working on my PHD and I have created this machine to collect information and research for my dissertation."

"So, I'm your science project at school." Billy added sarcastically.

"Time is like a spiral, Samuel." Smith said with a touch of irritation. "Each second lies upon another second in the large spiral. Imagine an old album record. Every one of those grooves is like a day upon a day forming a row. Each row is bordered by an energy field. If you were to start at the middle of the exampled record and spiral outward, you are traveling forward in time conversely, the opposite direction takes you back in time. As I said, each layer, or row, is bordered by an energy barrier. This barrier is constant and is easily calculated and can be broken through or over by exerting the necessary energy. The more energy, the further back or forward in time you travel."

He went on to explain that time and space are three dimensional and any point or date in time can be calculated as to its location in the three-dimensional spiral. Billy interrupted his explanation and had another question.

"How did you choose me ... I mean me, out of who knows how many?"

"I needed people to interview. I had already made two trips back in time but I hadn't sent anyone back. So, I did a search for people who were seeking information about time travel and I came across an old want ad in a paper in Chicago ... and here I am. So, about the money, can you, pay it?"

Billy wasn't worried about money, he had plenty of it. Between his mother's and Tim's holdings, Billy inherited well over two million dollars. He called his bank and had the money transferred. Once that was complete, the man asked Billy exactly what he hoped to accomplish. Billy explained how he wanted to reverse the damage Kevin Spencer had done to his family and how he wanted to get his family back.

His plan was to go back to the morning of the day Kevin destroyed his family and his life. He would shadow the man to the bar where he had gotten drunk. Before he could leave to hijack his brother's car, he would stop him perhaps challenge him to a fight. Since he had a record for violence, the police would arrest Kevin and return the man to jail.

Smith suggested that it might not go quite the way he planned and if he mistakenly killed Kevin, he might find himself in jail for murder, or he might be seriously injured or killed. Being this close to the possibility of changing the course of the past, Billy could not be shaken from his plan. He would be smarter than that he thought as he followed Smith to one of the suite's bedrooms.

Inside the room, Smith presented the time machine. Billy looked at it suspiciously. It resembled one of those security devices stores installed at their doors. On one side of the structure was an open box that contained a sphere about the size of a basketball. The sphere was dark but the exterior was rough, covered by hundreds of raised surfaces.

Before beginning, Smith made a cup of coffee. The traveler set to work and entered all of the dates that Billy had requested, into a glass covered rectangle he held in his hand and moments later the sphere lit up like lightning. He gave Billy a small controller that resembled a key fob. It had one button beneath a guard and he suggested to Billy that he put the controller in his pants pocket before beginning. Smith explained to him the sphere will travel first. Its purpose was to pinpoint the exact place in time and space where he would appear.

"When your task has been completed, lift the guard and press the button on the return controller, it will bring you back to here. If you need to leave immediately, depress the button and you will be returned to the present as you know it." Smith once again reminded Billy to put the controller into his pants pocket.

Smith next began to describe a fail-safe provision the program would initiate in the event he became separated from the controller. Billy was preoccupied by the closeness of ending the nightmare. He daydreamed about holding Lori in his arms and seeing his mother and Tim alive and happy. Unfortunately, he paid Smith little attention and as a consequence, Smith's words were but faint echoes in Billy's ears. He put all of his trust into a man he knew nothing about and a machine that was nothing short of science fiction.

Billy stepped between the two vertical structures. His heart was racing with the anticipation of ending the decade long nightmare. Smith touched the glass panel. The sphere had shown an even brighter light and then disappeared. He suddenly remembered the controller was still in his hand but before he could place it in his pocket an energy field enclosed him and froze his movements. A low frequency hum played against his eardrums and a pressure squeezed against every inch of his body. He felt the controller slide across his palm. There was a bright flash and then darkness

CHAPTER 12

The discomfort seemed to last for hours but only a second or two had passed. Billy regained control of his body and moments later, his sight had returned. The sunlight was bright and hot. The sky was a clear and beautiful blue. A hot breeze blew through is hair while wind gusts gathered sand and soil and pushed them along the ground. As his eyes took in his surroundings, panic began to grow within him. Something had gone terribly wrong. He wasn't in Sycamore Illinois ten years in his past but had appeared into some time and area that looked post- apocalyptic or just forward in time of pre-historic.

He immediately looked at the ground by his feet. The controller should be there. He had felt it slide across his palm as the time field enveloped him and he was sure it made the same journey as he had. Billy didn't see it by his feet. His heart began to beat faster as he reached down to sift through the dirt with his fingers but he found nothing. He feared to leave the exact place he landed because the controller had to be in this spot. He widened his search for the device, sifting in arcs as wide as his arms would allow. Anger was beginning to replace trepidation. In his thoughts, he was certain Mr. Smith had made an error in calculation and as soon as he found the controller and returned to Chicago, he would demand he send him to the correct place and time.

He dropped to his knees sweeping his arms in wide arcs trying desperately to find the controller. He realized he needed to know the exact spot he appeared so he could return to it after he widened the search. With his finger, he drew an X in the dirt. Panic and fear pushed him forward as he continued his search for the device crawling across the ground and muttering like a mad man, now admonishing himself for not placing the controller in his pocket as Smith had twice suggested. But there was something else Smith had said, something about a contingency for an emergency return. He was angry at everyone, and now, particularly himself for not listening. Perhaps his arrogance may have cost him everything, maybe even his own life.

Billy had searched a wide area, wider than the distance the controller might have bounced. As he stood he looked at his surroundings and the visual clues could not send any clearer message. He was lost somewhere and in some time and his last hope and chance to be with Lori and his family was gone. Grief returned in full measure as did the hopelessness of being stranded in whatever this place was and it forced him to his knees. He bent down to the ground, clawed at the dirt as both anger and agony filled him. As the tears streamed down his cheeks, a thought, no, a hope came to his mind.

Perhaps he was in the correct year, just the wrong country. He had added in an extra day so he could plan for unforeseen challenges. His anger for himself was now redirected back toward Smith. The man had made an incredibly costly error in his targeting. He may still have time, but he needed to know where he was and he would need to plan to get to Sycamore Illinois.

Billy stood and began wiping his eyes. The dirt on his hands mixed with his tears and had created muddy streaks upon his face. He walked to the closest of the structures that were most likely dwellings. He approached a door and knocked. There was no answer but the door was ajar so he pushed his way in. He called out and like before, there was no answer. He began to search for clues to tell him where he had landed. A newspaper, mail, anything that would tell him where he was would have been helpful, but there was nothing.

The moment he entered the structure, something happened outside and behind him, something he hadn't noticed. The Orb had appeared and was hovering where Billy had been standing when he had appeared from temporal transfer. His ears didn't hear the slight snap as the machine's lifeboat had returned to rescue him, for he now stood inside the structure. The orb hummed and flashed, but no one was there to touch it. Seconds later, it vanished leaving Billy trapped in the past.

Billy's search inside produced nothing of help and he returned to the outside through the rear door. The area was devoid of human presence. Dozens of similar structures stretched outward next to one another and many of the buildings appeared to have laundry hanging in the warm dry breeze, but no people seemed to occupy the area. Goats, dogs and chickens scurried about the grounds but these were the only things he could see alive. He decided to go back into the structure and wondered if the view from a front window would be any different. As the blind was pushed aside, the sight that met his eyes caused his mouth to fall open.

Thousands, perhaps ten thousand people were gathered some distance away. They seemed to be walking up a small hill to stop before three or four other people at the top. They were given something and they would move on. As Billy watched he wondered if he should walk over to join them. They would know where he was and at least someone, he hoped, should know English.

He turned away from the window to start for the front door and a thought crossed his mind. He would need money to hire a cab and purchase an airline ticket to Chicago. Habit caused him to reach for his cell phone. When he looked at the display, it showed no service. He reasoned perhaps ten years in the past this area had no cell coverage and it also appeared to have no electricity to recharge his almost empty phone battery. His wallet was almost as useless. It contained credit cards that hadn't been issued yet and the little cash it held was printed in a time that had yet to come. But there was money in the bank back in Sycamore he would only need to make a phone call to gain access to it.

Billy now had a plan he just needed help to put it into action. He returned to the window to once again look at the horde. As he watched, he noticed a single man had departed the crowd from the top of the hill and was walking toward the village. The man was getting closer and seemed on a course that would bring him to the house where Billy was standing.

"Oh no!" Billy said under his breath. He didn't want to get arrested for illegal entry into someone's home. He began to panic and started immediately for the back door. Several Pottery jugs offered a hiding place and he crouched down behind them and became as quiet as he could.

The man entered the house and made his way to the back door and stopped. He called out in clear English.

"Billy, it's okay, you're safe ... no one's going to hurt you."

Billy slowly stood and came out from hiding. He looked at the man who was smiling at him. He was about as tall as Billy, had curly black hair that landed about his shoulders. His olive colored skin and features bore the same resemblance to those from Middle Eastern Countries. Billy approached the man and began to speak to him.

"You sound like you're from the states. Do you know Mr. Smith?" He asked timidly.

"I know a lot of people." The man responded. He was dressed in the same loose robes everyone in the crowd had worn. "Come with me, you're hungry." The man started to turn to direct Billy toward the front but Billy stopped.

"Who are you and how do you know who I am? Where am I?"

The man looked at Billy and smiled. "Let me answer your questions this way. I know who you are because I know who everyone is ... because my father knows every one of his children."

The man spoke in riddles and Billy didn't have time or patience for childish games. His plan needed to be put into action very soon or he would fail to stop the murders of his family and friends.

"Look, cut to the chase! I need to know where I am, how I can get to a phone to call a cab and get to the nearest airport!"

The man considered Billy and rubbed his chin. "The airport, cab ... these things will not exist for almost 2000 years." The man let his statement settle into Billy's mind.

Billy's impatience was quickly evolving into shock. He looked at the man standing before him and the words he had taken for gibberish, started to make sense.

"Wait a minute. You're saying I traveled back 2000 years." He paused as if he was assembling a story in his mind. "And you know me because your father knows all of his children."

The man was still grinning at Billy as he was putting things together and he decided to help by adding one more piece of information—one that would tell Billy exactly where and when he had landed.

"This is spring in the Judean year 29."

Silence came over the room and soon Billy's face registered the shock of when he was and where he was, but also, who it was standing next to him. He looked down at the ground and began to sob and cry.

"It's over ... I'll never be able to save them ... to save her."

He fell to his knees and wept heavily as his only hope was now certainly scuttled. The man who stood before Billy Thompson was Jesus of Nazareth and he had landed in the middle of the biblical story of the feeding of the five thousand. However, Billy was not overcome with adoration of Jesus. Vitriol began to fill him.

He slowly looked up at Jesus and all the pain in his life began to flow out of him like hot lava. "You … you let all of it happen. You let my grandmother get sick, my little brother or sister die and you let my dad get cancer and die. Then you let that lunatic loose so he could kill my family!" Billy was looking directly into Jesus' eyes as he spoke through clinched teeth. His hands were balled into fists and he had the appearance of someone who was ready to attack. "I prayed so hard I put my heart into everything. I fasted so you would save my dad … but you did nothing!"

Billy had risen to his feet and was beginning to pace angrily around the room of the structure. Clouds of dust were rising as he kicked his feet onto the ground. The sunlight passing through the window openings created dimensional patterns as the dust played through the light. He Pointed at Jesus and hurled question after question. Jesus said nothing and let Billy continue to rage. He watched Billy move around the room, pacing as if he were a caged animal and once Billy had exhausted himself from yelling, he watched him fall to his knees and cry.

Jesus cautiously walked over to where Billy knelt and carefully placed his hand on his shoulder.

"I know you are hurting Billy and I did hear your prayers as well as the prayers of your mother and the pastor. While they touched our heart the will of the father was to be done. And your wife and mother, well, Kevin made a choice that unfortunately took many innocent lives, including your wife and mother's."

"I suppose your platitudes are supposed to make me all warm and fuzzy. I set out to save my family and nothing but that will make me happy!" Billy growled as he threw the hand of Jesus off his shoulder.

"Don't you want to know why you landed here and not in Sycamore Illinois?" Jesus asked.

Billy was still on his knees and rested his hands on his thighs as he panted from his crying and anger and looked hatefully at Jesus.

"I suppose you're going to tell me a stupid story about how you did this for my benefit."

"Your impatience and impertinence are not becoming. If you would be quiet for a moment and stop interrupting me, I'll explain why you are here." Jesus looked at Billy the same way his parents had done when he was in trouble for something. "When the time field began its journey, a solar flare hit the atmosphere of the earth. The intense radiation of that event reset the target of your destination and landed you here. Had you placed the controller in your pocket as you were told, you could have returned to Chicago and Smith would have been able to send you as you had desired. And, if you had listened to Smith, you would have heard him tell you of the built-in fail-safe that every trip, including the one you took, had."

Billy's face began to twist into a tight and angry grimace. He vaguely recalled Smith talking about an emergency return but unfortunately, he hadn't paid Smith any attention when he spoke. Perhaps Jesus' opinion of him was accurate. Maybe he was too sure of himself and in too great a hurry. Perhaps his ego had cost him his family. But he was not going to bury his anger toward God, not yet. He had an audience with Jesus and he was going to get his pound of flesh for the wrongs he felt had been delivered upon him.

"I get it now ... it's my fault that I'm here." Billy said as every word was laced with anger and sarcasm. "I've got a question for you, Jesus. If

God so loves me, then why didn't he hold the flare for just a couple of seconds? He's all powerful, couldn't he do that?"

"William, I advise you to think back to the lessons in your classes and watch your tongue. It is not right to test the Lord your God and anger toward the Father or me will not help you achieve your goal." Jesus paused but never broke his gaze from Billy. "There are worse places a man can land than Judea in the 29th year." Jesus then explained what Smith had said when Billy was not listening. "He was trying to tell you if you had lost the controller, the orb would have sensed the controller hadn't registered your body heat and it would automatically return to the place you had landed. You could have touched the orb and it would have returned you to the place you began this journey. If you had stayed in the same spot you had landed … for a few minutes longer, you would have seen and touched the orb and would be back in Chicago and not trapped here." Jesus paused for a few seconds as Billy absorbed the information. "So, yes, it is your fault that you are here, now trapped in the past."

Billy returned to his feet and both men stared at each other in silence but it was Jesus who broke it.

"William, you are hungry and you need to eat. Come with me to the hill. You already know what is happening outside so please come and sample the Father's love and power."

He was exhausted from yelling and numb from grief. His spirit was broken and all he could do was to nod his head and acquiesce to the suggestion of his new host. Before they left the building, Jesus looked at Billy and made a few observations.

"You cannot walk about this place attired as you are. Your machines and devices of the future cannot be seen here." With a single movement of his hand Billy's clothing had been changed into the same type of garment Jesus was wearing. His cell phone, watch and wallet seemed to have vanished into thin air. Billy took a breath as if to speak, but

Jesus hand gestured he should remain quiet. He placed his hands over Billy's ears and an odd buzzing hummed in them. Jesus then placed his right hand on his throat just below his jaw. "You will now be able to understand what anyone says and what you say will be understood by those who hear your voice. I suggest you use extreme caution before speaking."

"How is that even possible?" Billy asked.

"At one time in your life you would not ask that question, you knew by your faith that what is not possible for man, is possible for God. I must return to the people and you should come with me."

As Billy walked to follow behind Jesus, his new clothing was offering some challenges. His under pants were replaced by a loin wrap. It was bulky and felt like an old cloth diaper. The hot breeze was more detectable as the wind was flowing up the robe and around his legs. He imagined a strong gust lifting the robe forcing him to recreate Marilyn Monroe's famous iconic pose.

While they walked, Jesus instructed him about the culture he was now part of. The rights and privileges that were his advantage were not present here and the behavior of his recent past would get him killed. Billy stopped walking and wanted clarification.

"Committing adultery William is a crime punishable by stoning or beheading. It is the seventh commandment and dovetails with the tenth. I'm sure you remember them."

"Yea, I remember them ... but sometimes things happen and you don't care." Billy replied with a distinct edge in his voice. He then purposely changed the subject. "Where do we take showers, brush our teeth and where is the restroom and why are you calling me William?"

"The latrines are far over there. They are designated for women and men. Do not approach the women's latrines for any reason or you may be arrested and killed."

"What, a wrong turn or a mistake and you die? It seems kind of Draconian, don't you think?"

"It is Mosaic Law and it is the law of the Jewish People." Jesus paused and looked at Billy harshly. "Perhaps you would find a better life in Rome where your type of lifestyle is promoted."

"They sound like my kind of people." Billy answered with sarcasm.

"The grass seems always greener on the other side of the fence William. In the beginning you would fit in, but you would be found out eventually and because you are not a pure-blood Roman, you would be considered a savage and the privileges bestowed its people would not be available to you. Further, you would most likely be found guilty of a crime against Rome and crucified. If that is the path you wish, I will not stand in the way of your free will. Oh, and I call you William because as your teacher, we must do things … formally."

Billy looked at Jesus the same way he looked at his mother when she cornered him in an argument. He thought deeply for a response but the only thing that came out was equal to a child's whining.

"You know you're … weird and you don't look like your pictures in the Bible."

Jesus laughed at Billy's response. "William, I look like my mother's heritage not like the European renderings. Perhaps they thought the Son of God was supposed have the appearance of the most beautiful man alive. Beauty of the body is not what counts because as age diminishes it, the real inner beauty of the essence or soul is what we cling to. You were attracted to Lori by her beauty but it was her soul, her essence that holds your heart."

"Please don't talk about her … I'm never going to see her again." Billy said as his lip began to quiver and tears filled his eyes.

"William, I will help you find peace and help you grow in your faith and you will see her again, I promise."

Jesus placed his hand on Billy's shoulder and urged him to join the crowd at the base of the hill. He stood in silence as Jesus left him to return to the others at the top. This was now his life, trapped in a world he didn't know and one misstep from death. He wondered if death wouldn't be better, at least the pain of her loss would be gone.

CHAPTER 13

The queue moved faster than he thought it would and he reached the top of the hill quickly. As he stood before the people working at the baskets Billy looked at the surroundings and wondered about the details of this scene that were not written in the Bible. The woven containers were tiny and reminded him of two small wicker waste baskets. He looked in the first container and saw three fish that had the appearance of having just been removed from the sea. The other basket held two small loaves of bread. Billy looked up at the two very young men, almost boys, standing next to Jesus and figured they were two local boys caught up in the excitement of what was happening. As he took his food, Jesus smiled at him. Billy shook his head in disbelief and walked away. On his plate which was essentially a wicker mat, the fish became a prepared dish. He had no need to cut, clean and cook the fish for it had already been done and done to his taste. He sat on the hard ground in the company of many and ate until he was filled and began thinking of the miracle he had just lived through and began to wonder if Jesus would perform one that would send him to Sycamore … to save them and her.

The sun had made its journey to the hills beyond the village and the shadows of the afternoon were signaling evening was approaching. The crowd had been fed and Billy sat alone under a tree. Jesus and a man about the same age as Jesus approached him. He watched them silently. They both looked tired and Billy wondered what it was they would want from him. They stopped before Billy and Jesus made the introduction.

"Andrew, this is William. He will be traveling with us." Jesus said as Andrew greeted him. Billy elected to sit, reengaging his anger toward Jesus and did not attempt to shake Andrew's hand. Jesus acted as if Billy had done nothing wrong and continued to speak, making certain only the three of them could hear him. He had explained everything about Billy to Andrew and then forbade him to speak of his origins to anyone, including his brother Simon.

After Jesus had finished, he asked both men to follow him to the camp area where the other apostles waited patiently. Gathered together, Jesus introduced them to Billy. Some of the eleven were young men, very young, almost teenage boys. Billy had begun to feel awkward about the entire process and suggested he might be better off alone.

He was a stranger in this time and he didn't belong here, he thought to himself. His mind wandered back to the malfunctioning time machine and his arrogance and the heavy cost it levied upon him. There was no way he could ever be happy in this dust bowl of a land. Lori was gone forever. He was so close to stopping her death … and now he was stranded here. Here where there was no shower, no toothbrush and based on the data his nose had collected no deodorant.

Jesus walked over to him and sat beside him. Billy was indifferent to his approach.

"Turning your back to them was rude."

"What in the world are you running here anyway? Billy looked angrily at Jesus. "I mean it's like you're a cub scout master or something. These kids should be home with their families or in school, not running around the countryside with— "

"—Whom, the likes of me? Jesus asked. "William, you have a lot to learn about your faith and about kindness and selflessness. It would do your soul well to listen to the lessons that are taught and stop fighting what is right."

"Oh yea, what's right. Look, I'm not even supposed to be here, okay, so stop trying to make me into some goodie-two-shoe guy because I'm not!"

"I have instructed the twelve to take the boat to the other side of the lake and I suggest you go with them."

"What if I don't want to? What if I want to stay here and try to find the controller so I can get out of your hair … unless you can send me home?"

"William, you already know the controller is not there. And yes, I could send you back but you would fail in your plan." Billy's eyes brightened. "If I send you back now, you will not achieve what you desire because you are not the same man you were ten years ago. You would return to her as the man you became, not the man she knew as she died. Besides, there would be two of you there. You would be competing against yourself for her and everything about her. Because of what you had become, you would most undoubtedly fall into temptation and commit unbearable atrocities causing your own demise." Jesus looked away from Billy and over to the apostles who had gathered as a group awaiting his next direction. "You must first lean to be a better man."

"Look, I just want to stop Kevin from killing everyone and then you can send me back to where I was when I left." Billy said, almost pleadingly.

"You will return and take Kevin's life. Certainly, everyone will be saved but you will pay the price for taking his life." Jesus replied.

"Dude, he murdered them and the way I see it, I'm doing society a service by getting rid of a real masterpiece."

Billy turned and began to walk away from Jesus and toward the village. Jesus called out to him.

"You won't live to see tomorrow William. You will follow your lustful ways and you will be stoned for your crime."

Billy stopped walking, and turned slowly to face Jesus. His hands were once again balled into fists and he started back to where Jesus stood.

"Get into the boat with them. You know what will happen during the crossing and you will need to calm them. Andrew knows as well but you and he, being older, will calm them."

Billy looked at the face of Jesus and into his eyes. He didn't see anger and hate to be returned to him as he expected. A slight pang of guilt flittered within him. Jesus was trying to save his life and he fought him. Perhaps he was being rude but then maybe he had the right to be that way, he thought. Suddenly, Billy remembered something Jesus had said to him earlier in the day. He stated that he would one day see Lori again … he promised. He felt he needed an explanation as a glimmer of hope started to burn within him.

"So, will you send me back? You promised I would see her again." Billy asked as gently and respectfully as he could.

"I have already said you have much to learn before that can possibly happen. Now go with them before the light of day is completely gone." Jesus replied. He could tell by the look on Billy's face that answer didn't make his guest very happy.

It was a quiet ride in the boat, quiet in that all the apostles sat and stared at Billy. They may have been children, as far as he was concerned, but they had feelings and he treated them with the same lack of kindness that he showed Jesus. He hated to admit it but Jesus was right. They would keep him alive by preventing him from doing something stupid and he needed them. He decided to try and smooth things over.

"Look guys, I'm sorry for being a jackass. I … I miss being home and I was wrong to take it out on you."

He hadn't expected they would respond and certainly not one of the youngest, James.

"Can't the master help you get back home?"

James's young innocence made Billy smile. He felt he owed them something of himself but he was afraid to go too far. He looked to Andrew as a barometer of the apostles and noticed he raised an eyebrow showing some assurance he was on the correct path.

"My father's name was James. He died when I was only twelve. He was my best friend and I was very upset he was taken from me. After his death, I took out my anger out onto my mother and treated her horribly … she didn't deserve that."

Everyone in the boat was listening intently and watching him and all noticed the emotion come across his face. Simon stood and walked over to him, placed his hands on his shoulders and offered comfort. The others also greeted Billy, offering their feelings and support.

They had been on the water for a while and Andrew looked over to Billy, motioning for him to sit next to him. He seemed to need to get something off his chest.

"Simon is the one chosen to lead us after Jesus leaves. He chose him who is younger. He is not organized and is barely a man."

"Andrew, if I wasn't so sure, I'd say you're jealous of your little brother."

Andrew shook his head no as he stifled a short laugh. "You sound like Jesus. No, I'm not jealous, I'm just a little let down."

At the second Andrew finished his words the light breeze began to grow into a strong wind. The waves grew larger and washed over the boat, threatening to fill it and bring it to the bottom of the lake. The apostles were overcome with panic as the water washed over them. Billy and Andrew were now on opposite ends of the boat and urged the young men to bail as fast as they could.

Suddenly one of the twelve pointed to what looked like a ghost walking upon the water. Simon leaned over the rail and exclaimed it was Jesus. Billy watched as the story he had heard so many times as a child, was unfolding before his eyes. Although the event lasted much less time than was written, it still ended the same with Jesus calming the wind and waves and admonishing them for not believing in their hearts.

The crowd that had taken part in the miracle the previous day had followed Jesus to the other side of the lake. The group had come so that they could have their stomachs filled. Jesus stood before them and the exchange of words between them had gotten loud. Billy stood to watch and listen and was a little impressed at how Jesus handled the crowd that had become restless. Simon came to stand next to Billy and asked a question.

"Why is the master yelling at them?" Simon asked in his somewhat squeaky voice.

"Because he's pissed off at them, that's why. All they want is more food. They don't have a clue that something special happened to them." He let out a heavy sigh and left Simon standing to watch Jesus as he walked alone to sit in the shade beneath a tree.

A couple of the apostles were close by Simon and overheard Billy's opinion of the situation. Simon and the others re-gathered and they talked among themselves about the altercation using the adjective their new friend had used. They knew Billy was an educated man and decided the phrase was something learned men used and they found no harm at all using the word.

After things settled down later that day, Jesus was sitting alone in thought. He was running his fingers through the dirt, drawing pictures with them when Simon sat next to him.

In a voice so calm and innocent, Simon brought forth the fruits of the apostle's discussion of the altercation earlier in the day. "William said that you were pissed off at the masses. He said that you were this way because they only came for more food." He looked puzzled as he said the words. "I'm not sure why the people cannot see that you are the son of God but truly you are."

Jesus, slowly and deliberately, looked at Simon … his eyes locked onto Simon's. He said nothing for a moment, but when he did, the tone of his voice was seasoned with anger. "It would do you and your soul well to not repeat the things you know nothing about. Do not allow your innocence of heart be taken from you Simon. Your destiny is great and I will not allow one person destroy what the father has set forth." Simon looked confused and crestfallen. Jesus understood the questions in Simon's heart and before they could be asked he continued. "The words he speaks are sometimes from evil and should not be repeated. I will deal with William and ask him to not teach you any more of his special words. I tell you the truth Simon; if you continue to use this language I will leave you behind and find another."

Jesus stood and walked away from Simon in search of Billy. It didn't take Jesus long to locate him. There were three of the younger Apostles sitting by him and one young woman. Billy was getting rather friendly with her. As he reached the group of people sitting by the tree, Jesus stopped.

"Leave us I need to speak with William alone." He looked the few apostles away and then told the young woman to return to her father's home. His body language and the tone of his voice let everyone know, he was not happy. After the last of them had left them, Billy spoke to Jesus.

"Well aren't you a party-pooper." The sarcasm in his voice was not tempered, nor was his displeasure with Jesus for breaking up his moment with the young woman. Jesus could tell the thoughts in Billy's mind were not chaste as his guest watched the girl walk away.

"Simon has been listening to you and has added some new words to his vocabulary."

"Well, he's not the brightest bulb in the marquee, so it can't hurt him to learn something new." Billy said.

"You come to be with me and defile these men with your profanity and evil thoughts!" Jesus wasn't yelling but there was no mistake, he was not happy. "Simon is simple, that's the way I need him—all of them, to be! Do not teach them your ways, particularly the way of adultery." Billy began to protest but Jesus cut him off. "The woman you spoke to moments ago is not married and her father has not arranged for you to speak with her. You don't understand that he could have you stoned for what you had just done. I cautioned you the culture you left behind is so very different than what you are living in today." Jesus paused. "I will not allow you to drag their innocence from them and take them with you."

"Look, all I did was made a comment about what was happening. Simon wanted to know what all of the noise was about and I told him."

Jesus was getting frustrated and his voice was starting to rise. "There are more ways to describe what was happening. It is *not* necessary to use profanity to describe the events of our lives!"

"Great. If I'm such a disruption to the … plan … then send my sorry, cussing butt back to Sycamore so I can do what I wanted to do in the first place!"

Jesus raised his right hand and quickly closed his fist as if he snatched something out of the air. Billy felt a burning sensation in his throat. His vocal cords seemed to have disappeared and he could no longer speak.

"When you learn to use the blessing of voice responsibly, I will return it to you but not a moment sooner." Jesus said and then turned to join the twelve.

CHAPTER 14

Several weeks had passed since Jesus had taken his voice from him. Billy's normally clean-shaven face had grown a thick beard and his hair had become an itchy, oily mess. He wanted to take a shower so badly but there were no bathing facilities. His lack of voice was probably more of a blessing for the apostles than a punishment for himself for he knew he would complain incessantly about the lack of hygiene in the time. As they walked through the heat of the day, he looked ahead at Jesus. His mood had deteriorated greatly, not that he was ever happy there, but the distain he held for Jesus had deepened.

It was probably a good circumstance that his voice was gone because the apostles would have told him to take a hike, particularly Simon. His not so flattering thoughts, which they could not hear, would have certainly changed their opinion of him. Billy's actions toward Simon were not overly cruel, but they left no doubt he didn't like the young man. But most took pity on him and helped him through his situation and their acts of kindness touched his heart.

One evening after a particularly difficult journey, Judas came to sit with him. He caught up Billy on conversations that he wasn't included. Billy listened but the entire time Judas spoke, he could only think of what this one would do in the future. He was a rat and even now was tattling on Jesus and some of the others. It was a double-edged sword for him, he liked to know what was happening but he still believed secrets should be kept.

Jesus had come to stand behind them as Judas spoke. Neither had seen him approach and when he spoke, it startled them.

"Judas, please leave us, I need to speak with William … alone." The young man appeared to have been a little rattled as he left them. Jesus began to speak but all Billy could do was to think his words in his head. "Please stop interrupting me." Jesus said. "I can hear the words in your mind, and they are vile and should not be spoken by any man.

Billy was shocked and apparently his face showed it as well. Jesus locked eyes with him, blue into brown and he made one request of Billy.

"Explain what the Ten Commandments mean to you."

Are you serious? Billy asked in his mind. He hadn't been asked that question since he was seven years of age and it was his answers then that made Judy Jackson become impressed by his knowledge and understanding. Once he realized Jesus was serious, Billy reluctantly began.

He recited the first four and explained them without interruption from Jesus. But once he began on the fifth and on through to the end, his explanations had been heavily critiqued. Jesus reminded him how when he committed adultery, he not only broke that commandment, but three others.

"You dishonored your parent's teaching, you coveted what was not yours and you lied. You keep asking to be returned to save your family but it is the sin inside of you that holds you here. Open your heart to my teaching and grow. I am not your enemy for I want to save you from eternal damnation."

Jesus then stood leaving Billy alone to think. He watched Jesus walk to a quiet place where he knelt and began to pray. Billy began to wonder how he could soften his heart. He was so angry at Jesus for allowing all the loss in his life and he couldn't get past that. As he sat pondering his misery, he realized, Jesus had once again hinted that he could be returned to his time and perhaps save his family. His thoughts returned to Lori and back to when they were dating … to when she told him she had forgiven her father. Perhaps forgiveness was the key to all of this. But the pain, the pain of those he loved, ripped from his arms, from his heart. How could he transcend the hate that he had cultivated? *I am not your enemy,* Jesus had said but how could he push the anger away … to find the way back home? Billy yawned and decided tomorrow would be the place to continue his thoughts. He joined the others who had already prepared themselves for sleep.

The next day the same routine played itself to the same conclusion. The apostles knocked on doors to invite the people to the center of town. Once they arrived, Jesus would teach about the heavenly realm and how a man can gain access. While Jesus spoke, Billy noticed a young boy standing close by him. The boy looked as if he was starving and his heart broke for him.

A few days prior, a man had dropped three coins at Billy's feet, no doubt thinking he was a poor handicapped beggar. He didn't tell anyone he had the coins and had no idea what they might be worth. He walked over to a man who was selling bread from a cart. He showed the man the coins and pointed at the bread. Without voice, it took a second or two but the man came to understand that Billy wanted to buy as much bread as the coins would purchase. To his surprise, the man gave him four loaves.

Billy returned to the boy and placed the loaves in his young arms. The child looked up to him, smiled and said thank you and ran back to his home. Billy returned to join the others. Jesus had been speaking to the gathered people but suddenly stopped talking. The people looked puzzled at the break in his message. With a smile on his face, Jesus looked at Billy. Moments later, he continued to teach those who had gathered to hear him speak.

Once the crowd had dispersed, Billy went off to be alone. He hadn't brought attention to himself for his act of kindness and had no intention of doing so. Jesus approached him and started to speak.

"Why didn't you bring the coins to me?"

Because they would have been put into the temple bank and some fat guy in a big hat would have spent them on more food for himself. That little boy was starving and I decided it was better spent on him, not some fat … um … Guy in the temple.

Jesus laughed at Billy's thoughts. "He is called the High Priest and thank you for catching your tongue. It is best you never openly describe the High Priest that way." Jesus paused and looked directly at Billy. "You have taken the first steps of a long journey but you will make it."

Make it to where?

To your destiny of course William, it awaits you."

Jesus then walked away from Billy and joined the twelve. Billy sat alone and started to think about what Jesus had said. It was the first time since he had been in the company of Jesus that he didn't have feelings of loathing for the man. He stood to join the others. Once he arrived in their company the apostles began to whisper among themselves. Finally, Simon stood and walked to face Billy. It seemed he had something on his mind and it needed to be liberated.

"The master said you gave four coins to a seller on the street. You should have turned in that money to the temple and it would have been used to help the poor among us." He continued to admonish Billy for spending the money until Matthew came forward to stop him.

"Simon, you do not know the story and your criticism comes from revenge for the treatment this man has given to you. He traded those coins for bread and gave all of the bread to a family that had no food. He gave the money to the poor and does it make the money less effective because it did not touch the hands of the Priest? Open your eyes Simon, open them to what Jesus has been teaching ... Gods love can come through anyone!" He paused as he realized his voice has been getting loud. After taking a cleansing breath, Matthew spoke again but in a voice that was only loud enough for Simon and Billy to hear. "Jesus said you would be the rock he would build his church upon but if this is the church you will grow, I will not want anything to do with it."

Simon's head dropped in shame but so had Billy's. Even without voice, he was still cruel and Simon showed him. He wondered why Matthew had come to his aid and the answer came from Jesus, who had returned to the group, no doubt drawn by Matthew's raised voice.

"Most of you have taken my words to heart. The rest of you, it is time to let go of prejudice. My mission is greater than any one man and any one man who believes himself greater than any other may leave now. Go back to your homes, go back to your families and your work, I will not stop you. But if you stay, I need your heart to be with me."

Jesus went on to tell the apostles of what was to come in the time ahead. Billy knew he was talking about his death on the cross but the others had no idea what was being revealed to them. He could see the frustration on the face of Jesus and he wished he could help but with no voice, he could only watch.

Jesus stood for a few moments in quiet, apparently hoping the apostles would understand. Billy suddenly felt pity for Jesus and remorse had begun to replace distain. He felt uncomfortable about what he had said to him when they first met and watched Jesus walk to a private place to pray. Billy looked around to make sure he too was alone, also came to his knees and prayed.

Father God, I am sorry. Tears began to fill his eyes as he prayed. A flood of emotion washed over him as he relived every moment he had spent arguing with Jesus and blaming him for everything. Once again Lori came to his mind and his crying became harder. Help me, please help me. I need to have her, I need to hold her, and I need her.

He suddenly became aware of Jesus standing next to him. As he looked up at Jesus with tear-stained eyes, Jesus placed his hand on Billy's shoulder.

"I'm sorry for your pain but it is necessary for you to grow."

CHAPTER 15

Billy had thought he had been making progress. He was feeling more positive about his life in Judea. All this good feeling was fostered by several references by Jesus that his time there was temporary and he would eventually be sent back to Illinois. Unfortunately, the progress wasn't moving as quickly as he had hoped. Impatience was leading Billy to become irritated and this caused him a major setback. Jesus asked him to accompany him to a hill so they could be private.

"You are selfish and manipulative." Jesus said.

Billy immediately became defensive. What are you talking about?

"The bread was a true act of kindness but your actions since then have been premeditated and well-rehearsed in your mind. You may fool them but God sees what is in your heart."

"What is in my heart is I want to get home so I can save them.

"No William, what is in your mind is a goal and only a goal. You must fill your *heart* with love and until you can do that, temptation will take over your emotions and you will fail. You have a greater purpose and until you grow you cannot fulfill that purpose."

Anger filled Billy as he watched Jesus walk away. He had hoped his meeting with Jesus was about going home. It was just that, but his teacher's report card was not a passing grade. He believed he had changed. He was forcing himself to be on his best behavior and was taking every precaution to prevent argument and attitude with Jesus. What did Jesus want from him? He had no voice so he couldn't speak to anyone but Jesus and that didn't seem to be getting him anywhere. The distrust he had kept in control began to emerge and take over. Standing alone, he looked off to the surrounding hillsides. He hated being there and he hated Jesus for taking his voice. He was disappointed and needed to start the game again and wondered if he would ever be able to leave this horrible place. The sun was now low in the sky and the long shadows signaled the approach of night. It would soon be getting dark and he knew he would be stranded on the hill once the light of day was gone, so he sensibly returned to the group for the night.

Fires had been started at the camping area. Jesus was again alone off to pray and Billy sat by the spitting fire, thinking about what Jesus had said to him earlier that day. His brain processed the words and the more he puzzled over them the more depressed he became.

The crackling of the flames brought a memory of him and Lori at the same lake his parents brought him when he was a child. It was shortly after they had been married and were sitting at a campfire talking about the future. Lori wanted a daughter, he wanted a son. He remembered putting his arms around her and holding her so close, telling her she could never get away from him. All he had were memories of her touch, and he wanted more. He had to figure this out and how to give Jesus what he wanted from him.

The apostle's conversations in the background returned him to reality. He could only sit and think of what Jesus had said to him ... how he was failing to grow. It seemed the only hope he had was that Jesus had intimated on more than one occasion his destiny lay in the future but achieving the goal and returning to save her was beginning to seem so far from his reach. As he returned to thoughts of her, the world seemed to be closing in around him, choking off his breath and for the second time, he seriously welcomed death as it would certainly end his pain.

Jesus had returned from his prayer and sat next to Billy.

Did you come over just to rub it in that I can't go back?

"No, I came to let you know that this is where your wisdom begins. You have been *thinking* about how to get back. Your mind has ruled you. It is your heart and what is in it that needs to be cleaned and set straight. The pain you had just experienced is true and that is where you begin your journey back." Jesus paused and looked at the spitting fire. "You need to replace the selfishness that guides your decisions and replace it with love for her and everyone else.

What are you talking about? I have only love for her.

"You have love for yourself. Think back to why you called on Mr. Smith. You wanted to stop yourself from meeting Kelly Anderson and prevent her pregnancy and then at the last moment changed your plan. You proceed from a place of selfishness and dishonor. You have committed adultery to ease the pain of loss and in doing so you have dishonored not only your parents who had taught you right from wrong but Lori herself." Jesus never took his gaze from Billy, but *he* turned his red and embarrassed face toward the fire. "You cannot run away from your sins William as they will follow you like a team of donkeys with each sin adding one more donkey to the line." Jesus changed the subject. "I will return your voice when you have learned your lessons. It's best to get some sleep because we have a long journey tomorrow." Before he got up to leave, Jesus spoke again. "Remember what your father told you after your grandmother died? Only the brave and strong of heart can love. Because you know that someday the person you love more than anything in the world will leave you … not because they want to but because they have no choice. You now feel that pain, the same pain your mother felt when your father left this world. And what did she do? Did she envelope herself in pity? No … she buried herself in her love for you." Jesus let his words sink into Billy. He then added a few more. "You know your mother would give her life to protect and save you. That is where your heart must be."

Jesus stood and left Billy alone by the fire. Billy's mind began to process what Jesus had said. He tried to justify his actions during the last ten years. Then there were the thoughts he held about the apostles. He was especially hard on Simon. He thought he might start calling him Peter since everyone else did—except his brother Andrew. His treatment of *Peter* was less than nice. He had thought the young man a fool and a moron. That would need to change and tomorrow would be the best time to begin. He grew tired and went to make up his area for sleep and as he rested, he looked over at a man who, a distance away, again knelt in prayer. He rolled on his side and in his thoughts, he told Lori goodnight and he loved her.

The day's journey began at sunrise. Billy's back was starting to feel the effects of sleeping on the hard ground. The endless walking exacerbated the pain and caused him to fall behind and thus slowed the progress of the group. Jesus walked back to help and placed his hands in the small of Billy's back. There was a crack, some pain but then relief came. Jesus smiled and suggested he should now be able to keep up.

As they came into another town, Jesus was quickly set upon by some of the elders visiting the area from Jerusalem. They questioned him and weren't at all nice. Billy started to come forward but Andrew pulled him back. He whispered in Billy's ear.

"Do not attack these men as they will have us all put to death. Jesus knows what he's doing." Billy offered a look to Andrew that suggested he didn't agree with the man's opinion.

Later that day, Billy bore witness to another passage in the Bible. Peter and a few of the apostles came to Jesus and suggested he may have gone too far with the Pharisees. Calling them hypocrites was not the way to gain good favor with important people. When Jesus offered a parable and they didn't get the meaning, he became frustrated with them and explained it clearly. "It matters not if your hands are dirty when you eat. What defiles you is what comes out of your heart." He looked toward Billy as he said the next words. "For out of one's heart come evil thoughts: Murder, adultery, sexual immorality, theft, false testimony and slander."

Jesus was clearly irritated and everyone gave him plenty of room. As Billy sat alone, he had only his mind to keep him company. The horrible words Jesus spoke while he looked at him were an assessment of his recent life. Jesus had judged and found him a little short of where he needed to be, at least in the eyes of God. Suddenly, he began to realize what Jesus was trying to teach him. He needed to be guided by his heart, not his mind for the mind, at least his mind, was filled with prejudice and avarice. That evening around the fires, he could only listen as the apostles spoke of their families and their future with Jesus. It seemed cruel that he could not speak but then, he understood it was his fault his voice was gone. Another door had opened a doorway to humility and he cautiously walked through it.

The sun brightened the morning sky. The small group gathered their belongings and moved onward. The tension between Jesus and the apostles from the night before was still evident. As they proceeded to Tyre and Sidon the usual conversation and laughter was not present as it had been on other journeys. Billy walked near the back of the pack and had a good view of Jesus, Peter and Andrew. They spoke very little as they traveled.

Some distance into the town, a woman came running over and dropped to her knees before Jesus. She pleaded for him to cure her daughter. Jesus was not interested because she was not a Jew and he dismissed her as he walked on and away from her. She continued to pursue Jesus and would not leave him alone. Finally, he stopped and obviously agitated, he spoke to her.

"Woman, I was sent to this place only to the lost sheep of Israel." Again, she begged as she knelt before him and sobbed. Jesus then said to her, "It is not right to take the children's bread and toss it to the dogs."

"Yes, it is Lord." She answered. And through her tears she added, "Even the dogs eat the crumbs that fall from their master's table."

Jesus looked at the woman and at the people around him. He took a cleansing breath, looked skyward and then back at Billy. "Woman, your faith is great. Go home to your daughter … she has been healed."

The woman thanked Jesus, kissed his feet and ran off to join her daughter. Billy stood at the back of the group and realized a smile had come across his face. Jesus looked over in his direction and motioned for him to join him and when he stopped, Jesus placed both of his hands onto Billy's shoulders.

"William, I realized that my time here is not just for the Jews. How could I have kept that position when your knowledge of my life is a proof of this fact?"

Jesus raised his hand and held it in front of Billy's face. A warm, tickle filled his throat. He coughed several times trying to dislodge the feeling of something trying to force its way down his throat and realized he could speak again.

With the blessing of speech returned to him, Billy verbally apologized to all the apostles, particularly Peter. His apologies were from his heart not from his mind. Billy was welcomed as a friend into their circle and Peter called him the thirteenth apostle.

Billy looked to Jesus and wanted to speak to him privately about the woman and the miracle that had been performed. They walked several yards to maintain their isolation, something that Peter and Judas had noticed.

"This event was written in Matthew's, 15th chapter. I wasn't here the first time it happened but your comment confuses me." Billy said with a look of complete bewilderment on his face.

"True, you wouldn't have been here. My father told me the answer … you just happened to be the cherry atop the sundae." Billy laughed at the turn of phrase and the sense of humor Jesus displayed. He wondered if it had been there all along and he had missed it because he had been so engrossed in his own misery. As he looked onto Jesus, a new attitude began to emerge. He seemed more of a man than God, and he began to develop feelings of friendship.

Darkness was falling and the usual camping preparations had begun. Once the fires were burning, the apostles, Jesus and Billy sat by the fire and listened as Jesus once again predicted his death. As it had happened the first time, the young men didn't understand what they were being told. They had begun to discuss what they thought was the meaning of the parable Jesus had presented. Clearly frustrated, Jesus stood and walked away to pray. Andrew approached Billy and asked him a question.

"Why does he pray all of the time?" Andrew asked while several of the young apostles looked their way to hear the answer to the question; Judas was front and center.

Billy thought before he answered. "Prayer is how we connect with God. Jesus kneels in worship and respect. He is the son of God and even *he* kneels to speak with God."

As Billy spoke, he looked in the direction of Judas. He didn't care for the young man. Judas had his nose in everyone's business and he was a rat. He had the personality that suited him to be the one to betray Jesus in the future. Billy knew he couldn't speak of those things so he cleverly changed the direction of the conversation to something as mundane as the weather.

Indeed, the weather was changing, fall was approaching and so were the rains. The local people had begun to dig deep holes in the ground and set out large vats to catch the water. Billy was curious why all of the excavation was happening and Simon or Peter as Billy had now referred to him gave a lesson.

"William, as you have seen, the sun shines almost every day and it is hot and dry. The people know to prepare to gather water for their crop and flock this time of the year. Just as the Lord had provided water for Moses and his followers in the desert, he provides for us still. It is up to us to gather it and hold it through the year."

It seemed a plausible explanation but he wondered if a hint from the future, to educate them to build a reservoir might be helpful. That idea was quickly squashed by Jesus. He reminded Billy that man's inventions must proceed on their original schedule. Billy suggested reservoirs were hardly an invention of the future as Rome had constructed them and aqueducts several times. Jesus simply cocked his head and smiled kindly, suggesting they end the conversation about the future.

The next few weeks they walked to and through villages and towns. Some places had a large Roman soldier presence. Billy looked at them and took notice of the spears and swords they carried. He also noticed how muscular and how they seemed to be all business. Peter was quick to pull Billy's attention away from the soldiers. He told Billy that men who stare at the soldiers usually die a slow and painful death. He was advised to keep his eyes to the ground and his mouth shut.

Because Jesus had given Billy's ears the gift to understand any tongue, the insults the soldiers spoke were clearly understood by his ears. Inside he became angry and wished he could confront the soldiers. He followed the advice given him by Peter and kept his tongue for all of their sakes. A man in the town directed them to a small building so they could spend the night out of the rain. When he, Jesus and the apostles were safely behind the door and private, Billy voiced his opinion. He and Jesus got into an argument about pride.

"And I say to you to show love not hate. Do you not remember this from when you studied it as a child?" Jesus asked angrily.

"Of course, I remember. Look I'm on your side Jesus. Those guys are jerks." Billy said as he pointed his finger in the general direction of where the soldiers congregated.

"Jerks who are well-trained in the use of sword and spear and Jerks that would have no problem dragging you off to be crucified!" Jesus said.

Peter quickly came to them. "Master your voices carry and I fear if this noise continues the solders will come for us."

Jesus looked at Peter and then to Billy. "Peter is correct. Our raised voices will attract them. It is best to bring quiet to this place."

Billy walked away and left Jesus and Peter to themselves. Shortly afterward, Peter caught up to Billy.

"Why do you put all our lives in jeopardy?" Peter asked.

"I didn't mean for this to turn into an argument." Billy said. "I just want to go home and fix the problems so I can get my wife back."

"So, the life of your wife is more important than ours." Peter was challenging Billy. "Please tell me, why is this so? Are you so selfish that only your desires matter? Jesus had said you were making way along your journey but I don't see it."

"Look Simon, Peter or whatever you want to call yourself, I have only one goal and that is to get out of here and get back to save my wife and family and that's all. You and your gang can travel the country side and sing hallelujah as much as you want. You have fun with that!"

Billy stomped away from Peter and sat on the stone floor with his back against the wall. He pulled his knees to himself and rested his arms on them as he watched Peter gesture with his hands, occasionally pointing in his direction. He wasn't in the mood for a pep talk from anyone, especially Jesus. As he sat alone, frustrated and angry, the words Jesus had spoken to him several days ago replayed in his memory: *"No William, what is in your mind is a goal and only a goal."* A goal ... he had used that exact word to Peter just moments ago. His disappointment with himself began to grow as did the feeling of dread that he would never make it back home. He rested his head on his arms and in his mind, he asked God why he had to suffer so much, and how could he clean his heart of the dirt that Jesus said filled it?

Billy didn't expect an answer and wasn't surprised when Jesus said nothing. He fought the urge to respond with sarcasm and anger, trying to tap into the love in his heart, as Jesus had suggested. With little else to do, he joined the others as they were already wrapped in their sleeping blankets and like them, prepared himself for sleep. As he lay on his side, Billy whispered to Lori he loved her.

Sleep came and he had a dream. He had entered into a room where each wall contained a window. The walls and furnishings were white and everything seemed to produce light. Outside there was bright sunshine and beyond the windows was a child, a young girl, playing on a swing. It was a peaceful place. He saw a woman standing with her back to him, watching the young girl play. The woman wore a white dress and her long black hair fell to just past the middle of her back. It was Lori and perhaps this was his unborn daughter. His heart beat with excitement as he approached her. He opened his arms to embrace her. She turned and smiled at him but wouldn't touch him. She had begun to speak but the words she spoke were not verbal but in thought.

Billy, please stop fighting with Jesus. He only wants what is best for you and if you continue to have this aggression, you and I will never see each other again. I love you and I need you to save yourself in that world so we can be together in ours. Always remember I love you.

CHAPTER 16

I n the next days, there were more run-ins with the Pharisees and Sadducees and Jesus stood his ground and made his point. Billy tempered his enthusiasm for Jesus, especially since he had been told his progress to his desire was not progressing as quickly as he had thought. He intended to confront Jesus when things settled down later that evening.

Jesus' brother James had managed to catch up to them and his presence scuttled Billy plans to speak with Jesus. Andrew had announced the man's arrival.

"Look who has come to join us. It is James the brother of Jesus."

"Great, now were going to have a sibling rivalry here in the stone ages." Both Andrew and Peter looked at Billy oddly because they didn't know what siblings were but then remembered what Jesus had told him about the words Billy used weren't always good ones.

"Where is my great brother? Is he healing the sick and saving the world?" James asked rather sarcastically.

Billy's eyes fell upon James and a look of disgust must have been painted upon them. James walked straight toward him and when he stopped in front of him, he looked Billy up and down.

"This one seems under fed. Perhaps my brother should make you a feast out of thin air." He laughed at his joke.

For some unknown reason, Billy became enraged and an involuntary urge surfaced. He punched James in the face, between the eyes. He had seen his father do the same thing so many years ago at the fifth-grade school dance. A fight erupted between his father and the father of his date, Linda William's. Like his date's father, James fell to the ground.

"I SHALL HAVE YOU STONED FOR YOUR CRIME!" James yelled at the top of his lungs.

Suddenly Jesus came to them and broke up the fight. "James why are you here and how is mother?"

"Aren't you God? Don't you know?" James taunted. "And who is the animal that dares to strike my face?"

"His name is William and he is one of my people. You will not touch him or you will suffer my father's wrath."

"Joseph was your father you fool! You believe you are so important and so special but all I see is a smelly man who walks around in the desert causing riots wherever he goes."

After Billy apologized for punching James, Jesus went off by himself and left the two men alone. As James stood rubbing the pain out of his face, Billy had pondered some questions but he was concerned if he asked them he may provoke another fight. He paused thoughtfully and then began.

"James, haven't you heard of the things your brother has done?" Billy asked.

"They are simply stories, just stories and fables of great things that Jesus, my famous brother has supposedly accomplished."

"Then why are you here?"

"Because my mother has been bothering me to come and spend time with my brother so that I may believe in him."

"What do you expect to gain from this trip?" Billy asked.

James laughed at the question. "Absolutely nothing my misguided friend … well almost nothing, I'll get sore feet."

Later that evening tents were being erected to shelter them from the rains that were now unceasing. James had been such an irritant that no one wanted to invite him to their tent so he was on his own and as he struggled to erect his shelter, he called out for someone to help him. Billy started walking toward James to help. His assistance was more of a peace offering to James than anything else and as they worked to put the final touches on the tent, the heavier rains came.

It had rained all night and by the morning almost everything they had was soaked through. Billy was awakened by the sound of Peter's voice, telling him it was time to get up and start moving to the next town. Billy protested and suggested they wait until the rain ceased but it was James who informed Billy, they would need to wait until the spring for that to happen.

Once they were into the journey Billy noted the transformation of the landscape. Just days ago, the sun was shining and the ground was dusty but now the skies were gray and the ground had been transformed into a deep layer of sticky mud. The mucilage made travel slow and difficult causing him and several others to often slip and fall. Most of them were covered from head to toe by the sticky mess and whenever they walked past a heavy stream of water flowing off a hill, they would attempt to wash it out of their hair and robes.

As they walked through the rain, Andrew caught up to him. Since Andrew was close in age to Billy, they had to become closer friends. They talked about Simon particularly how the younger brother was hand-picked to lead after Jesus had left them. He was still disappointed with that decision since he was so much older than his brother and felt he should be the leader.

"Jesus has a mission and a plan. Your brother is a well-spoken young man and he can get the attention of crowds quickly." Billy began to explain. "You can organize people but Simon can close the deal. You need to teach him how to manage people. I'll tell you this, if you help your brother, you will be held in high regard by God."

"High regard doesn't ease my heart." He changed the subject. "And you … you and my brother seem to not agree on anything. He has been trying to lead the others against you and says your actions are dangerous to everyone." Andrew shook his in disagreement with his brother's actions. "I told him one day he will make a huge mistake and will expect to be forgiven."

Billy wondered if Andrew knew what was to come in Jerusalem in the future. He thought it best to not engage that conversation and simply thanked Andrew for having his back. But there was a lesson in this and that was the acts of contrition and forgiveness. His thoughts began to work the words Andrew had spoken and he remembered forgiveness was a way to soften the heart. James had said it and so did Lori. Perhaps once he learned to forgive, his time here would be ended.

CHAPTER 17

B illy had lost track of time and couldn't remember exactly how long he had been in Judea. With confession and forgiveness on his mind and heart, he had spoken with Peter about his feelings and short comings. They came to understand one another and moved closer as friends. Billy also pulled Andrew into the mix and together they helped Peter grow. He would become the leader in the future but he needed to be taught. As they walked from village to town, the lessons continued.

Walking was getting him in better shape and the effects of the last ten years of poor diet and lack of exercise seemed to be disappearing. They followed Jesus into the region of Caesarea Philippi. Jesus had gathered his followers to a private area. Before he spoke to the twelve, he asked Billy to remain silent. Once again, he was reminded that he was living though the New Testament and he was going to witness one more recorded passage. What wasn't written was the long discussion and argument that took place between the apostles and Jesus.

Not everyone in the group was on-board with the idea of Jesus being the Messiah. James had departed the group and went back home but his disbelief tainted the conviction of some members of the twelve. This caused some commotion in the ranks. Several of the twelve had openly doubted Jesus and had cited comments made by James, the brother of Jesus. After those comments, Peter stood and demanded quiet. His voice carried over the hum of their individual conversations and the others fell silent. He looked at them for a few seconds, and then began to speak.

"What fools you are!" Peter came forward and took over the front of the area and continued to admonish them for falling in their faith. As he continued, he looked in Billy's direction. He paused for a moment and a confident smile came to his face as he stroked the beard on his young face. He then continued. "You take the word of a man who has seen none of these things that Jesus has done and trust what he has said. I tell you to trust what you have seen with your eyes. The kingdom of heaven is coming and you must prepare your hearts and minds or … or you will be passed by."

Jesus looked to Peter and then to Billy. He had waited for Peter to begin to assert himself as the leader of the group and apparently Billy had helped him. Jesus approached Billy whose face wore a proud, almost fatherly smile.

"I see you have been talking to Peter. He has found his strength with your help."

"Actually, Andrew did most of this. You know, he's so young to be the leader of the church and I kind of need to agree with Andrew. Shouldn't someone older take command of the operation once you leave? They're all so young."

"It is not for you or Andrew to question the wisdom of God. What has been set in motion will be and no man should dare to change it."

"Alright I accept that. But answer this, please. I wasn't here the first time and Peter wasn't stepping up. How did it happen if I wasn't here to make it happen?"

Jesus rubbed his chin before answering. "Your presence here is not without effect. Had you not been here, Peter would have risen. You intimidate him and he fears that your association with me threatens his position."

"He's jealous of me, is that what you're saying?" Billy asked as he tried to not smile.

"Let me just say he feels a little inadequate around you. If you recall the night of your argument some days ago, I said nothing to you. I needed you and Peter to come together and you needed to soften … and you have."

Billy felt a little awkward and embarrassed and as his face turned scarlet, he was reminded of the dream he had.

"The night Peter and I argued, I had a dream about Lori. I tried to touch her but she wouldn't take my hand and she told me to stop arguing with you. It seemed so real so my question is, was it real or was it in my head?"

"Sometimes man is permitted to see inside of a situation that he could otherwise never see. You have reached an intersection. Choose the narrow road for the wide road is filled with beautiful wonders that will lead to your destruction."

"Can't you ever answer a question with a simple yes or no? You'd be horrible on a witness stand." Billy let out a sigh as Jesus looked at him. "So, the dream was prophetic?" Billy asked.

"If you ask that the dream was a message through the Father, yes. It was real and Lori was permitted to speak to you. You were granted the sight of paradise. Your heart needed a little push and Lori was the one for that task. Remember William, everything happens at his order. The grass and flowers will again grow once the rains that feed them stop. Keep that message close to your soul and your heart as a guide."

Jesus stood from him and brought everyone together. The quarrels from earlier had been subdued and the apostles were once again united in purpose and faith with Jesus. They gathered their belongings and moved to another town.

The continuous rain made travel difficult. Because they were constantly slipping and falling into the mud, everything they possessed was covered by the slick and heavy, clay-like material. They passed a body of water and scrubbed the gray mess off themselves. Billy wished he had a bar of soap, his razor and some deodorant, but did as the others and got himself as clean he could. He knew being clean would be short lived as the mud was everywhere and each step spattered the oozing goo. As they walked, Billy came along side of Jesus. He asked him about the frustrations from the day before. He felt as if he was partly responsible for the heated discussion and he apologized.

"We have talked about this, already. If you were not here, it would have still taken place for you knew it was going to happen." Jesus said.

"That's just it … I don't know. All I know is what was printed in the Bible, and that level of conversation was not covered."

"As I have said, there are many things we have done that are not recorded … many things you have seen and will witness to; there will be more to come."

Jesus had once again suggested that Billy had a destiny but he wouldn't say if this destiny was in Judea with the apostles or in the future and when he asked Jesus to clarify the situation, he received a rather nasty look from Jesus.

"Once again your mind takes over your heart and selfishness overtakes you."

Immediately Billy bristled and spoke his opinion. "What are you talking about … I have been thinking of my actions to others, I have been making sure I don't step on anyone's toes. What do you want from me?"

"I want your heart Billy. You give me your mind and your mind is filled with the ways of the life you left behind. Your mind, it overrides your heart. You need to lead with your heart. Until you learn to do this, you will remain in Judea with me!"

Jesus left Billy to stand alone. John, one of the "Sons of Thunder", approached Billy. He could see Billy was both confused and hurt. His young age helped Billy reconnect to something he had lost as an adult.

"William, why do you have so much trouble being guided by your heart?" The young man asked. "I believe that Jesus is going to make everything right and the sun will come out and the grass will grow again."

Billy began to laugh at the absolute innocence of John. But he wasn't laughing at John specifically and made sure John was made aware of that. He had found humor in the simplicity of the answer and perhaps the key to solving his problem. He remembered that Jesus had, on more than one occasion, suggested he look at the world and the people of the world through the eyes of an innocent child. He told him to love everyone as he loved Lori and his heart would rejoice. He had told him, that pure feeling was the filter for how he should make his decisions. What Jesus had been trying to tell him was starting to make sense.

CHAPTER 18

The rains had stopped and the sun had returned. With the clear weather came new grass and leaves on the trees. Flowers were beginning to open and the surrounding hills and fields were awash with the colors of spring. Fields were plowed and crop was planted. Billy sat on a hill looking down into a valley where men toiled under the fresh sun and hadn't noticed Jesus approaching. In his thoughts he remembered the book of Genesis and the story of man's fall. God had promised Adam that he would need to work the ground for any benefit of it for his sin had taken away the blessing of food without labor. Billy began to reflect on his own life and he began to realize what all those lessons in Sunday school were teaching him. He understood that he was placed on the earth to serve mankind and that would in-turn serve God. Jesus startled him when he spoke.

"William, your thoughts, they touch my heart and the heart of the Father. Your wisdom has been growing."

"I wish you would let me know you're there. You almost gave me a heart attack."

Jesus laughed but only briefly. He placed his hand on Billy's shoulder and sat next to him on the hard ground. After a short silence Jesus began to speak. "Billy, as you know my time is getting shorter. I will be moving toward the final destiny."

"They still don't understand yet … do they?" Billy asked as he stared off at the men working the field.

"As you know, I have tried to explain it to them but they fail to understand it." He paused as if he was looking for the correct words. "I can't just say it, they need to find the answer in their hearts because without their hearts, their minds will make them falter and they won't be able to do what they must. You of all people should know this."

"I see your point." Billy said as he let a few seconds of silence come into the conversation. "I have another question. Why do you pray alone? Shouldn't you include them?"

"I will, soon, teach them how to pray but for now I pray alone because my time has not yet come." Jesus stiffened as the words came from his mouth. "My Father's will, shall be done and I need his strength. He reminds me every day why I am here. As you looked down into the valley and watched the men toil as they prepare the fields you were reminded of man's fall. You know I was sent here for that reason."

As a child, the story of Christmas and the crucifixion were tales of faith. But here, sitting next to him was the man who was the product of that first Christmas and would be the one to endure real pain and agony. It was suddenly more real and cruel and his heart began to break for Jesus. Billy winced slightly as the memory of Christmas at his grandparent's house in Florida played in his mind.

"Your grandfather didn't care much for your Santa joke as I recall."

"Neither did my mom and dad … and you either, I'm guessing." Billy answered as his face turned a shade of pink. He then changed the subject. "Since God is more powerful than … you know … him, why can't he just wave his hand and fix it that way?"

"It's complicated and I'm sure you studied the fall of Lucifer." Billy nodded his head, yes. "Before the universe and all that it contains was created, the angles praised God at his throne. And they had duties during creation. Lucifer worked very hard and the angels he watched over, he directed them with skill so they would prefect that which God directed them to do. Lucifer was the protector of the throne and as such was given great power so he could fight off challengers."

"So, why would there be challengers?" Billy asked.

"Every being created has a free will and they have the ability to choose to follow their creator or to ignore him. As it is with man it was with the angels. Many had tested their power against the throne and were defeated by Lucifer. After God placed man on the earth Lucifer became jealous and used his power for his own purposes. He believed that mankind was not worthy of the love of God and wasn't worth all the doting. As you know he interfered and in his thoughts he proved his point by showing that mankind was weak, easily manipulated and should be relegated to slavery to serve the angles. God disagreed and Lucifer was removed from his closeness to the throne. He was enraged and vowed to destroy man by driving him away from God. Then a way for man to atone for sin was decided. Because the wage of sin is death, death must be part of the process. An innocent lamb would be sacrificed and its blood would pay the price for its owner's sins. So, it shall be with me. For the power of the curse set upon man by the deceiver must be broken by one more powerful than the deceiver. He will bruise my heel but I shall bruise his head. The blood of God's lamb must be shed to break the curse."

Billy sat listening to every word Jesus had said. He thought for a moment before he spoke.

"So that's why you had to be born as a human … so you could die because if you had just appeared, you could not be sacrificed."

"There is more but that is a lot of it." Jesus said as he let out a sigh that was more of a sign of trepidation than exhaustion.

Jesus stood and held out his hand to help Billy stand. As Billy looked up at him he offered his understanding and gratitude for what was to come. Several quiet seconds passed and a new thought came to his mind. Something bothered him since his arrival in Judea … when he first met Jesus.

"You know, you never did answer my question why you never answered my prayers about saving my family."

"You never asked me, you simply told me I never lifted a hand to help."

"Okay then, why didn't you help?" Billy's brow began to furrow.

"God could have let your father live longer but his agony would have been excruciating and it would have devastated you even more. And your wife, she was kept in this world until she could profess her love to you one final time. Free will is given to everyone and we cannot interfere with it and evil had entered Kevin's heart and mind. Come let us join the others."

It wasn't the answer he had expected. He didn't know what he expected but he realized that in those tragedies, God was being merciful and had spared him greater pain. His father would never get better and Lori, well, she was kept with him long enough so she could tell him she loved him and say goodbye. A twinge of guilt passed through his stomach as he realized his pain and selfishness had ruled his life not just when he met Jesus, but for ten years prior.

Billy had followed Jesus back to the twelve and as he walked behind him, he was thinking over everything he had been told, just moments ago. This put him into a quietness that almost everyone noticed. While Jesus talked and directed the plans for the next day, he sat by himself.

Anger started to build inside of him, but he didn't know why. Nothing Jesus had said would cause this to rise and the apostles hadn't said anything to him. Yet hate was emerging in his mind. He had made so much progress and now something in him was threatening to set him back. He turned to his heart, where the love for his wife resided, where the friendships of Peter and Andrew lived and where his love for his parents stayed. He focused on that love and let it argue with this anger. He was in a drunken state but he hadn't consumed any wine and he heard voices. They were telling him that Jesus was never going to send him home. The voices told him everything was a lie and he was going to die here. He wondered if he was having a heart attack or stroke. Jesus had said it was his mind that was keeping him here and would never let him return. No, he thought, this couldn't be possible because Jesus had promised and God doesn't break promises.

Suddenly he felt a hand on his shoulder and he heard another voice speak with the power of a massive explosion. "Leave him Satan for he belongs to me and the Father!"

The disembodied feeling went away and he realized he was shivering uncontrollably. His body was wet with sweat and he felt as if he would vomit. He opened his eyes to find Jesus and all the Apostles looking at him. Their faces shown pity and concern for he had just had a close encounter with the dark angel. As Jesus looked at the faces of his closest followers, he had decided that this was the time to teach them to pray and another story in the Bible unfolded before Billy.

The remainder of the day was much quieter, at least for Billy. Jesus had congratulated him for not giving into his mind, but Billy was curious why the hate returned as it had and Jesus offered a simple explanation.

"You want to return to save them and the lessons are not moving along as fast as you hoped. Satan knows this and turned up the heat on your impatience. It wasn't as easy as it was in the beginning and he needed to fan the flames of those doubts that remain. Had I not been here he would have succeeded and you would have started from the beginning."

"Will he try this again … and how do I fight it?" Billy asked as the fear of failure painted a troubled look on his face.

"He never stops but, you know how to fight him. Love is your weapon. He cannot endure the pain of love for he is obsessed with himself and his desire to take heaven from the Father. Love is the flaming sword he cannot pass through and it is the only great power that God has bestowed to mankind."

"Love is more powerful than the ability to will things into creation?" Billy asked with one eyebrow raised.

"I must caution you William do not delve into magic or open your heart to it. Mankind has not the capacity to handle those powers. But yes, Love is a very powerful force when one learns how to use it."

The next day they continued their journey to and through villages and as the summer blazed on and so did Billy's witnessing of more unrecorded miracles. He and the apostles, with Jesus, would help land owners tend to their crop and as payment they would be fed and given a place to sleep. During these times, Jesus preached about the Kingdom of God. Billy found it amazing that these people had no idea that God was sitting in the same room with them but then it was only recently that he fully opened his heart to the same reality. He realized the hypocrisy and didn't know how to handle it.

As they prepared for sleep that night, Peter came to him to talk to him.

"You are thinking about something, something that troubles you."

"Tonight, as we ate and Jesus taught, I judged these people as fools because they had no idea who Jesus is. But then I was reminded of my own actions and I was no different. I am a hypocrite and I have no right to stand to preach." Billy said quietly as shame quieted his voice more than the darkness of night.

"The master said we all need to grow in him and although we will make mistakes, we should learn from them and share them with others so that they may not take the same course as we."

Billy smiled and a short laugh came from him. "You should write some of this stuff down because it might come in handy someday." Peter looked at him oddly and he continued. "Someday, you might find yourself writing to a group of people and telling them the same thing you just told me."

The summer moved quickly and the work in the fields became to harvest the crop that was planted back in the spring. Soon the clouds gathered in the skies and the rainy season returned. Their work continued as they followed Jesus through the country. More miracles were performed. The previous day, Jesus had given a man the blessing of sight and today they walked by a very dirty and terrible looking place. A man covered in leprosy fell before the feet of Jesus. No one would touch him, even Billy was a little cautious. He watched as Jesus bent down next to the man. The hard rain was dripping from Jesus' hair and with each drop of water, the sores and bruises on the man's skin began to clear.

"Rise and rejoice in the water of life. Go and find your family and tell them that your faith in God has healed you." Jesus said as the man stood, looking at the clean skin on his arms and hands. This happened dozens of more times and in each case Jesus sent the healed to proclaim what God had done for them. Perhaps Jesus was increasing the frequency of his miracles because the time was getting shorter.

Billy and Jesus had begun to spend more time separate from the apostles and the men becoming curious as to why. Jesus told them, preparations for Billy's departure were ongoing and he needed to make sure his student would have all that he needed to succeed. This was the first true confirmation that Jesus would send Billy back, but he still didn't know if back was to Chicago to continue his life there or to Sycamore to save his family.

This caused a little jealousy to rise in a few of the apostles and Peter was left to sort it out. Andrew stood behind his younger brother and offered his full support. Peter had grown considerably since Billy had first met him and he was becoming a man the same as his brother. His demeanor had changed to suit his position and the lessons and guidance of Andrew enabled him to gain control of the men who were soon to become his responsibility.

As they entered the next town, a group of tents was the first thing that they had seen. They would need a tent to shelter from the rains so arrangements would need to be made. When the owners of the tents had heard Jesus had arrived, they began to bicker among themselves as to who would be the one to offer shelter to the Lord. Jesus looked at the men standing in the mud, arguing about who was the best and purest among them. Billy looked on as Jesus stepped toward the group of men and began to address them. As he had learned, Jesus never wasted an opportunity to teach and this was certainly a teachable moment.

"You worldly men, your self-proclaimed righteousness does not bring the light of God to you. You are so impressed by your own deeds that they blind you to what is right. You welcome only the elect and turn away the common. But one among you is greater in the eyes of God and that one, I will accept his shelter."

Jesus had placed his hand on the shoulder of a man who stood away from the group and had not joined in the contest between the others and had bowed his head and had come to his knee once Jesus had touched him. The other tent owners looked on as the man knelt in the pouring rain and the cold sticky mud at the feet of Jesus. They were embarrassed and enraged, but the other men said nothing.

"Rise, the Father's blessings will be upon you." Jesus said.

He led Jesus and his followers to a tent that was not large but adequate to shelter about twenty people. With the addition of fourteen people to the few that were already there, the tent suddenly became crowded.

Billy looked around at the accommodations and he suggested it wasn't quite "Five-Star" but it would do. Although they were out of the rain it did wash under the walls of the tent and the ground was the same sticky mud as was everywhere else. However, planks of wood had been laid on the ground to provide a dry surface for the guests to set up their sleeping areas.

Once they were settled, Jesus continued to teach Billy in the ways of the heart and during their conversation Billy offered something from his childhood, something the innocence of that time had been buried by the responsibilities of adulthood. He looked around him to make sure no one was close to hear what he was about to say. "When I was a boy, about four years old, I remember Grandma Velma Anne telling me the story of your death and resurrection. I cried when you died but I was so happy that you came out of the tomb. I wanted to see that and I felt that one event would be the greatest thing I could ever see."

Jesus looked out into the rain, almost emotionless. He didn't comment on what Billy had said, he acted almost as if he didn't hear him.

"Are you alright?" Billy asked Jesus.

"Yes … I'm fine. The rains will soon end and it will begin. I am finding myself troubled. The will of God shall be done and I need his strength. For I know what will happen on that day. The suffering and indignity that will be unleashed upon me will be great and I need his strength." He paused. Billy could see a tear stream down his cheek. "Does the childhood desire still fill your heart?"

"Believe it or not it does and now that I'm here, in this time, I'll actually be able to fulfill that dream." Billy said as his face looked to the ground.

Their time was interrupted by three Roman Soldiers. The men entered the tent to shelter from the rain and because of its smaller size the space became even more crowded. They were probably passing through and as Billy remembered from last year, it would be best to give them a wide berth. One of the soldiers looked over at Jesus. He and the other solders approached Jesus and Billy. The soldiers stopped short of them and in unison, fell to their knees.

"You are Jesus of Nazareth. We have traveled to see you." The solder said.

"And how may I serve Rome's finest?" Jesus asked as he came to his feet.

"It is I who should ask how to serve you." The soldier replied as all three had bowed before Jesus. "You are the one sent from God. I have heard what you have done and I wish to follow you."

"You know you will be killed for treason to your duty if you follow me." Jesus told the soldier.

"I … we, accept that risk." He said as the three soldiers looked up at Jesus.

Billy watched as the faith of the soldiers was on display. They were willing to die for a man that they had never met and knew the reward for following Jesus would be great. They led with their heart and this is what *he* needed to do. As he looked onto the three soldiers, it was as if another door had been opened for him to walk though. He could see his selfishness and could see the line that separated what was right and what was right for him and him alone. He understood what Jesus had been telling him since their first meeting almost two years ago.

The day was getting long and small tent had become overfull most of the day. Jesus had been teaching for hours and his voice was beginning to break from fatigue. Billy and the apostles had been forced to act as a security force to give Jesus some room to breathe and to take a few breaks. The pushing and madness of the people reminded Billy of a time he and Lori had attended a concert in Chicago. Then, the throng had pushed to get to the stage to see the band at the arena. Billy was extraordinarily unimpressed with the progress of mankind in two thousand years. Suddenly, Jesus told the people in the tent they must go home and surprisingly, they obeyed. The people's sudden change of behavior caught Billy and the apostles off guard. They believed they would need to use force to literally push the people from the tent and as the last man walked out, Jesus suggested the apostles, and Billy should pray with him. It was a short prayer, mostly of thanks for the blessings of the day. After he finished, he suggested they retire for the night and then did what he had always done, he left them to pray alone.

Billy didn't go to sleep with the others, he had too much on his mind and it threatened to keep him awake through the darkness. He quietly moved from the apostles and approached Jesus from behind. Once he knew Jesus had ended his prayer he asked if he could sit next to him. Jesus nodded approvingly. Silence surrounded both men for a few moments until Billy broke it.

"I heard one of the land owners say the rains will be ending soon because the buds are starting to swell on the trees." Jesus again nodded in agreement but said nothing. "We're heading back to Jerusalem, aren't we?"

"We are and we will take the long way. From this day forward, I will go where my father tells me to go. It is his will that shall be done." He swallowed hard after he spoke those words. Jesus was clearly showing stress and fear and they were beginning to change his mood.

He abruptly ended their conversation but Billy wanted more. He had questions surfacing in his mind. Was he going to Chicago to spread the word there, or would he return to Sycamore to save everyone? A light seemed to switch on inside of him as he realized he was concerned only for himself. The man he sat next to knew what was ahead and knew unimaginable pain would touch every nerve of the human body he agreed to occupy. Every sunrise brought that moment closer. He remembered the dread he felt as that September approached so long ago, but this ... this was so much more than his little inconvenience. He felt shame for his selfishness and bowed his head. He knew Jesus could hear his thoughts but he verbally said he was sorry.

"Thank you, my friend, for softening your heart. Go back to the others, you will now sleep well." Jesus said, as a tear streamed down his face.

CHAPTER 19

Sunlight woke them from their sleep and the soggy, muddy men gathered their belongings and began their journey to the next village. They bathed in a river they had passed and for a while, they were clean of the mud. As the afternoon wore on, the rain fell on them again as they walked. Billy was used to it by now but he was amused when he thought about his mother and if she had made this journey with him. He imagined her constantly complaining about being wet and how much she hated it. His thoughts were interrupted by a man who met them on the road.

James, the brother of Jesus had returned. This time Jesus seemed to be happy to see him and James was seemingly more receptive of his older brother. They talked and laughed at the head of the line and although Billy couldn't hear everything they said, he knew, at least from a Bible Story point of view, James was turning the corner on his faith in Jesus.

Judas came along side of Billy and began to ask about James and why he was there. He tried to bury his prejudice for Judas but it was one of the most difficult things for him to do and he wasn't very successful.

"Why do have your nose in everyone's business?" He paused, almost expecting an answer to his rhetorical question. "James is his brother … they probably miss each other and are reconnecting. Do you have a brother and wouldn't you miss him?" Billy asked as he walked quicker, hoping Judas would take the hint.

Peter unwittingly saved the situation by approaching Billy. He asked to speak privately with him and that meant Judas needed to leave.

"Why do you despise him as you do?" Peter asked.

"I have my reasons and someday you'll know why and … "

"And what William, why didn't you finish your words?"

"I can't talk about it." Billy answered. He moved nervously as he tried to redirect Peter from the previous conversation. "So, what do you want?"

"How is it that our Lord had invited his brother back among us?"

Billy looked at Peter. He cocked his head to the side as if he puzzled over a question. "Peter, you of all people should know this. Jesus is all about forgiveness and salvation. He is the key to heaven and anyone who believes in him will have life eternal."

"That's profound William. Did Jesus tell you this?"

"Actually, John did. But Peter, haven't you been listening?" Billy moved his gaze to the ground. "He has shown me that the past is just that and as long as I'm sorry and don't repeat my errors, God will forgive me of my sins."

"And he says this of everyone that listens to his words?" Peter asked.

Billy shook his head yes and then placed his hand on Peter's shoulder. "There are great things ahead my friend and you will be part of them, all of us will."

As they talked the village came into view. The children of the area ran toward them as they got closer and they clamored for Jesus and surrounded him. He fell to the ground laughing as they piled onto him, kissing his cheeks and laughing. Some of the adults in the town came to gather their children and ordered them to return from the stranger. Jesus looked at them and then stood to face them.

"Suffer little children and come unto me and forbid them not, for such is the kingdom of God." Jesus said as he began to walk toward the adults. Jesus continued to speak at the adults as he walked ever closer to them. Billy was sure a fight was about to erupt and as he looked to his left and right, some of the apostles thought so too. Jesus stood considered the faces of the adults and a silence that seemed to last for hours stretched between them. Finally, one of the men began to laugh and the others joined in the laughter. This seemed an odd conclusion to a standoff but it was far better than getting into a physical fight with the village men.

Jesus led them to the center of the town and immediately began to preach and heal the sick. Billy noticed he hadn't even so much as grinned since the children hugged him and he began to worry about him. As a child, Billy was taught that Jesus walked toward his death with bravery and poise and in complete compliance with the will of God. In the last few days, he was seeing something that was different, something more human. It made complete sense, after all. The man was becoming overcome by the fear of the intense pain the iron spikes would cause his body as they were driven through his flesh and bone. Billy recalled that just days prior, Jesus had pulled a thorn from his finger and had commented of the sharp pain it caused him. The fact that Jesus still walked toward *that* destiny bordered on insane but at the same time, it showed him, Jesus was the bravest man he knew or probably ever would know.

Through the following days, Jesus prayed and seemed to be praying more. Billy could only stand and watch the man he had grown to call friend, suffer with fear. Peter and Andrew saw it too and they asked Jesus about it and he told them it was soon coming, the fulfillment of the scriptures. They still didn't get it and Billy felt compelled to explain it to them. But Jesus forbad him to speak of the near future and threatened to take his voice again if he went against his wishes. As a consequence of his knowledge of the future, Jesus kept Billy close to his side and confessed what he had been communicating in prayer.

"The flowers, they and the leaves of the trees are my sign." His lip quivered with fear as he spoke. "God's strength is with me but my human body fears the suffering … I don't know if I can go through with this." Jesus said as he looked down at the healing red spot the thorn had left on his finger. His breathing was not smooth but labored and raspy. He was fidgety and started to bite his finger nails.

"You told me that God's will, shall be done and I know you'll do it. I'll tell you this though, you have guts. I will cry when I watch you die, but on the third day, Mary and I will be in the garden. I might camp out in the garden so I can see everything."

"You will not speak of future events and the people that are in them." He paused and then softened. "I might suggest you stay far from the garden. The guards will be looking for anyone who might be there to steal my body and proclaim my resurrection. You would be dragged before the Sanhedrin and sentenced to death. I feel great love for your faith but I will not have you sacrificed and wasted." Jesus said as his face showed no emotion.

"What do you mean wasted?" Billy asked as his head tilted to the side.

Your destiny awaits you. I took the long way back to Jerusalem so you could grow further in your faith. That growth is reaching the point it must. We must rest for the journey will be long tomorrow."

They set out the next morning in the darkness. A thin fog hovered just above the ground and as the sun began to rise, the landscape took on a surreal appearance. The saturated grounds were beginning to dry and new grass transformed the gray mud into a green velvet blanket.

Soon the shepherds would be filling the fields with their sheep and other livestock. They walked beside fields that were being plowed and readied for the planting of crop. Billy thought about the men who labored and watched them pass by and wondered how their lives might change if they knew the man walking by their fields would be taking them to the precipice of eternal life.

Over the next several days, they moved to and through town and village. Each stop was the same in that Jesus healed the sick and preached about the coming glory of God. Jerusalem was not far away and Billy figured within a couple of days, he would become part of the great entrance to that town and begin the week of preparation that would see his friend nailed to a cross.

CHAPTER 20

Darkness was in control of the sky when Billy heard a sound that brought him out of his sleep. He opened his eyes to find the face of Jesus looking down at him. Billy sat up quickly.

"Is something wrong? Do we have to leave?" Billy asked.

"We are leaving for Jerusalem." Jesus answered.

"Why didn't you wake me ... I could have been ready to go with everyone else."

"We, will not include you ...you can't go with us." Jesus said with some tension in his voice.

Billy paused and said the next words quietly. "So, this is it ... Jerusalem is the next stop ... and you're not going to let me come. I'm not going to see your resurrection, am I?"

"Billy, you can't go because you were never supposed to be there and your presence could, as your society says, screw-up everything. I have told you several times, you know what happens, they don't." Jesus sat beside Him. "I cannot risk your life or delaying what has been set by God so long ago."

Billy looked down at the ground as a tear swelled from his eye and ran down his cheek. He wiped at his eyes, still saying nothing.

"Why do you weep?" Jesus asked.

"I've only had a few friends … real friends. And each friend has been taken from me … and it's happening again. But I've never had a friend like you." Jesus sat saying nothing, letting Billy continue to speak. "You have been patient with me while I've been here and you've helped me find myself and fix myself."

"Billy, you've definitely been a challenge, but God's wisdom, love and yes patience is infinite. I wish you could go with us but the truth is you cannot."

"Why can't I go … I have no place else to be but with you. You could still have twelve after Judas does his thing."

"And that's it in a nut shell." Jesus said.

"What, do you mean?"

"How are you going to be able to keep your composure when Judas *does* leave to meet with the Sanhedrin? Currently, you talk very little to him because you know what he is going to do; you will know that he is in the process of betrayal. I see a fight breaking out and both of you thrown in prison." Jesus paused. "You are as strong in your faith as you ever have been and I believe I could have two Peters at my disposal. But Billy, this is not your destiny."

"I want to see your resurrection. I want to see the stone rolled away and you walk out of the grave."

"Someday when your time comes to bring you home, I will show it to you … I promise, and I never break a promise."

Billy's tears continued to come. He wiped at his eyes and told Jesus he was sorry.

"Why are you sorry? You better than anyone but me, knows this is a time of triumph and coming glory of the power of God." Jesus asked.

"I cry because I'm never going to be able to talk to you again. You'll be gone and this place will drive me insane. You are my only link to civility. I know that sounds stupid and condescending to the others, but they don't know or understand where I came from."

An awkward silence fell between them but Jesus broke it. "It is time for you to go back to where you came from. You have learned well and grown into a respectable man."

"Jesus, how can I return? The control has been missing since I arrived and even if I had it, I would go back to a life of misery."

"What is impossible for man is possible for God. I can send you back without the use of the machine, and summon the part you need."

With a deliberate movement of his right hand, Jesus changed the clothing Billy wore. No longer was he attired in robes and a head scarf but the blue jeans and button-down shirt he wore two years ago. His watch, wallet and cell phone appeared to the last places he remembered them. His beard and long hair remained and he puzzled over why. The modern clothing, he now wore was much tighter than the robes he had become accustomed to and the undergarments seemed rather uncomfortable.

"I wish you'd give me some warning before you do that." Billy said. "Why didn't you give me a shave and a haircut?"

"They will be necessary for what you will do next." Jesus began. "You must do exactly what I tell you to do. If you let your thoughts drive your actions, you may jeopardize everyone's lives, including your own. You have a destiny and job to do and it is not here."

Billy's heart began to beat quickly. He didn't quite know what Jesus had in mind for him but he hoped he would be going to Sycamore to stop the massacre.

"Please stand with me." Jesus asked.

Billy stood next to Jesus, and then followed him to the center of the room. "Billy do you accept me as your Lord and Savior, and believe in me as the son of the one true God?"

"Yes, I do."

"Your faith has become strong and because of that I absolve you of all sins. Now it can begin."

"What can begin?"

Jesus then said one word: "Behold."

The room faded into blackness. The sounds of the world went silent. A small point of light formed in the darkness and quickly grew into a mist and within the swirling bright mist, a doorway formed. He could see the future. It was a bright sunny day and he watched as automobiles and people went past the misty door way. He could see people shading their eyes against the bright early afternoon sun. He was looking at Sycamore Illinois, two blocks from where Spencer and Associates office was located.

Billy fell to his knees as he was in such proximity to God. He bent down to worship and started to once again weep. He was so close to achieving his desire but would his acceptance of the deal show him as a selfish person?

"Rise up and stand before me." As Billy stood, Jesus began again. "This is where your heart needed to be so that you could return to your home and be the servant of God that you were meant to be. But you need to choose your destiny and choose wisely. I know your heart yearns to be with your wife so I will ask you to tell me how you will stop the murders without committing murder."

"If I can go back to the Jail, an hour before Kevin hijacks his brother's car, I can have a police officer check out the office." He stopped and shook his head. "Wait a minute, that's not going to work because he'll just drive by because nothing is happening." Jesus smiled at him and encouraged him to continue to play out the scene. "How about: I know the approximate time Kevin hijacks his brother and when he gets to the office. What if I get to the office ten minutes before Kevin? I can warn everyone to get out, have the police alerted and save … almost everyone." His voice trailed off because he knew Tim would still die. He turned his face toward Jesus. "It's impossible to save everyone isn't it?"

"Yes, you're right, Tim will still die." Jesus said. But you will have saved others.

Tears came once again from his eyes as shame came over him. "It would be selfish of me to cast one life aside so I can have what I want." Billy felt dejected and began to sob. He was so close to going back to save Lori and the others. He felt ashamed as he stood before Jesus. "Your wisdom is great and my heart is still filed with the love of self." Billy said through tears.

Jesus placed his hands onto Billy's shoulders and turned him so they faced each other. "Billy, your heart sinks as you realize that Tim may still die and you feel shame such that you will choose to be alone here, rather than act out of selfishness. This is not a sign of selfishness, it is a sign that you have grown, that you will sacrifice yourself for the better of others." He paused for a moment. "It is true that someone will need to die so that Kevin can be stopped. He will need to succumb to the evil that resides in him or else the police will not stop him." Jesus shook Billy as he started to look away. "Listen to me. Tim's love for his daughter, wife and you, will cause him to lay down his life. That selfless, love-powered sacrifice will bring all of his sins to the top and they will be boiled away. He will be forgiven and he will join me in paradise with those he truly loves."

"You just told me I needed to give you a plan that doesn't put my life or my soul in jeopardy and I can't see how hate for one man will not over-ride my decisions." Billy said.

Jesus didn't acknowledge what Billy had just said and began to provide a detailed plan. "You will return to a phone booth where you will call the police. By the time you walk to the office, Kevin will be on his way and you will have just enough time to get people out. When Kevin does arrive, the police will be there and they will stop him." Jesus then handed a small oval device to Billy.

A huge smile covered Billy's face as he took the return controller from his hands. "Thank you, Jesus." Again, he fell to his knees and praised him through the tears streaming down his face.

Jesus bent over, placed his hands onto Billy's shoulders and continued. "You must listen carefully." Jesus said. "You will first be sent by me to that place. Once your task is completed, you will press the controller. It will return you to the time you left. Do only what you must … your destiny awaits."

"My destiny … whatever that's going to be." Billy said as he stood and wiped at his eyes.

"Your love for Lori is great and strong. Follow that which you have learned to trust and you will be fine. It won't always be easy Billy, but it will be worth it." Jesus then laughed. "You do know you will be unique of all mankind in your time. You will be the only man who can truthfully say he has walked and spoken with the Lord." Billy laughed as he looked over at the face of Jesus.

"I need to thank you for everything you've done for me … for all of us."

"Satan's grip on the souls of those who accept me will not hold. They will be with me, the Father and the Spirit. But there are countless others who will not be as lucky, please pray for them that they may see the truth." Jesus looked at Billy and at his hand that still contained the controller. "Be sure to put that thing in your pocket this time."

Billy made sure the guard was covering the button and then placed the controller in his pocket as Jesus had suggested, he wasn't going to make the same mistake twice.

"Hey, one more thing I need to ask you. The solar flare … was it really a freak of nature or was it created by God?"

"As they say in your time and country, I'll plead the fifth. May peace and God's blessings be with you William Thompson." Billy gave a wave as he smiled appreciatively at Jesus and then stepped into the mist and through the door.

He was suddenly in bright sunlight near a phone booth. He looked behind him, expecting to see the room he had just left but there was nothing but the brick wall of a building. Billy looked around and had seen no one. He reasoned God had delivered him at a rare moment when no one was in the area, eliminating the chance of someone witnessing his appearance out of thin air. There was work to do and no time for him to reacquaint himself with the small city and time where he was the happiest. He needed to act immediately. He entered the phone booth, looked up the phone number of the police department. He remembered he rarely had change but when he pushed his hand into the pocket he discovered Jesus had thought ahead and provided coins for the call. He inserted the money into the phone. A familiar ring sounded as the coin passed through the switch. He dialed the number. When the phone was answered on the other end, he spoke.

"Hello. I have solid information there is a man with a gun who is going to kill everyone at Spencer and Associates. He is on the way now. He is driving a dark gray BMW and will park that car in the alley next to the building. Please hurry." The voice in the receiver asked his name. "My name is William Thompson … Please hurry."

Billy ran to the office which was two blocks away. When he arrived, his appearance startled the occupants. He cleared his throat and began to speak. "Everyone needs to leave the office now. Please, leave now." They recognized him and started asking questions. "Please leave now, there is not much time, don't ask questions, just leave the building."

Most of them stood from their desks and started for the door but a few lingered. Those few would cost him precious seconds as they demanded to know what was going on. He told them sternly that they must leave because Kevin Spencer was on his way to kill everyone and he needed to get to his mother and wife so they too could get out. The few stragglers took his warning and left him alone in the office. He immediately turned for the hallway to where their offices were located. He quickly reached the first room that was Lori's and found her and his mother talking. His eyes saw them both, alive and beautiful. He smelled Lori's perfume and looked at her face and her green eyes. He had not seen this blessing in twelve years and now struggled with his heart. He wanted to rush forward and hold her, kiss her lips and profess his love and he wanted her to respond. Her arms, her lips, how he missed them and now she was only steps from him but he could not give in to the passion and desire that burned inside, for a mad man would soon be there to unleash his fury upon them.

When he approached the door, Lori was apologizing for knocking a coffee cup over and splashing it onto Kathleen's skirt. His mother seemed only slightly irritated as she wiped at the stain. Once they registered his arrival, his appearance startled them and they began to ask questions.

"Billy, I thought you said you were going to the market. What's with the wig and the beard? And why did you change clothes?" Lori asked. She and Kathleen looked at each other, wanting an explanation. Precious seconds were evaporating.

He had no time for this. "Kevin's on his way, he's coming to kill us for sending him to prison. Everyone else is already out. We need to leave now!"

"Where is Tim?" Kathleen asked as she looked at her son and understood the urgency in his voice. "Come on Lori, let's go. I'm sure he'll explain the costume stuff after we're out of here and we catch up with your father."

Billy looked away from them. Because the two women knew him so well, the knowledge of Tim's death would be in his eyes. He decided to wait until they reached safety before he would divulge that news.

Both women started walking for the door of the office to join Billy, when all heard the unmistakable voice of Kevin Spencer.

"Come out come out wherever you are. Uncle Kevin's got something for his favorite niece. I've been storing it up for ten long years."

They stopped walking immediately. Billy realized he was too late. The time he spent moving everyone out of the front may have cost them their lives. Where are the police, they should be here by now, he asked himself? There was no back door in the building and the only way out was through Kevin.

Billy was so focused on a way to disarm Kevin, he had almost forgotten about the pistol he had, ten years ago, given to Lori. He went to her desk, opened the drawer and found the pistol. He quickly loaded the weapon and held it in his hand. He knew Kevin was trained and would be ready. Billy figured Kevin would shoot him the moment he saw the gun in his hand so he needed another approach.

Lori suggested she would place the pistol behind her, near the small of her back. The maternity skirt she had worn that day had an elastic waistband and made it easy to store and retrieve the weapon. They were now armed and had a plan as they waited in silence.

Kevin looked around the deserted office. The desks were covered by papers and open books so he knew they were there recently. He looked forward to an open archway that led to other offices. Rows of desks created a maze that blocked his direct path. He reasoned they were hiding in there and he would find them and kill them all. He started walking slowly to the archway talking at them and mocking them. He was drunk, his words and steps were compromised by the effects of alcohol. He thought, that would be the only advantage they might have against him but he was trained to be a soldier. He had worked efficiently through other challenges in Viet Nam and overcame them. The desks slowed his progress, but only slightly.

Kathleen turned to look at her son and daughter-in-law. Neither Billy nor Lori liked what they had seen.

"He'll kill you Mom. Don't go out there. The police are on their way." Billy said as he pleaded with his mother to stay where she was.

"And he'll kill us all if we wait for the police. He's drunk and we together might be able to disorient him enough that we can take him down."

Kathleen took a deep breath and without saying anything she rounded the corner of the archway and came to face her husband's brother. Billy and Lori immediately followed her. Kevin stood quietly and waited until all of them had assembled as one group.

Billy looked at the man who stood before him. His clothes were stained with his brother's blood but it had dried and was no longer bright red but a deeper brown. Kevin leaned to one side, perhaps because he was drunk or maybe Tim had indeed hurt him during a struggle before he was shot. Billy thought, like his mother, they may be able to disorient him and take him down. The police should be there at any second so all he needed to do was to stall him.

Kevin looked at all of them but his first words were to Billy. "Well if it isn't Jesus Christ himself. Has the messiah come to save his children?" Kevin mocked.

Billy was angered but remembered what he was told by Jesus and Peter. He kept his cool. He looked at Kevin and calmly replied. "It's not good to mock the Son of God ... that's not going to show well on your resume' Kevin."

"Well maybe I don't give a hoot about Jesus or anyone else and as far as I'm concerned *he* can go to hell!" Kevin said as he slowly reached to his right and pulled a pistol from his right pocket and pointed it at them.

"You don't have to do this Kevin, you can leave now and no one needs to say a word." Billy said as he started to move in front of the women to shield them.

Kevin laughed and taunted him. "You see that's what people always say before they die. They try to bargain and beg for their lives." Kevin's eyes turned toward Kathleen. "So, Blondie, what will you give to save your life?" He smiled as thoughts of lust boiled to the surface." I've got an itch that needs scratching." Kevin said and then used his left had to gesture vulgarly. "You're a pretty thing … my brother always liked pretty women." He looked at the wedding rings on Kathleen's finger and a devilish drunken grin came across his beard-stubble face. "I supposed your knight in shining armor never told you or Lori why he got married to Kelly. He never told you he got her knocked up on a sales trip. He never told you I took the knife blade for him because her old man was going to kill them both." He paused and looked away from them for a moment, as if he was posing for a hero's photo. "Now that he's out of the picture, you're available." He waited for the meaning of his words to sink in to the three that stood before him.

Kathleen broke from behind Billy. "You … you killed my husband!" She was now in plain sight of Kevin and he would have a clean shot at her. Billy tried to pull her back behind him. Her sudden movement had caused Kevin to stiffen and ready the weapon. She knew the man would pull the trigger and her son would be killed. She had to protect Billy so she broke from behind and rushed forward. Billy and Lori both yelled for her to stop but it was too late.

The bullet struck her in the chest. She stopped, stood motionless for a second, and then fell to the floor. Billy quickly dropped to his knees and held her in his arms. A dark red stain immediately began to pump through her blouse and with each beat of her heart, the stain grew wider.

Kevin spat on the floor as she lay in her son's arms, bleeding heavily. His focus was on Kathleen as he watched the blood soak into her clothing. He was transfixed and seemed to be excited about what he had done.

"You're going to suffer a little first Blondie, because those wounds are painful as you slowly die from bleeding to death." Kevin said it through clinched teeth. Evil fueled his revenge and it consumed him completely as he took pleasure watching her die.

From behind Billy shots rang out. Lori had removed the pistol from the elastic band of her skirt and pulled the trigger. Two bullets hit Kevin. One grazed his head and the other penetrated his left shoulder. As his body reacted to absorbing the round, he twisted and intended to return fire. At the same moment, a police officer rushed into the room. His gun drawn, he ordered Kevin to drop the weapon. Kevin turned his weapon toward the officer. Alcohol and the pain from the bullet in his shoulder degraded his performance. Two shots from the officer's weapon hit Kevin squarely in the chest. He moaned as he clutched at the wounds and collapsed to the floor. The pistol he held rattled across the ceramic tile and a dark red puddle began to form around him. He died within seconds. His body lay motionless on the floor ... his eyes were open and showed a terrified expression.

"Officer Phillips? Is that you? Lori asked. Her hands and body shook with fear and adrenalin. "Thank you." She said has she looked at the lifeless body of her uncle who had caused so much tumult in her life.

"Ma'am please put the gun on the floor." The officer asked politely.

Lori complied immediately and then rushed to Kathleen's side.

As she knelt next to Kathleen and Billy, Lori looked at the front door that was now being filled by more police officers. In her mind a thought played: This was the same officer that had arrested Kevin ten years earlier. The justice of it playing out this way seemed to be fitting. She turned her attention to her husband, kneeling next to her. She hadn't been this close to him since he had arrived and she could see the beard he wore was not artificial. It would have taken an experienced makeup artist several hours to achieve this effect and he had been away from the office for perhaps only half of an hour at the most. His face was different too. The skin seemed to be aged more than when he had left for the store. She pondered the changes but then brought her attention back to Kathleen.

"Can someone call an ambulance? My mom needs to get to the hospital now!" Lori frantically called out. She knelt beside Kathleen and tried to render aid as Billy held his mother in his arms. Tears were running down his face and falling onto his mother's cheek. He brushed her long blonde hair and through tears, begged her to hang on.

"Where's that ambulance!" Lori yelled frantically as she too began to cry. The blood stain now completely soaked Kathleen's blouse and the top of her skirt. Billy held his mother in his arms, still crying and brushing her hair with his now, blood stained fingers. A thought, no a request, played through his mind. He had seen Jesus perform so many miracles with his own eyes and he prayed and asked God for just one more as Lori tried to put pressure on the wound in a futile attempt to stop the bleeding. The officers stood by and watched the family grieving for their loss that was moments away. Lori had been kneeling in Kathleen's blood and her clothing was covered by it. Her hands and face were smeared red and she too had the appearance of someone who had been shot. Billy wore his mother's blood as well. And as she lay in his arms he remembered something Jesus had told him: *You mother would give her life to protect you.* Her sacrifice was out of love and he knew had she not jumped as she had, it would be him who would be dying in Lori's arms as they watched him and wept.

Kathleen looked up to her son and Lori. "I love you both." She said through a labored breath. Her forehead glistened as beads of perspiration formed. She was in shock from the loss of blood. Another deep breath and she continued. "Be sure to raise my grandchild right." She stopped speaking to them, turned her head to the side and she smiled. "It's Jimmy ... can't you see him ... your daddy's over there ... his hand is out and he's standing with Jesus ... he doesn't look the same as in his pictures."

The end was moments away and through his tears Billy replied. "I know Mom ... I told him the same thing when I met him two years ago. I'm sure you and dad will love the stories he's going to share with you." Lori's face took on an odd expression as she looked at Billy. He knew he had said something he shouldn't have but it was too late. Kathleen squeezed Lori's arm and told her she loved them both. Her grip slacked and her arms fell limp to her side as she died in the arms of her son and daughter-in-law.

Billy was devastated but he knew he had to leave. His counterpart from this time would be arriving at any moment. He gently rested his mother's body onto the floor and stood. Lori looked at him but said nothing however her eyes were asking so many questions. "Look, I can't stay ... I think you know why ... I'll explain everything to you ... in about ten years. I need to go now. I love you Lori, I love you so much."

She looked up at him with tearful green eyes as she watched him walk away and quickly leave the building. Seconds later another Billy, one with short hair and no beard, was standing outside of the doors demanding to get in. My wife and mother are in there! She heard him yell. She watched him force the doors open and run toward the archway where she and the bloody body of Kathleen lay on the floor. Lori watched as this second Billy fell to his knees and cried over his mother's lifeless body. He reached down to pick her up into his arms and cradled her, rocking back and forth to sooth her as she had done to him when he was a child. Her lifeless arms splayed out to her sides.

Lori looked away from the sight of the other Billy holding his mother's body. She looked at the bloody footprints that led to the door and understood who the other man was. He had somehow traveled back in time and he had apparently met Jesus. This day seemed to be the center of all of it and for a second time, she consoled her husband for the same death. She said nothing as he wrapped his blood-covered arms around his mother's body. Inside, she felt pity for this version of her husband because he didn't get to hear his mother's voice for the last time. At least one of the copies of her husband would have that memory.

She struggled with the possibility of two men living there, both the same person, one older than the other, both in love with her, and she with them. Perhaps he went back and in ten years she would get the answer to all the questions that were filling her mind. There would be time for that later but for now, just processing Kathleen's horrific death would be enough.

As Billy knelt next to his mother's body he could only speak incomplete sentences. "No, it can't be ... she can't be dead." Lori hugged Billy with all her strength as they both continued to cry. Moments later, Billy wiped his eyes and looked at his wife. He had been so overcome with his mother's death that he hadn't noticed Lori's appearance.

"My God ... You're covered in blood! Where did you get shot? I need to get you to the hospital!"

Lori's face, arms, hands and clothing, were smeared and soaked with blood but none of it was her own. She could see the panic rising in Billy's tear-swollen blue eyes.

I'm ... I'm alright." She answered. "I think I can probably toss this outfit though." She said attempting to break the tension with humor. Billy smiled and was reminded of one of the many reasons he fell in love with her. He gently rested his mother's body onto the blood covered floor. He and Lori both reluctantly stood and stepped back from Kathleen's remains.

Officer Phillips asked them to leave. They needed to collect photographs of the scene and evidence. The request was met with almost maniacal laughter from Billy.

"With all due respect, I don't think there's going to be a trial—not in this world anyway." Billy said as he looked down at the body of Kevin Spencer. Quietly, he and Lori walked out of the building.

Once they reached the outside, the surviving members of the office staff surrounded them. Blankets were given to them so they could cover their blood-stained clothing. Most cried for Kathleen and offered their condolences to one another. But there was still someone missing. Kevin had alluded to killing Lori's father but it had yet to be confirmed. Several police officers were standing in the area and all of them had radios. The words she feared would come were heard through their speakers. A body of a man was found in a ditch just outside of the western edge of town. There was a single gunshot wound to the chest. The identification found on the body was of Timothy Spencer.

No matter how tumultuous their lives had been together while she was growing up, she still loved her father. "My Daddy's gone." She said as Billy pulled her to him. She buried her face in his chest as her tears flowed. She began to hyperventilate and became dizzy. Billy caught her and helped her to the ground. "A hand full of years is all I had. Because of his stupid brother, he'll never get to see his grandchildren." Lori was stringing her thoughts together and as she spoke them, they didn't make much sense to most people listening. But Billy understood and held her. Lori looked up at Billy as a thought entered her mind. They had both lost a parent when they were children and that common thread started their relationship. Now they would begin a new phase of their lives as parents and the death of her father and his mother would be a thread to start that life. The strangeness of it seemed to comfort her, but she didn't know why. Perhaps her husband felt it too. It was just one more thing they would need to talk about.

Officer Phillips found them and confirmed what Lori had heard on the radio. He delivered the news and he too broke down into tears.

"I'm so sorry. If I had gotten here just five minutes sooner, at least your mother could have been alive." The officer said as he looked shamefully at the ground.

"But you did come and you saved my wife and for that I will be eternally grateful." Billy said as he placed his hand on the officer's shoulder. "We keep crossing paths … maybe there's a reason."

Officer Phillips smiled at Billy's words, regained control of his emotions and then returned to the business at hand. He began to ask Lori questions.

"The man that was in the office when I arrived, the man with the long hair and the beard, have you seen him? I'd like to get a statement from him since he witnessed everything."

"He left. I don't know where he went." Lori answered. Billy looked at her oddly and she cut him off. "I'll tell you about it when we get home."

Billy turned his attention to something that was happening in the distance behind Officer Phillips. He watched as a tow truck was removing Tim Spencer's BMW. The police were taking photographs of the interior. A dried smear of blood stood out against the gray color of the driver's side, car door. He knew it was Tim's blood and he shielded Lori from the sight of it.

He quickly walked out of the building he turned to his right and ran to the end of the block. From a safe distance, he watched as the Billy Thompson from ten years past, came running toward the office doors. He watched and listened as the other Billy yelled at the officers blocking the door, and saw him go in. Billy stroked his beard with blood-stained fingers as he reflected on the painful loss of his mother but was thankful that Lori was unharmed. It was a better outcome than the one that he had been faced with those years ago but the costs were still too high.

He closed his eyes and played the memories of his life when he was young. How so full of love and life his parents were. He continued to page through the years as he and his mother were alone and how he disregarded her and finally came to his senses when he thought she had tried to take her own life because of his stupidity. He then thought of the wedding on the beach and the new beginning as his family expanded. That brought him to the present and this horrible tragedy. He offered a prayer of thanks for those earlier blessings and he asked for strength for his family to get through this terrible time. He knew his mother, father and Tim would be fine. Jesus was there to make sure they got home safe. Billy knew he would make good on his promise that they would all be with him in paradise.

Emotion was trying to take hold of him but there was still more to do. He turned and walked down the street until he came to another phone booth. Billy looked around to make sure he was alone and pulled the controller out of his pocket, walked into the booth and closed the door. He lifted the guard and pressed the button. He clasped both hands around the controller.

Billy could hear a buzzing sound and as the energy field surrounded him, he became frozen and could not move. Seconds later his eyes focused on a wall in a motel room in Chicago Illinois that he hadn't seen in two years.

CHAPTER 21

The time traveler looked at Billy, his face showed shock and horror. Billy was covered with blood and his appearance was a fright. As he stepped out from between the two vertical generator plates, Smith could only look; he was speechless. Billy said nothing but walked toward a chair in the room and sat down heavily. This was the first opportunity since he had left the presence of Jesus that he had time to process and feel what he experienced from the moment he woke that morning.

He placed his face into his hands began to cry. The death of his mother cut him deeply through his heart. He remembered what Jesus had said, not all could be saved and thought that would only include Tim. He fought the temptation of selfishness and turned to his heart. It was there he realized that love, when used properly, is a very strong force. The bullet his mother took was intended for him and love, true deep love, saved his life. Perhaps God too had intervened to save them as he directed Lori's hand with the weapon. The bullets that struck

Kevin changed the outcome. He offered a silent prayer for strength against temptation and hate and remembered the words of Jesus when he scolded him about judgment of others: Spend more effort worrying about your soul and less of others … it is not you who have been chosen to judge. It was out of his hands and he knew the one for that job was his friend who was now in heaven.

The man named Smith recovered from his initial shock and placed his glass rectangle-shaped control against the left side panel of the machine. Instantly lights began to blink and the control started to register data that scrolled down the front of its display. Seconds later, the lights went out and he removed the device from the generator plate. His finger danced across the surface of the glass. Billy was far too engrossed in his own thoughts to pay much attention to what the time traveler was doing but when the man let out a whistle, it caught his attention.

"That doesn't make any sense. It says here, you traveled back to the spring of 29 and then left just ten years ago. You would be almost two thousand years old. How is that possible?"

Billy explained how a solar flare had overloaded the time machines circuits and sent him back to Judea and how he spent two years walking with Jesus and the apostles. He further explained Jesus had sent him back to his original target of ten years ago and how he saved his wife but could not save his mother and Lori's father. He told Smith, the blood that stained his clothing and flesh belonged to his mother and how she died in his arms.

After he finished, Billy looked at the man. Something came to him.

"I can't believe you stayed here for two years." Billy told Mr. Smith.

"Subjectively, I have only been here for about maybe two minutes." He looked sympathetically at Billy. "I had enough time to use the restroom and finish drinking this cup of coffee."

"You're saying that is the same cup of coffee you made before I left?"

"Yup." Mr. Smith said as he shook his head yes.

The traveler pulled another chair over to sit next to Billy. The man was obviously repulsed by Bully's appearance and was overly cautious about getting too close. However, once he sat down, he touched his fingers to the glass surface of the device. Each time he touched the glass, a different color light would blink through its face.

"This is a normal debriefing after any time travel segment. I compare the historical data before you left and after you have returned. The differences, if there are any, are in this list." As he looked at the right-side margin, he said, "There are a few changes."

"Like what … what has changed?" Billy asked.

"Well for openers, you are two years older, physically, than you should be because you lost two years in Judea … I told you there were consequences to time travel and … you no longer live in an apartment in Chicago you live in a house in Hannover. You and your wife Lori are the parents of two children, a daughter named Kati and a son named Tim. Kati will be nine in December and Tim is five. The company has expanded greatly with offices in Illinois, Ohio, and Georgia and there are plans to open an office in Florida." The man rattled off dozens of changes that had occurred and when he finished, Billy sat shaking his head.

"I don't remember any of this. I wasn't there for my kid's births, or birthdays. I'm a stranger in my own life."

"That's normal." Smith said. "You need to sleep. Once you sleep, all these changes will become your memories. They will be as real as any other memory you may have had in your life because they will be … real." He stopped and began to chuckle. "This room that we're in is actually registered to you. Apparently, you're on a business trip to meet with, or rather have met with executives of Braggerton Incorporated. You have cut a major deal with a logistics chain, allowing Braggerton to cut its operating costs by ten percent. You are also quite wealthy … Mr. Thompson."

"So, I need to take a nap."

"Yes."

"Will I remember my trip back to Judea?"

"You should because of the way things played out."

"There are parts of my last ten years I'd like to forget, like all of the women I was with."

"You won't remember it because it never happened. As I said, once you take a nap, you will only remember what history says you will remember. But, if there is something you do want to remember, you can force that memory by taking notes. When you wake from your nap, read the notes and those memories will stay with you."

He stood from the chair and walked toward the two generator plates, stood between them, turned to face Billy and made one last statement. "So, Jesus is real and the stories in the Bible are real."

Billy stood, smiled widely and walked toward the man known as Smith. "Yes, they are real. There are or were so many things that weren't written that I thought should have been but as Jesus told me, a rewrite of the Bible wouldn't be cost effective. Billy was still grinning, especially as he remembered Jesus' sense of humor. "I know it sounds cliché, but I made a really good friend in Jesus and I know he'll always be with me ... not because it says so in the Bible, but because he told me."

Billy reached out to shake the hand of the time traveler but Smith declined to touch the blood-stained hand however, did raise his hand in farewell. Shortly after pressing some buttons on the glass controller, he fixed the device to his leg. Billy backed away. Seconds later, the orb lit brightly and the machine and its operator vanished. Two impressions in the carpet were the only evidence of the time machines' presence.

He was alone and decided he needed to get cleaned. He walked to the bathroom and realized it would be the first shower he had in two years. He stopped in front of the mirror and looked at his blood-stained skin and clothing. As he reverently touched the dried blood, he told his mother he loved her. The faucet was opened and he stepped into the shower fully clothed and let the water wash his mother's blood off him. As he looked down at the crimson river flowing between his feet, his tears mingled with the water from the shower head.

After he had finished, he took all his soiled wet clothing and placed it into a garbage bag. He tied it tightly closed. He looked in the mirror and decided it was time for him to say goodbye to the beard and long hair that he had grown over the last two years and he recalled seeing a barber shop on the first floor when he entered this building two years ago. On his way to the elevator, he placed the garbage bag into a trash chute. He listened as the bag fell, bouncing off the sides of the chute. After an hour in the chair, the barber had transformed him back to what he had looked like two years ago before he met the man named Smith.

On his return to the elevator, he encountered a woman with long dark hair. She smiled at him as she got into the elevator car. She was a very attractive woman and was quite friendly. It was just the two of them as the doors closed. A shiver ran down his spine as he recognized her. He needed no introduction because he had already met her in the past … her name was Kelly Anderson. He thought it was odd that she should be there. Perhaps she was awarded that job she was interviewing for last year. He pressed his floor and asked which one she needed, she offered the floor number and he pressed her request using his left hand.

"A gentleman … That's rare these days." The woman said as she smiled at Billy and looked at the wedding band on his finger.

"You remind me of my wife. She has hair just like yours." Billy said. He then thought: She doesn't seem to know me. It appeared circumstances had indeed changed.

"So, you're married …. I saw the ring." She feigned a laugh. "I got divorced about a year ago." The woman looked sadly at the floor. "I can tell you really love your wife."

"How's that?" Billy asked.

"Because you, you lit up like a Christmas tree when you talked about her." She said. She continued to look at the floor and then added more. "One year into my marriage, my *ex*, started to pay attention to women other than me, so it's a blessing I never had … your wife is a lucky woman."

He wondered, since the time line had changed, did she ever become pregnant? He'd ask some questions, just to be sure. "I'm sorry to hear about your marriage. Do you have any children?"

"No, luckily we didn't have any children." She paused and then looked directly into his face. "Do you have any kids?"

Her gaze made him uncomfortable, but he answered. "Yea, Lori and I have two children, a girl and a boy." Her eyes telegraphed sadness. The smile on her face was false and was only there to be polite. Silently, he offered a prayer for her, and asked Jesus to bless her. Suddenly, an idea popped into his mind. "I met my wife at church. I don't know if you go to church, but it's a much better place to meet people than at a meat market like Casey's Place, in town."

She laughed at his statement. "How did you know I met Joey, my ex, in the *meat market?*"

The bell chimed and the elevator came to a stop. The doors opened and the woman walked out into the hallway. She stopped and turned to face him.

"Hey, like I said before, tell your wife, she's a lucky woman. But if she ever gets tired of you, let me know." She smiled and disappeared behind the elevator's closing doors.

When the bell chimed again, the doors opened and Billy exited the elevator and quickly went to his motel room door, opened the lock and went straight for the bed. As he lay there, he thought of holding Lori in his arms. It had been twelve years since he had that precious gift. Even earlier in the day, when he went back to Sycamore to save them, he hadn't been able to touch her the way he wanted, but now he would have the rest of his life … that is if the kids would leave them alone long enough.

Suddenly, a thought occurred to him, something Smith told him about the past. He would only remember what history dictated. That would mean, he would be saved the memory of the parade of women through those years, but he would probably not remember Lori dying in his arms. He wrestled with the idea of saving that memory and quite soon decided that it was important to remember what had happened. The pain of those years would strengthen the love he had for Lori and his children. The lessons of Jesus and the apostles would not have the same weight if he let those memories fade.

Billy quickly rolled off the bed and went to the desk in the room. He started to create an outline of the events from ten years ago. It was easier to write about it now that the circumstances had changed, but the pain of his mother's and Tim's loss lingered. Once he finished, he placed the paper into a briefcase that apparently was his and returned to the bed.

Sleep came without him knowing it had arrived. The sound of the phone roused him from his slumber.

"Hello." He said. "Lori, I have been thinking about you all day long." They talked for a short time. "Yea, I'll be home tonight. Pick me up at the airport?" He laughed. "I love you too."

He looked at his watch. It was nearly dinner time. He needed to get his bags packed and check out. He looked at the carpet and noticed the two lines and a smile came to his face. He remembered the man named Smith and his trip back to Judea and his time with Jesus. I wonder where he went … I hope he gets a passing grade.

The last shirt was folded into the suitcase and the zipper was closed. He made one last check of the room and gathered his luggage. After waking to the hallway, he closed the door and headed toward the elevator. His trip to the lobby was uninterrupted and his check out was quick.

Outside a car and driver waited for his arrival.

"Mr. Thompson." The driver said as he touched the tip of his cap in a pseudo salute. The trunk was opened and Billy loaded the luggage. He sat in the back seat of the car and watched the city blocks go by as the driver worked his way through downtown Chicago and toward the airport.

It took about an hour to get there but once he arrived he didn't go to the airline stands, they drove to the private aircraft parking area on the west side of Chicago O'Hare field. He collected his luggage, tipped the driver and walked to the business jet that waited. A flight attendant and the captain greeted him as he approached. He noticed the other pilot was busy inside the plane, on the flight deck, preparing for the flight.

Billy climbed the stairs to the jet, turned for his seat and he made himself comfortable. Minutes later, the attendant came by to check on him and ask if he desired any refreshment. The captain closed the door and walked to the flight deck and took his place. Billy asked for a plain cola. Moments later she returned with a small plastic cup filled with his request. He thanked her and then began to reflect upon his life.

It seemed that God had indeed blessed him. His successes and blessings were no less than those of Job. The company had grown so well that he was able to have the luxuries of a nice home, a family and this Jet. His ministry, as it turned out was not to stand before a church every Sunday, but to reach out to children to help them through organizations which were set up in each of the cities the company had offices. He donated large sums of money to these places to not only feed the children's stomachs but also their souls. They learned about Jesus in a way that no other children had been taught. Naturally a few religious leaders scoffed at his words however, most did not. Billy would laugh at the few and remind them they were exactly like the Pharisees that tried to dissuade the people away from Jesus. He always spoke with the confidence of someone who was there, someone who had walked with Jesus and the apostles.

As in the past, his thoughts always came back to Lori and his family. All the memories of his family's past ten years were there, at least most of them. He could remember the birth of his children, the work everyone put in to build the company and make it successful and he remembered holding Lori. Oddly though, he still felt as though he hadn't seen her in over a decade and he looked forward to her touch and the taste of her lips.

The engines were started and the plane began the trip to the runway. The taxi time seemed about as long as the car ride to the airport but once they lined up with the runway the engines spooled up and Billy felt the pull of acceleration as the jet gained speed. The sound and vibration of the jet's tires against the runway grew faster and suddenly went quiet as they were off the ground. A few turns and twenty minutes later, the wheels touched down onto the runway at DeKalb County airport.

Billy watched out the window as the plane slowly taxied to the parking place. As the pilot brought the jet to a stop on the ramp, he looked out the window and saw his wife and his two children. They were joined by another man who was the head of security, John Phillips. His heart beat strongly as if it was trying to break through his ribs so it could run ahead to be with her. She was ten years older and had changed slightly but Lori looked as beautiful as ever. Her hair was shorter but was still past her shoulders and her smile was just as he remembered it. Although he couldn't see her eyes behind her sunglasses, he knew how beautiful and green they were.

His daughter was a combination of his mother and Lori. She was as smart as her grandmother, had Kathleen's blue eyes but she had her mother's dark hair and smile. Timmy was similar in appearance to Billy except he had his mother's green eyes and her father's smile.

He felt like he did as a child on Christmas morning. His heart continued to race with excitement and after the attendant opened the door of the plane, he stood from his seat, grabbed his brief case and walked quickly to the open door. He looked over at his children and waved hello. He jogged down the steps and he ran toward them. His arms were outstretched and he hugged them both. He kissed them each on the cheek. As wonderful and warm as Kati and Timmy made him feel, he yearned for Lori. He took the two steps required to stand in front of her. Billy picked her up in his arms and spun her around and kissed her like he hadn't seen her in decades.

"Somebody's happy to see me." Lori said as she laughed with her husband.

"Spin me too daddy." Timmy said as he bounced up and down. Billy picked up his son and spun him around as he had done his mother. "Did you bring me something from Chicago Daddy?" He asked.

"Welcome home Dad." Kati said as she stood almost emotionless.

"You know it is okay to hug your dad more than once, your Mom's not going to get jealous."

"How do you know?" Lori said as she laughed.

Mr. Phillips stood back and watched the Thompson children climb into the back seat of their car. Billy thanked John for watching over his family. As they fastened their seatbelts Billy and Lori closed the doors. When they reached their own doors, Lori looked over the roof of the car at her husband and asked him a question.

"You know tomorrow is the tenth anniversary, don't you?"

"Yes. And I believe I told you I'd tell you everything on that anniversary." Billy said.

After they got in and closed the doors, he started the car, kissed his wife again and they began to drive toward home. Billy looked at the trees and houses and felt as if he was being greeted home by nature itself. Once they turned into the driveway of their house, Billy pushed the button on the garage door opener. He watched as the door made its progress upward. He pressed the button again and the door started to close. Kati asked him if he had too much to drink on the plane. Her mother hushed her by a stare. He began to think about all of the times he grumbled to his mother about opening the garage door by hand. He put the car in park, and turned off the ignition, walked to the side door of the garage and seconds later opened the garage door by hand. After walking back to the car, he got in and started the engine. A slight tear had formed in his eyes.

"I never told you kids how I used to give my mother so much grief about having to open the garage door by hand." The tears ran down his cheek as he remembered her. "It seems we tend to make the stupidest things so important."

"I'm sorry Dad, I forgot what tomorrow was." Kati said.

That evening before bed, Billy walked into Timmy's room to say bedtime prayers and to tell him goodnight. Lori stood at the doorway, watching. Timmy was on his knees praying while his father knelt beside him.

"And Jesus thank you for bringing my Daddy home safe because me and Mommy really love him … Amen."

Billy tucked his son into bed and kissed him on his head. Lori followed and told her son goodnight. They next went to Kati's room. She was already in bed and was waiting for her parents.

"What took you? It's like going to be morning soon so please tell me goodnight." She smiled as she said it. She had certainly inherited her mother's sarcasm as well as her beauty. Billy thought that it will take a strong man to handle this one. After they said goodnight, Kati called out. "Dad, it's good for you to be back home … I missed you."

"I missed you too baby girl, Goodnight." Billy said as he turned out the light and pulled the door closed.

Alone at last, they slipped into their own bed. Billy followed through on the promise he had made a decade ago. Lori was very interested and followed his story closely. She learned the details of the alternate time line, where she had also been murdered, how he came to be there ten years ago wearing long hair and a beard and how he met Jesus. He told her about his life with Jesus and how he argued with him … at least at the beginning. He shared his amazement of living through the New Testament of the Bible and how he had been, sort of, written into the Bible.

"You know how it says Jesus led them to Jerusalem but they took the long way? Well, he did that for me so I could get my heart straightened out. He finally got me to stop feeling sorry for myself and to start believing in my heart." He continued after a short pause. "For me, the murders of Mom and your dad were earlier today." He paused as the emotion of their loss filled him. "Inside, I haven't been with you in twelve years … and I really missed you."

Lori looked at her husband with amazement and gratitude. "You did this, all of this … to save me?" Her green eyes began to sparkle with tears. Then Lori did what she always did when too much emotion washed over her, she injected levity. "Well you definitely look better with a good haircut and a clean face." She reached over and kissed him lightly on his cheek.

That's not a kiss." Billy said. It had been over a decade since he had seen or touched her and he wasn't going to settle for a peck on the cheek. He reached for her and pulled her to him, held her tightly and pressed his lips to hers kissing her passionately. "Make love to me." He whispered as he reached over to turn out the lights in the room.

CHAPTER 22

The anniversary date was a holiday at the company. Most of the people that lived through that horrible day ten years ago still worked there. Billy and Lori had the year after, authorized a paid holiday for all of the employees so that they could spend time with their families and give thanks that their lives were spared.

The office was completely remodeled. Hanging on the wall was a large photo of Kathleen and Tim, taken shortly before their wedding day and on the floor where Kathleen had died, a star was placed. It had no letters, no pictures or any markings whatsoever, but everyone knew its meaning. Along the road that led out of town, an Iron cross marker identified the place where Tim Spencer gave his life for his family and employees. It was a simple cross, but again, everyone knew its meaning.

The Thompson family went to the cemetery to place flowers on the grave of Kathleen and his father. Billy remembered the funeral where both he and Lori had stood by, as emotion gripped them. He had replaced the original headstone with a larger, granite stone that bore a picture of his parents from when he was about eight. He never realized how beautiful his mother was and became emotional as he looked upon the stone. They both looked so alive and young in the granite. Engraved in script beneath their picture was something his father had always said to his mother.

You Always Make My Heart Melt. Together Forever

They placed flowers on the graves of his family including his grandparents. Mr. Phillips kept a watchful eye over the family as they remembered their moment of grief. After placing the flowers, he walked over to his head of security and suggested he take the day off so he could be with his family. Nine years ago, a year after the tragedy in the office, Billy offered him a new position within the company created primarily as a reward for his part in saving both Lori's and his lives that day. Since that time, he was always there watching over them and making sure they were safe

When they had finished at the cemetery, they drove to the airport and boarded their plane for Ohio. Once they landed at Cincinnati, they drove up to Lebanon and were met by Lori's aunt and cousins. As a group they traveled to the cemetery where Tim and Kelly Spencer were buried and placed more flowers. Emotions got the better of Lori more than once but she managed to get through it, as usual, with humor and sarcasm. As the group walked away from the graves, Billy and Lori were flanked by their children. She stopped suddenly, almost causing Timmy to run into her and Billy.

"Roller coasters Billy, we need roller coasters." Lori said as she looked at her husband. Her tears had transformed her makeup into dark, spidery trails spilling down her cheeks.

"I think you're right." He replied as he looked at her green eyes. "But before we go over to Kings Island, you need to look in the mirror." He chuckled after he said it.

Once they got back to their car, Lori repaired the damage her tears had done and after a short drive, they were at the gate of the amusement park. Timmy had grown since their last trip but was still not tall enough to ride the roller coaster known as the Beast so his great aunt stood with him as the rest of the family rode the coaster.

Kati and Lori took the front car of the *Beast* while Billy shared the second car with one of his wife's cousins. The train rounded the bend and began to climb the hill. The chain clanked out its two-note song as the cars climbed. They reached the top, the cars started down the steep grade. Everyone screamed as the train picked up speed. It was freedom from the memory of the day, freedom from the pain. They rode almost all the rides that day and stayed for the fireworks that evening.

The trip and the amusement park left them tired and ready for bed. After they settled into their motel room for the evening, prayers were said and goodnights exchanged. Billy and Lori curled up together in their bed, he on his back, his arm around her and her head on his shoulder ... her hand rested on his chest. He turned his head and kissed her. She yawned and then asked Billy something.

"Do you miss Jesus?"

"I miss talking to him, but I know he's here."

"Do you think you'll ever talk to him again ... here?"

Billy smiled as he answered, "Time will tell. Goodnight Lori."

"Goodnight cowboy, I love you."

About the Author

The first writings from J.E. Rechtin, were short stories while he was in the sixth grade. While nothing he had written ever made it past the teacher's desk, it was a preview into what would come later. A boy with an imagination, fueled by the events of the late 1960's and early 1970's, he watched longingly as a seemingly, endless parade of rockets left the Earth for the moon. Sadly, he could never qualify to be an astronaut, but around a decade later he did obtain his Pilot's license. Of course, between that achievement, he became a firefighter and EMT and took part in one of the most tragic fires in the history of the country: The Beverly Hills Supper Club Fire. It was here he bore wittness as loved ones found their spouses bodies and watched as their grief exploded. Four decades later, the ability to connect a reader to deep emotions they themselves have, was discovered ... it will only get better from here.